THE GOBLIN OF ADVENT

WALTER FIRTH

Ark House Press
arkhousepress.com

© 2025 Walter Firth

Cataloguing in Publication Data:
Title: The Goblin of Advent
ISBN: 978-1-7643577-3-9 (pbk)
Subjects: [FIC042100] FICTION / Christian / Contemporary;

Design by initiateagency.com

This book is dedicated to

KATHERINE and GEORGIANA

Remember:

there are stories within stories;

worlds within worlds;

truths within truths;

and loves within loves.

"Long ago, when the nights grew long and frost crept upon the windows, the people would wait for Christmas not with impatience, but with reverence. Each candle lit, each small gift opened during Advent, brought them nearer to the holy day. But beware... For when hearts grew greedy, or when joy is taken for granted, a shadow creeps in. A goblin with crooked fingers and a hunger for cheer — the Advent Thief."

CONTENTS

PROLOGUE

THE LAW OF ADVENT

They do not speak of him openly, not even in the coldest of winters when the wolves grow thin and the bread runs black with mold. They whisper instead, as though the very frost upon the glass has ears, as though the icicles might lean inward to listen and drip their secrets into the night. They speak in tones so hushed and so quietly muttered, that the very name of the thing has been long forgotten: thus, this ancient goblin is known only as the Advent Thief. On nights when snow buried the roads and frost climbed the windowpanes like pale fingers, people counted the days of Advent with trembling joy. Each night they lit a candle, each morning they opened a gift, small and simple, to mark their journey toward Christmas Day. The fire glowed warm, and hope carried them through the long dark or winter.

But not all nights are safe. For in the cold silence, when a heart turns sour with envy, or a hand clutches too tightly to what should be shared, the Advent Thief stirs, for he is still around: bound to ways and laws older than the Church; older than the great bells that toll for Christmastide: THE LAW OF ADVENT. Its ways are not written in any scriptures of men, but in the marrow of the land itself: carved upon stones now long-lost beneath snowdrifts, passed from dying lips to frightened children. He creeps low beneath the rafters, his limbs long and crooked, his teeth like broken shards of ice. He does not strike on the first night, nor the second. He waits until the third, or fourth, or fifth, when people have grown careless, or when bitterness has already begun to gnaw, and family members are tired and want to squabble. On those nights, when suspicion whispers or eyes glance jealously toward another's gift, the Advent Thief comes. He does not steal every gift. Only one. But with it he steals your hope, the warmth from your fire, the light from your candle, and the joy from your heart.

And there is a rule, old as frost:

If the stolen gift is not found before the next sunrise, then Christmas is lost to you forever.

Your fire will not burn, your tree will wither, your joy will turn to ash, your days to shadows, and all laughter to silence. You may live to see the day, but never again will you taste Christmas warmth.

Once, long ago, when kings still rode with antlers nailed to their helms, the villagers tell of a woman who awoke to find her candle guttered out. Her child's gift was gone — no ribbon, no wood-carved toy, nothing but the dark hollow of its absence. She searched, but her feet froze into the snow. When dawn came, she was found upright in the drifts, eyes wide open, her mouth full of ice. Her house never saw another Christmas. Others tell of worse. Of men who followed the trail of their vanished gift into the trees, only to meet hungers that wear the faces of friends. Of children lured by voices sweet as sugar, only to vanish in the mists. Of entire families whose hearths were found extinguished, doors frozen shut, the smell of rot seeping out long before the thaw.

The priests call it superstition, or dismiss it outright as the raving tales of primitive peoples; but some grandmothers know better. They remember too much. They remember the nights when the wind did not merely blow but howled in laughter, when the Advent candles sputtered with no draft to blame. They remember the change in their childhood friend, of strange footprints pressed deep into the snow outside the doors of those unlucky or cursed by a visit from the Advent Thief.

Children, for their part, laugh at the candles glowing in every window, giggle at the bells that toll dusk like frightened old hens clucking in the dark. They think it is only holiday merriment, pretty flames to match the songs, a ringing to call the faithful to prayer. Their parents, eager to appear wise and pious, nod along with the priests and insist the lighting of candles is tradition, nothing more. But the old women — the ones with smoke-roughened lungs and fingers cracked from years of cold — they know the truth. This is why candles are lit in the windows through December, and why church bells ring at dusk. They insist the candles are not for cheer, but, warding; that the bells are not a summons, but a warning, their peals meant to scatter the shadows from gathering too thick at the village edge. They watch the young smile knowingly, mock their fears, and they do not argue. For they know the Advent Thief feeds not only on envy and bitterness, but on disbelief. And so, the village lives divided: children who laugh, priests who scorn, mothers who pretend not to hear, and grandmothers who sit silent at their hearths, staring at the flames as though each candle is the last small weapon keeping the dark from rushing in.

And always there is the chain. For the goblin carries with him the gifts of centuries, each wrapped in sorrow, each link forged of stolen joy. Those who have seen it and lived long enough to tell, describe the sound: a dragging, rattling music in the night, like bones on stone. But like all old magic, the rule is simple: find what is taken before the sun rises and touches the horizon. But the journey is not. For in the dark of Advent, winter births its monsters. But once, and sometimes still, a child or a fool or a stranger must face the night alone. And then the law is tested anew. Though no child wishes to test the law, one winter it fell to Morana, the girl at the village's edge, to step into the shadow...

This is the tale of Morana, who dwelt at the edge of the village with her grandmother. It was she who awoke one Advent to smoke curling from a dead wick, and to a missing gift.

And I tell this tale to protect you. Not to sweeten the long nights, but to remind the shadows that we still know their names. For the Thief walks with destroyers and howlers, with the forgotten broods of frost and famine, with those who creep into houses and leave hearts desolate. Such spirits fall upon men without warning, seeking not flesh alone but understanding, hollowing the soul until only weariness remains.

Remember this, listener: the tale is told so that your heart does not grow careless, so that your fire does not gutter out. These are the days of waiting, when the air itself listens, when the frost presses close, when joy must be guarded like a flame cupped in the hand. That is why the story is spoken — that you may keep it close on your journey, and learn to read the truth of the world more deeply.

And thus begins Morana's walk into the dark...

CHAPTER ONE

THE EDGE OF WINTER

The village lay nestled in the hollow of the valley, rooves bent beneath the weight of snow, their chimneys coughing threads of smoke into the starless night. The streets were narrow, cobbled, and crusted with ice; lanterns swung at corners, hissing when snow blew against their flames. From within the houses came the warmth of voices — laughter, songs, and the rustle of gifts being hidden away. Each window glowed like a jewel against the encroaching dark, Advent candles in their rows marking the steady passage toward Christmas. In the village square, the last of the market stalls had shuttered, their fabrics frozen stiff, their meats salted and hung high away from prowling foxes. The villagers lived close, pressed shoulder to shoulder by both stone walls and necessity. In the nights, they found safety in the nearness of others, in the shared warmth of a fire that belonged to more than one household. There was comfort in the knowledge that if a shadow slipped between two houses, someone else's eyes might see it too.

But at the farthest edge of the village, where the cobbles gave way to brittle dirt paths and the last lantern's glow was swallowed by darkness, stood Morana's home. Beyond her gate stretched the woods — tall, skeletal pines whose tops clawed the clouds, their trunks dark with sap that oozed like old wounds. It was a place the villagers called the margin, where the safety of hearth and company bled into something else: the silence of the trees, the growl of wolves at night, and the feeling that unseen things watched from just past the line of vision.

Her grandmother's cottage sagged there like a weary sentinel. Its roof bowed under snow, its shutters warped, and its stones damp from ceaseless frost. Moss grew thick in its corners, and in summer the weeds grew high as if eager to reclaim the land. Children from the village dared one another to touch its gate but rarely lingered — they said the shadows there were darker, the air colder, as if even the light hesitated before stepping in. Inside, the warmth was hard-won. A single fire struggled against drafts that slipped through the cracks, and though the hearth was always lit, its glow barely chased the chill from the corners. Each evening her grandmother tended it with slow, deliberate care, as though every ember were something that could be bargained with. Morana often woke to the old woman crouched at the hearth long before dawn, whispering over the flames as if coaxing them to stay.

The morning began before the sun dared rise. Frost thickened the inside of the window, lace so intricate Morana thought even the angels might have admired it. She scraped it away with her sleeve, her breath fogging the glass, but all that showed beyond was the endless black of the forest. Her grandmother's voice broke the silence. "Wood."

That was how each winter morning was: one word, a polite command as plain as the wind. Morana wrapped her scarf twice around her neck; the wool stiff a little with yesterday's snow. She stepped outside, boots crunching through the crust. The trees loomed. Collecting wood was a daily ritual, one that kept their fire alive. Once, her grandmother said, people used to help each other; and there was never any shortage. Now the fire lived on a diet of carefully selected wood. Her grandmother had taught her to choose carefully — not green branches, not heavy logs, but brittle limbs, already fallen, already given to the earth. "The forest offers what it will," she'd said once. "Take what it gives, no more."

Morana's arms ached as she dragged the bundle back through the snow, but she never complained, even as she hauled the wood across the threshold, snow still clinging to her skirt. Inside, the air was close with the mingled scents of smoke, damp wool, and something sharper, more inviting — the sour-sweet tang of *Piimäpuuro*: a sour milk porridge, thick and filling, and it had just finish thickening over the fire. Her grandmother knelt at the hearth, lips moving in low murmurs; lips moving in the strange whispers Morana could never quite catch, as she coaxed the coals to glow, one hand steady on the iron pot as though it might slip away without her. \ "What are you saying?" Morana asked in curiosity.

"Words older than these stones," her grandmother said, eyes not leaving the fire. "Wards against what waits in the dark. Not for your ears yet."

Morana bit back her questions.

The cottage always smelled the same in winter: of pine logs drying by the wall, of moss ground into the stone floor, of smoke that clung stubbornly to the rafters no matter how often the shutters were opened. But on mornings like this, another note joined the chorus — *Rieska*: a simple flatbread that added scents of ginger and earthy oats; a faint edge of rye It was a gentle scent, and filled the cottage the way music might fill a church, humble and whole. But today that chorus of scents had a new refrain — *Rieska*, the flatbread of oats and rye sat toasting on the flat stone by the fire. The dough had been pressed by her grandmother's hands rather than a spoon, her thumbs leaving little valleys where the ginger and butter had been worked in. A root of ginger was a treasure, kept wrapped in cloth at the very back of the pantry, and brought out for Advent, so that its perfume could rise like a rare spice in the humble air. The smell was at once earthy and sweet, bright enough to cut through the smoke, and it made Morana's stomach twist with longing even before she tasted it. Her grandmother ladled the porridge into a small wooden bowl, its surface steaming, then pressed into Morana's hands a portion of *Rieska*, crisp at the edges and soft in the middle where it had baked against the stone. She tore a piece carefully, as though it might vanish too quickly, and the warmth against her fingers felt like a secret gift. Steam curled into her face as she lifted it, and she let herself breathe it in before daring the first bite. The bread was nutty, almost sweet, and the ginger bloomed sharp on her tongue, chased by the faint smokiness of the firestone. She thought then that if home had a taste, it would be this. Her grandmother set a dollop of warm berry preserve in the centre of the porridge, and Morana watched it sink and spread in; colouring her breakfast with blues, purples, and reds.

"Eat before it cools," the old woman said. Her own bowl sat untouched a moment longer as she stirred the fire with slow care, whispering words Morana had learned not to question. Morana wrapped her fingers around the warm bowl, breathing in its scent before lifting the spoon. The porridge was tangy, comforting, the sourness cut by the faint sweetness of some of the berries. When she broke the bread and dipped it in, the flavours met in a way she thought might be remembered even in dreams — tang, smoke, spice, and berry, all dissolving together until the cold outside seemed very far away. Outside, the snow blew against the shutters; inside, for a fleeting moment, it felt as though the world could be held together with nothing more than grain, milk, and fire.

The rest of the day passed in its small rhythms. Morana fetched water from the half-frozen stream, her breath smoking in the air. She mended a tear in her skirt with clumsy stitches, while her grandmother's hands — though bent and gnarled — flew quick as sparrows over her own repairs. At midday they ate a thin broth with two slices of bread, each piece measured as if by weight. Nothing wasted, not a crumb.

Sometimes her grandmother spoke; often she did not; instead humming gentle old tunes whose words only she seemed to remember. But when she did, the words lingered. "Never leave a candle to die alone," she told Morana that day, placing the Advent candle in its holder: "its flame carries prayers you cannot see. When it dies, darkness listens — and things without names draw close."

Morana shivered, though the fire was strong.

And so, they lived: not in ease, nor in plenty, but in a rhythm as steady as the swing of the lanterns in the village. To Morana, it was both comfort and cage. She longed for laughter that did not come with a warning, but she also knew this life had shaped her. Every splinter, every shiver, every whispered word of her grandmother's was part of who she was becoming.

Morana often sat by the small window, wrapped in wool too thin for the cold, watching the other children parade through the village with song and laughter. Their hands clutched sugared fruits, their voices rang in harmony, and each night's candlelight flickered from their windows like little promises that tomorrow would be brighter than today. Her hands itched to join them, but her feet never carried her down the path; she knew well enough that no invitations would come. Sometimes, when the carols floated through the woods, she would press her palms to her ears, not because she did not want to hear them — but because the ache of being left out was worse than silence. Her grandmother said little about it, but grandmother would notice, and without a word she would place her gnarled hand over Morana's, the skin papery, the grip surprisingly firm. It was not comfort exactly, but a reminder to Morana that she was not alone. Morana's grandmother was bent with age, her eyes sharp as flint beneath a tangle of white hair, her voice low and clipped. Sometimes she muttered to herself — old prayers that Morana could not recognize, words not meant for her ears. Morana had once asked if they were church prayers, but her grandmother had only shaken her head and said, "Older." That single word seemed heavier than any hymn, and it left Morana uneasy, though she dared not press further. And when the girl asked why they must live at the margin, away from warmth and company, her grandmother would only shake her head and say, "Because the dark must always be watched."

Yet even in the quietness of their routine, moments were full of tender fondness. The old woman's hands seemed never to still. If not cooking, they were mending. If not washing, they carved. Always from broken branches, snapped, crooked: she teased life from what others would discard. She never touched wood cut in greed, anger, or arrogance; only the discarded, the storm-broken, the seemingly useless. In her hands even these assumed ruined pieces remembered life, her knife teasing out lines so simple and clean they seemed almost to breathe. And of these Morana knew her grandmother loved to carve birds most of all. Morana loved to watch her most on nights in a hypnagogic haze, when the fire burnt low, the shavings curling like pale feathers to the floor. A bird was taking shape now, its wings only half-suggested, its body no larger than her palm, and yet it already seemed to breathe. 'Why birds?' Morana sometimes asked, because her grandmother always gave a different answer. With careful thought, lips pursed, her eyes reflecting the firelight she would respond: *"Because no matter how small they are, birds always find the strength to lift themselves. They fall, they scatter, the winter tries to silence them — but still they return to the branches come spring,"* or *"Because when you carve a bird, it carries a song with it. Not one we can hear with our ears, but one that lives in our hearts. When you hold it, it's as though silence itself remembers a song."* The saddest though had been: *"Because I can't follow them anymore, child. My bones keep me here. But when I carve them, it's as though I've sent them ahead of me — flying over rivers and mountains, carrying tales I'll never walk to find. And sometimes I like to think they might bring a little of those stories back, if only in their shape"* On the mantle above the hearth rested some of her earlier treasures — a fox curled in eternal sleep, a crooked star, a tiny horse so finely cut that Morana swore she could feel its gallop in her hand. A piece of the forest, rescued, remembered.

So it was there, at the very edge of the woods, that night fell and Advent turned. The wind had fallen silent, and the snow no longer fell but swirled in thin plumes from the ground, curling like smoke. From far off came the faint toll of bells — not bright and joyful, but cracked, dragging, as though rusted chains struck against iron.

Her grandmother was at the window, her face pressed close to the glass. Morana had never seen her there before, never seen her so still, so intent. "Too quiet," the old woman muttered, her breath fogging the pane.

"Isn't quiet good?" Morana asked softly.

"Not when the dark listens." Her face shifted, and for the first time Morana saw fear there — not sternness, not weariness, but true fear, sharp enough to hollow her chest. She turned, and for an instant her eyes met Morana's — and there it was, a look

Morana had never seen before. Not sternness. Not weariness. But fear.

Morana's chest tightened. She wanted to ask more, to press her grandmother with questions, but the old woman had already turned away, lowering herself onto the stool by the hearth. She snatched up the half-carved block of wood and set her knife flashing again, as if the scrape of steel against grain might drive whatever lingered in the silence back. Morana, restless, could not leave it. She crept to the glass, and leant closer to the window; her own breath joining the fog.

Her mind drifted back to other nights — the ones where her grandmother had seemed untouchable: splitting frozen logs in the yard while snow rose to her knees; muttering at prowling wolves until their yellow eyes slid back into the trees; stuffing rag after rag into the shutters until the draft gave up its fight. If even she could be shaken, then what stood between them and the dark pressing at the shutters? Morana thought of the first carving her grandmother had ever given her — a fox curled tight in eternal sleep. She remembered holding it against her cheek, warm from her grandmother's palm, whispering her secrets into its wooden ear. *Keep me safe,* she had begged. And somehow, she had believed the fox was listening.

But now, as the knife began scraping, she wondered if even the fox had fallen silent — if the dark had swallowed it, too. The blade stilled. "The goblin feeds on gifts," her grandmother's voice came, soft, almost to herself, as if she believed Morana already asleep. "But it feeds most hungrily on hope."

The words slipped through the dark like a curse. Morana clutched her blanket tight, her pulse loud in her ears. Her grandmother had never spoken such a name before, never dared shape it into sound. Now it hovered in the air like smoke, heavy and unanswerable. And in that silence, Morana realized her fear was not only of the forest, or the window, or the Advent Thief itself. It was of the day when her grandmother would no longer be there at all — knife in hand, whispering the old wards, holding the dark at bay.

For a brief moment Morana fell asleep.

The sound of a dragging, rattling chain broke the night with its music.

The dark pressed close, swollen and thick. The pane rattled. For a heartbeat, something stirred within it: a lurching shadow, bent and crooked, its limbs too long. She blinked, thinking the frost was playing tricks. But then the face slid into view — thin as leather stretched over skull, with a mouth that sagged far too low, teeth jagged as shattered ice. Two eyes bulged, wet and colourless, but glistening in the dark. She gasped — and it was gone. The room's single Advent candle guttered and died. Smoke curled upward in a twisting ribbon. And the small wrapped gift ready for the morning — a wooden bird she had watched her grandmother carve with aching hands — was gone: the sound of a rattling chain retreating off into the night

The wooden bird had not been carved from fine timber, but rather from a snapped branch brought down in a tempest months ago, gathered from the forest's edge: as all her grandmother's gifts tended to be. The bird was no ornament, no trifle: its wings folded close, its grain flowing like feathers in quiet rest, as if it might take flight when the fire cracked just so. Morana had been looking forward to unwrapping it and holding in in her hands. Whilst each gift was meant to be a surprise, she had not been able to hold back from peaking as each one had been carefully wrapped and set aside. Two other offerings still lay open beneath the Advent wreath, small tokens already unwrapped in the days before: a carved spool, wound with thread dyed from crushed berries, and a little whistle that sang clear as the wind through the pines. They were not lavish gifts, not like the gilt ribbons and sugared cakes in the village, but they were alive with care — each shaped by hands that knew both the frailty and endurance of wood, and by love too deep to speak aloud. And yet the one gift she most longed to hold—the one she had hoped might soften her apartness from the village children with their sugared cakes—had been taken.

Her grandmother's chair creaked as she rose, stiff with fear. "The Goblin has come," she whispered. Her voice cracked as though naming it might break her tongue. "If you do not find the gift before sunrise, Morana, there will be no Christmas. No joy. Only the cold, without end." Her eyes, sharp as flint in every ordinary hour, now glistened like a child's. Morana had never seen her afraid, and that made the fear all the heavier. The house seemed to exhale with her words, the wind rushing hard against the shutters as if in agreement.

And Morana knew: something had stolen not only her gift, but the promise of warmth itself. Looking out into the snow, she saw strange tracks, clawed and uneven, and the drag of a heavy chain leading toward the village. The footprints were jagged, imperfect, yet deliberate, each one a silent herald of a cunning, relentless presence.

It had begun with her, but it would not end here — the Advent Thief was hunting gifts, and by dawn there might be none left. If she wanted Christmas to come at all, she would have to follow.

Her heart hammered in her chest, half in fear, half in determination. The snow crunched beneath her boots as she stepped onto the path. She imagined the creature ahead, nimble and merciless, perhaps whispering to itself as it claimed joy and light from every doorstep. Each shadowed corner of the village seemed poised to conceal it, and the once-familiar streets now looked alien, twisted by the threat looming over them.

She glanced once at her grandmother, who stood rigid by the guttered candle, lips moving in some ancient prayer. The flickering flames cast trembling shadows across the lines of her face: as if the old woman herself had been weathered by years of guarding against the unseen. For the first time, Morana understood that her grandmother could not step into the snow herself — the watching, the waiting, had already cost her too much. It would be Morana who must carry the burden.

Hopefully in the village, thought Morana, she would both find the creature and some help to catch it. But even as she considered allies, her mind wandered to the solitude this task demanded. No one else could feel the loss in the same way; the absence of her gift was not just empty hands, but a hollow ache that reached into the chest. The snow seemed to hush around her, the world holding its breath.

She drew a deep breath and squared her shoulders, steeling herself for what lay ahead; determined to follow the tracks wherever they led. If the Advent Thief thought to outrun her, it would find her footsteps relentless, her resolve colder than the frozen ground she now followed.

CHAPTER TWO

THE BELLS IN THE FROST

The village sparkled like a storybook jewel in the snow. To anyone standing at its gate, it was perfection: to a passing stranger it might have seemed enchanted: golden firelight spilling from windows, smoke curling upward in fragrant ribbons, the sound of bells and carols feathering the night as they wove through the crisp night air. But from the shadow of the tree line, where Morana and her grandmother lived, it was only ever a mask — and tonight, as she entered the narrow lanes, the mask began to crack.

She stopped before the baker's house. The door was garlanded with ivy and bows; the windows steamed with sugared warmth. The home was swollen with fine spices, nutmeg, and ginger: the scent of sugar and honey clung to the walls; sweet as memory itself. Inside, the family sat around a long table groaning with pastries: gleaming gingerbread houses, loaves split open like golden hearts, sugared apples, bread crusted with almonds and raisins, sugared nuts and pies glossed in amber glaze and oozing dark fruit. Shrieks of laughter rattled the rafters: the children shrieking in delight, as their sticky fingers clawed and tore at the bounty with their hands, crumbs flying, lips slick with syrup. But laughter tilted into something else, shrill and wild. It was not laughter born of joy — it was vicious. The eldest boy, red-cheeked and wolfish, grabbed a fistful of his younger sister's hair, twisted it and shoved her head down until her face smashed into the custard tart. She thrashed, cream flooding her nostrils, choking her as tears cut pale grooves through the sugar crust as her small fists pushed back against the table while her other siblings howled: "Pig! Pig at the trough!", pelting her with crumbs.

Their mother clapped her hands together and laughed - laughing as though this humiliation was a new game: as though pain were a party trick, urging them on; her own mouth twisted with merriment. Children should be grateful for the bread in their mouths, no matter how it is given. The girl's sobs were muffled by sweet, heavy filling as she gagged on sweetness, drowning on a holiday meant for delight. The father watched with eyes like cold flour dust, and when the girl finally coughed the tart back up, gagging on yellow cream, shoved another bun into her hand and hissed: "Don't waste the feast. You'll eat what's given." Morana realized then that the table was not abundance — it was punishment. Every sweet was a weapon, every pie a tool to humiliate. The feast was no gift. It was a spectacle of power, of watching who could gorge, and who must choke. Hunger is not the worst cruelty, her grandmother had said once. Being forced to eat what poisons you — that is the truest famine.

The next window glowed red with lamplight. She pressed her face against the warped glass of the cobbler's home. A fire crackled, casting shadows over shelves lined with leather hides, boots, and scraps of half-finished soles. The smell of pitch and tallow stung her nose. Inside, the cobbler bent low over his bench, hammering nails into a heel with rhythmic violence — *thunk, thunk, thunk* — each strike like a heartbeat gone wrong. His eldest son, a boy not much older than Morana, stood barefoot in the corner; arms trembling with cold; his bare feet bleeding in the cold stone dust. Every few moments, the cobbler snapped his fingers, and the boy shuffled forward on raw, blistered soles to hand him tools. His steps left smears of blood like dark petals on the floor.

When the boy faltered, when his limp slowed the rhythm, the cobbler snarled and seized a boot. Without hesitation, he pressed the iron heel hard into the boy's shoulder, driving him against the wall.

"You think shoes are made for standing idle? For resting, like some prince?" the cobbler hissed. "Be Still!" the cobbler barked whenever the boy twitched or shifted. "You've not earned your shoes: Shoes are only for those who earn them." The boy whimpered, shoulders curled inward, tears dripping silently into the dust. *Shoes are not for the idle. Shoes are for those who earn the right to walk. The lazy deserve bare feet on stone, so that pain teaches them where pride cannot.*

The boy nodded desperately through his tears and shuffled back to the corner, and brothers and sisters danced gleefully in new boots across the floor; boot heels cracking against the boards like whips, the soles thick and new. His fingers trembled as he lifted another awl, the iron slick with blood from his hand. Morana watched as his lips moved — not a prayer, not a cry for help, but the hollow mutter of a child who knows there is no rescue.

And then she saw the boy's gaze fix on the neat row of shoes lined up along the wall: finished pairs gleaming with polish, soles stitched tight with care. Not a single one belonged to the boy — his father's skill in every stitch, every gleam desired by many— and none would ever be his. His feet, purple with cold and raw against the icy floor would never know the leather he had assisted in crafting. Morana stumbled back from the window, bile hot in her throat. To the families who passed by, the cobbler was generous — his shoes lined the feet of half the village. Yet inside, generosity was a blade, carving obedience from a boy too small to resist.

The innkeeper's tavern was an inferno of noise. Candles guttered in greasy sconces, shadows jerking across the walls. The warmth of the hearth carried even through the pane as they rattled from the carols within. The heat inside was so thick that frost melted from the eaves. Fiddles screamed a jig, boots stamped the planks, the beams above shivered, mugs slammed on the tables, male voices roared with laughter, their cheeks flushed crimson with wine. Glasses spilled, hands slapped the table, fists pounded in rhythm to a bawdy song. At the centre of it stood the serving girl, forced onto the tabletop to dance barefoot among puddles of drink. Someone pressed a jug to her lips, forcing it down her throat until she gagged, crimson liquid staining her chin and bodice: her face as pale beneath a mask of rouge, and cheeks painted redder than the wine forced down her throat. Her hair was tangled in one man's fist, her arms wrenched by another as they spun her like a doll between them. When she faltered, when her foot slipped in the ale and her knees buckled, hands clutched at her waist, shoving her upright again, dragging her into the circle of jeering faces. A customer's hand gripped her wrist, another's her waist. She tried to pull away, lips forming no, but it drowned beneath the chant of the room. "Another! Another!" they bellowed. She stumbled as men dragged her into their circle, spinning her between them like a toy. Their song rose louder, drowning her gasps as a hand slid up her thigh. The innkeeper poured another jug, grinning his hollow grin, far too wide, and his eyes too flat. In the corner his wife sat rigid pretending not to hear, her gaze focused on her folded hands with eyes like stone, lips pressed thin enough to bleed. Above the noise, Morana thought she heard, or hoped she had imagined it; a muffled cry under the fiddle's shriek. The girl's voice had splintered, small as glass breaking.

Farther on, children's shrieks filled the mason's house. At first Morana's heart lifted, mistaking it for joy as it bled warmth into the snow outside. But then she saw: one boy locked inside a hanging cage, pounding the bars with fists, his muffled cries echoing in the rhythm of play. Around him, his siblings pranced in a circle, chanting: "No gift for you, no gift for you!" Their father, pipe smoke thick around him, smirked into the shadows. He did not stop them. He did not even look. When the boy's shaking of the bars grew frantic, the father rose at last — but only to fasten another chain to the cage, lowering it so it swung nearer to the fire. The heat licked the boy's skin, blistering him with its breath, and his screams cut higher.

"The stone teaches patience," the father muttered, drawing on his pipe, eyes half-closed. The siblings clapped their hands, delighted at how the cage rocked, each sway branding the boy in the fire's glow. The man leaned back into the shadows, smoke curling like mortar between his teeth. *A house of stone births hearts of stone. Remember,* Morana recalled her grandmother's teaching: *when cruelty is left unchecked, it hardens, just as lime hardens to rock.* Once, a mason would build walls to keep the frost out — but in his children's laughter, you hear the frost creeping in. To lock away a child is to mortar cruelty into the very foundation of a home. Morana realised the boy beat against more than wood — he was beating against a legacy that will not open.

The butcher's home was worse and Morana nearly gagged at the thick, sweet reek of roasting meat. On the spit turned by his eldest son, fat dripped into the fire, hissing, smoke clinging to the rafters like a ghost. The family sat round the table, their mouths shining with grease, gnawing at thick slabs of flesh. Raising a gleaming knife, the butcher carved slices of roast meat with a flourish, laying the thickest, fattest portions on his children's golden plates. At his elbow knelt his apprentice, a pale boy with hollow cheeks: his clothes hung in tatters, his belly shrunken, his eyes wild. He gnawed on the ends of charred bone, stripped of all meat and tossed carelessly to the floor. His eyes burned with hunger as he watched the golden cuts pass him by, his stomach groaning. Once, he reached for a crust left on the platter. The butcher's hand shot out, striking him sharply across the knuckles with the carving knife. The child recoiled, his lips pressed shut against tears. The family laughed. But then Morana saw what the roast truly was. The ribs, pink and small. The curve of a delicate hand where the flesh had shrivelled in flame. The skull, its teeth bared in a silent, twisted grin. It was no pig upon the spit, no lamb. It was a child. A child she thought she recognized — pale hair, now singed, mouth stretched in a silent scream that had hardened in death. And by the fire, another child sat bound to a stool. He was being fattened — soft white bread stuffed into his mouth, fat dripping down his chin, his belly swelling while tears slid down his face. He forced down the bread, each bite a gasp and a plea; knowing soon he would be next. He sobbed as he chewed, hiccupping with each swallow, gagging when he slowed. The butcher's wife crouched before him, cooing like a mother to a babe, shoving more into his mouth with her thick fingers. At the other end of the table, a girl lay curled on the floor, her body wasted and thin, her wrists like twigs. She clawed weakly at the scraps, but each time her brother reached to help her, the butcher roared and slammed the knife into the table between them. "Fatten one, starve the other," he growled, his grin slick with grease. "Balance."

At the weaver's, song mixed with sharp cracks. A carol spilled from her lips, sweet enough to charm the night, but her daughter's knuckles bled where the switch bit them raw. The girl's fingers faltered over the loom — just once, just long enough to ruin a thread. The girl's fingers were swollen, her skin torn open where the cane bit bone. Her mother sang louder, hiding the screams in her melody. The weaver's hand descended again, punishment blending seamlessly with song. "Faster," she snapped, "finer, or we shall have nothing to sell come market." The girl sobbed quietly, but her hands did not falter. The child's tears slid silently down her cheeks, disappearing into the warp of wool. Morana watched until she realized the tune itself was warped — not praise, not carol, but something closer to a lullaby sung to the loom, not the child. The child was only a tool. Cloth is made of patience, but here it is made of pain. Once, a weaver spun blessings into garments to keep her children safe from the winter — but this one spun only curses. The red in her thread is not dye, but blood. And what is woven in cruelty will clothe no one in warmth: only bind them tighter to sorrow.

In the alderman's hall, all was radiant. Candles blazed on a towering tree, apples gleamed like jewels, gold ribbons shimmered. The air trembled with song and clapping boots. But at the threshold crouched a beggar boy — bones beneath his skin, eyes raw with hunger.

"Come in, come in!" the alderman boomed, beckoning with grand, false warmth. Gasps of delight rose from the crowd as the child, trembling, stepped into the light. "At Christmas, we share with all" they cried as they began anew their yearly custom.

They drew him to the table, his face lighting as they placed before him a plate piled high. He reached for it with both hands — and in an instant, the platter was yanked away, the feast scattered across the floor. The guests roared, stamping, clapping, shrieking with laughter. "Look! Look how he scrambles!" The boy clawed the ground, gathering crumbs, shoving them desperately into his mouth. Boots kicked them from his reach, knocking him sprawling. A man grabbed him by the collar, held him aloft as though he were vermin caught in a trap. His legs kicked, his hands tore at the air. "Another round!" the alderman crowed. "Bring him bread — and snatch it away again!" The boy's sobs cracked through the revelry. His cries echoed in the rafters, mingling with the bells, and no one hushed him. They laughed louder. The alderman's laughter still echoed in her ears as Morana stumbled back into the street. The beggar child's cries—shrill, desperate, then suddenly silenced—hung heavy in the frost-laden air. The village seemed to pulse with it: cruelty masked as festivity; delight sharpened into a weapon. Her breath shivered in her chest. She pressed her hands against her ears, wishing to shut it out, but the sounds carried still—choking sobs, giddy laughter, the muffled strike of a blow followed by applause. Hospitality is the mask of power, and here it grins wide. Once, to share a loaf was to honour the holy — but now bread is thrown like stones, and the hungry are made sport of. *Beware the hall that laughs too loudly,* Morana recalled: *the louder the mirth, the sharper the knives. To humiliate the poor is to salt your own feast with ash.*

Morana's stomach twisted, a knot of hunger and revulsion. The villagers had always called her family strange — witches, hermits, outsiders unfit for the joy of Christmas. Yet in every glowing window, she saw the truth: delight fattened by cruelty, pleasure sharpened with teeth. Her grandmother's words whispered inside her skull: It is not only the woods that are dark, Morana. The darkness waits inside men, too. And sometimes, men feed it gladly.

At the end of the lane stood a narrow house. Morana hesitated, for she knew it well. Once, she had trudged here each Sunday, hands scrubbed raw, to sit in stiff rows and learn hymns by rote. She peered through the crooked pane. The room was dim though the hearth glowed faintly, embers collapsing into ash. Her former teacher sat hunched in his chair, his robe unbelted, his collar askew. A Bible lay open on his lap, but his eyes were closed, lips slack, as though the words had long since soured to silence.

Candle stubs melted into greasy puddles around him; flies drifted lazily over plates of crusted food. The walls were papered with old scriptures, curling, their ink faded. Once they had been copied out in careful script, words bright with reverence. Now they drooped like withered leaves.

Children sat at the long table, but there was no song, no lesson. Their slates were blank, chalks untouched. Some dozed with heads pillowed on their arms; others stared dully into the dark, their hunger quiet, their boredom deeper than sleep. A small girl tugged timidly at the teacher's sleeve, but his hand only twitched and fell back, limp, as though even the weight of kindness was too much. Morana remembered how he had once spoken with fire, eyes alight when he told of angels and judgment, of the narrow way. But that flame was gone. What sat in his chair was only a husk, slumped in shadows, waiting for time to pass. A boy coughed, thin and sharp in the silence. No one turned. No one answered. The teacher did not stir. The cough came again, swallowed by the hush, until it sounded like nails tapped gently against a coffin. Morana shivered and drew back. *To forget cruelty is dangerous*, her grandmother had said, *but to forget hope is worse. For when fire dies, the night does not even need to fight — it simply waits, and fills the void.*

By the time she reached the square, the festivities had bled away. The market stalls, so full of trinkets and toys only hours ago, stood empty and skeletal, their awnings sagging under frost. The snow was littered with debris: splintered wooden dolls, ribbons trampled into mud, gnawed bones stripped of their meat. An overturned bench gaped like a jaw. The old beggar who had once slept upon it was gone. No one knew where. No one cared. And now there was certainly no one who would care for her plight. Deep down she had always known that no help would be found in the village; but she had gone and now knew this was her search alone: and if others wanted their gifts that would be their story. Looking around, only a stray dog remained. Gaunt and trembling, it nosed at the frozen earth where scraps had been. When it looked up at her, its eyes were round with a hunger that was more than animal — it was hollow, desperate, pleading. Then came the bells.

They tolled not from the church tower but from deep in the woods: slow, heavy, uneven, each note dragged like a coffin across stone. Morana's blood ran cold. These bells carried the weight of malice; they were both a summons and a warning. The sound carried no joy, no rhythm of worship, only doom. The dog stiffened. Its ears flattened, and whimpering, backed away with its tail pressed to its belly. Then, with a strangled yelp, it vanished down the alley, lost to shadow.

Her gaze wandered to the shadows between the houses and down the alley. Black seams in the snow where no torchlight reached. And there, for the barest instant, she thought she saw it -something else. At the edge of her vision, something darted across the lamplight: a shadow of a figure, stooped and thin, long fingers scraping along the cobbles as if counting them one by one. Its head jerked toward her, and two eyes caught the light, red as dying coals. Smaller than a man yet moving with animal speed. She turned, heart hammering. The thing crouched at the end of the lane, its outline twitching, its head cocked unnaturally to one side as though it were listening to her very heartbeat. She blinked. Gone. It had fled. Without thinking, she followed. The laughter of the alderman's hall faded as she plunged deeper into a narrow, crooked alley between the tavern and the alderman's stone wall. The ground was slick with frost, the air colder here than anywhere else, carrying a sour stench as though the alley itself were rotting. The shadow skittered ahead, just beyond reach. Each time she thought she'd lost it, a faint giggle echoed—high, childlike, but distorted, as though played on broken strings. The alley twisted, darker and darker, until the lamp-light no longer reached. And then, it opened. Before her stood a great arch of stone: weathered, strangled with dead ivy, blackened as if scorched. Beyond it, across a field, loomed the forest. The bells rang again. In their hollow metal throats, she thought she heard words, faint and warped, as if something were trying to speak through rust and cold: *Find it... or be lost.* The firelight of the village glowed behind her: warm, golden, false. Ahead, the trees stood like black spears stabbing the sky, their branches clawing upward, their roots drinking deeply of darkness.

The bells fell silent. The forest opened like a mouth, waiting.

And Morana stepped forward.

CHAPTER THREE

INTO THE FOREST OF HUNGER

The village fell away behind her as if swallowed by shadow, its dim lanterns blinking out one by one until the black line of the tree-line loomed like a serrated mouth. The air shifted there—colder, heavier, laced with pine resin and the faint iron tang of frozen blood. Snow muffled every sound until even her own footsteps seemed a trespass. The branches rattled in the wind like bones in a sack, and Morana felt the oppressive weight of stories told in whispers: the forest did not merely shelter wolves and storms; it bred hungers older than man. The forest remembers every famine. The trees grew tall on graves, and the snow kept count.

Once she paused and glanced back. The village was gone, devoured by distance and snowfall, as though it had never been. She thought of the Advent candles that still burned in the children's windows, and of the carols they might be whispering as they were put to bed. But here, in the breathless dark, there was no carol, no candle, no child. Only her — and the forest. The silence felt so total she almost believed she had walked out of the world entirely. This silence pressed upon her like a second skin. Even her breath seemed an intrusion, a trespass the trees themselves resented. Each pine was black as iron, its needles whispering with a voice too low to be wind. A weight lived here. It was not the silence of peace, but of watchfulness, as if the forest itself drew breath and waited. Morana shivered, for she thought she saw faces in the bark — sunken mouths, hollowed eyes, a thousand gaunt visages layered into the trunks, all turned toward her in mute hunger. She blinked, and they were gone, yet the sense of their need lingered like a cold hand upon her chest. She pressed her own hand against her chest, as if to feel proof of her own heartbeat.

Every child knew never to enter the woods alone; especially not at night. Morana knew this too. But like all characters in a fairytale, commonsense gives way to narrative need. Mundane rules were meaningless now, for the goblin had taken her Advent gift, and the law of the season was absolute: if she did not recover it before sunrise, she would never again see the glow of Christmas morning, never again feel warmth in winter. She stepped forward into that maw of darkness, heart thudding, breath clouding in ragged puffs. For a while, all was still—too still. The path bent downward into a hollow where the air thickened with mist. Frost glistened on the ground. Then came the breathing.

It was not sudden. It arrived as though it had always been there, a ragged undercurrent to the forest's silence, only now she noticed it. The sound grew with each step, a wheeze that rose from the earth itself, as though the ground beneath the snow possessed lungs and strained to draw her scent into them. The mist curled strangely, pulled in time with the sound, coiling around her boots like pale fingers. The air sharpened, acrid, and the faint coppery sting of blood caught at her tongue. Her heartbeat throbbed in her ears, yet beneath it the rasp grew clearer, wetter, a slow rhythm of need. She gripped her coat tighter and moved forward, though every instinct screamed to turn back.

She stopped; straining to listen. The sound did not come from one place but seemed to shift among the trees, first behind, then to the left, then just ahead. Her grandmother's words returned to her in a whisper: "If ever you hear breath in the forest that is not your own, do not answer, child. For hunger listens, and hunger learns your voice." Then a childish memory surfaced — how once the village boys had dared each other to call the Chenoo's name into the snow-fields. They had jeered when she refused, but now, with that ragged rasp rising and falling in the mist, not unlike cloth tearing across a seam, she felt a dark gratitude that she had kept silent.

Still, she clung to hope it was only the groan of ice-sodden trees in the wind. But the sound thickened: breath, wet and laboured, swelling louder, deeper, as if drawn through lungs crusted with frost. Then the smell hit: rot and frozen marrow, mixed with the sharpness of old iron. A shape shifted in the fog ahead. Not yet form, only a vertical shadow, too tall, too restless to belong to any tree, as if the mist itself exhaled. She crouched instinctively, her knees breaking the crust of ice. The cold bit through her stockings, but she dared not move. Her mouth opened as if to scream, but only a thin puff of steam escaped, devoured by the dark.

The creature finally emerged from behind a cedar, impossibly and monstrously tall, smashing the tree aside as though it were no more than a reed. A man once, perhaps, but corrupted beyond anything human. Its limbs were thick and swollen with frost-bite, purple and blue skin split to reveal slabs of frozen muscle; icicles jutted from ribs like knives. A Chenoo! The Chenoo's face, once human, was locked in a perpetual grimace, but hunger had carved it monstrous: teeth broken into tusks, lips peeled back and torn away so the gums showed raw. The sockets of its eyes leaked frost and pus, yet when they fixed on her, she felt herself marked for slaughter. On a cord around his neck hung bones—finger bones, she realized—some gnawed clean, others still clotted with blackened sinew. The growl that rumbled from him was not hunger alone; it was need, ancient and endless. She remembered then another scrap of lore, told to her at the spinning wheel: that the Chenoo could weep like a man and speak like a friend, but every word was only bait. Look too long at his tears, listen too closely to his voice, and your pity would serve him better than your fear. Morana clenched her fists, as if to hold her compassion inside where he could not find it. For a moment, the Chenoo did weep. Frost cracked along his cheeks like frozen tears, thin rivulets of ice spilling down his ruined face. His voice broke, not with rage but with grief, and he whispered into the trees as though speaking to someone lost: "Daughter... wife... mother... forgive me." The words rang with such human sorrow that Morana's heart lurched, but even as she felt it, she saw the hunger behind his eyes flare brighter. The tears froze before they touched the ground, brittle lies that shattered as soon as they fell. This was no man's mourning. It was hunger wearing grief as a mask.

Morana froze, for to move was to draw his gaze. But the Chenoo had already smelt her. His chest heaved with a snarl, the steam from his mouth billowing as he lurched forward. He towered, gaunt yet grotesquely swollen in the gut, like a famine victim who had gorged on ash and stones. His lips were split; gums black with frostbite; teeth jagged and thick as icicles. Where its chest heaved, she could hear, unmistakably, the gurgle of emptiness — like a stomach eternally rumbling, but magnified to a hollow thunder.

It was hunger made flesh.

"I smell..." the Chenoo rasped, each syllable a cough of ice. "... the living."

The words struck the clearing like stones hurled against glass. The sound was too loud for a voice, too deep, as if spoken by something hollowed out inside. Each syllable carried the weight of a tomb being pried open. Morana felt the vibration in her ribs, in her teeth. Her mouth went dry. The Chenoo leaned lower, its great body groaning as frozen sinews cracked. Its breath rolled over her in waves of sour rot and marrow-stink, so thick she gagged and pressed her sleeve to her face. Behind that stench lingered something worse — the faint sweetness of roasted chestnuts, of sugared cakes, of all she had ever longed for at Christmas. It was as if the monster breathed both death and false comfort, luring her toward it even as every instinct screamed to flee for its voice also carried the weight of every starving winter. Of children with bellies bloated and eyes sunken, of mothers burying babes in the snow, of fathers gnawing leather straps and bark in place of bread. The sound made Morana's own stomach knot, as if her body remembered famines she had never lived. The monster bent low, breath blasting her face in a cloud of steam that stank of rot. She gagged. Within its gullet she glimpsed a lump of black ice — a frozen heart beating slowly and unnaturally. She had heard whispers of it in her grandmother's tales: the cursed heart of hunger, planted in the chest of those who ate human flesh to survive the winter.

One of its hands reached forward, fingers as long as kindling-sticks, nails curved into talons rimed with ice. The claws scraped the bark of a pine and peeled it away in one curling strip, as easy as skinning fruit. The sound made her stomach twist. In its other hand, it carried something like a staff, though she realized with horror it was no staff at all — but a femur, thicker than her arm, gnawed hollow at one end. The Chenoo used it as a club, idly striking the ground so that sparks of frost burst upward in pale plumes. Each blow left a hollow, rimmed with blue ice, as if the very earth recoiled from its touch.

"I eat," it groaned. Its claws flexed, curling like scythes. "I devour. And still I starve. Nothing fills me. No flesh. No bone. Not even the marrow of babes." As if to prove its point, it bent suddenly, scooping something half-buried in the snow — a femur, yellow and gnawed thin. With a snap like breaking firewood, it bit through the bone and sucked greedily at the splinters. Ice and gore dribbled down its chin. Morana stumbled backward, boots slipping in the drifts. Her eyes widened as she saw what littered the ground around them: bones upon bones, some animal, but many unmistakably human. Children's skulls, their jawbones cracked. Ribcages hollowed like bowls. For the Chenoo leaves no graves. It makes the earth a table, and the forest a feast.

The Chenoo howled, the sound like a thousand corpses exhaling. It lunged, claws scything the air. Morana flung herself sideways into the brush. The beast's hand smashed into the earth, shattering stone like glass.

Morana stumbled back, nearly tripping over a combination of roots hidden in snow and the remnants of the Chenoo's previous catch; a half-devoured corpse lying splayed upon the frost, its jaw still frozen open in a scream. Her hand closed instinctively on a broken branch jutting from the drift — no thicker than her wrist, stripped of bark, pale and jagged where it had broken free from a branch. She clutched it like a dagger, though she knew it would be as useless as a straw against this monster. Only later did she realize it was rowan. Her grandmother had told her such wood turned spirits, that red berries warded hunger and rot. But here it was only a stick, trembling in her fist, as pitiful as a girl's hope. Still, she clutched it, for in a fairy tale the smallest thing might be the hinge of all fates.

Stories of the Chenoo said they were once human, transformed by famine, cursed to eat endlessly and never be full. She thought of the butcher's house, of the fattening child, and understood the echo between man and monster. The Chenoo clawed at the trees as if to wrench them apart, closing the gap. His voice was a gurgling howl, not words but a sound of bottomless craving. She darted aside as his hand—massive, with nails like daggers—slammed into the earth, sending up a spray of ice and dirt.

Her belly ached with sudden hollowness. She remembered nights when food was scarce, when her grandmother rationed crusts of bread and boiled nettles into weak broth. Yet this... this was famine without end, a hunger so deep it twisted the world into meat. *Hunger is a contagion — it leaps from body to body like fire, from winter to winter like a curse. Once you smell it, you are never rid of it. Once you hear it, you begin to starve.* The Chenoo leaned close, its lips splitting in a rictus grin.

"You too will starve. One night. One winter. One snow too deep, one fire too cold... and you will eat as I ate. You will eat your blood, your kin. And then... you will be me. As it was with the first Chenoo. So too will it be with the last. Hunger always makes kin of us all." Its words struck her deeper than its claws ever could. Was this her fate? Was this the curse hidden beneath Advent's cruel delights — that joy was only ever borrowed, and hunger waited at the door?

The Chenoo lunged. She scrambled, darting into the trees, branches whipping her face. Behind her the ground shook with its steps, slow but relentless. She ran. Branches lashed her face, breath tearing her throat, until the forest itself seemed to conspire against her with twisting paths and thorns. Pausing to catch her breath, she ducked down and pressed herself against the trunk of a pine. Her lungs burned, her breath too loud. The Chenoo's shadow moved through the fog, vast, patient. She thought he had lost her — then came a low whistle, soft as a lullaby. Her grandmother's voice again, rising from the mist: "Hush now, little bird... hush, before the cold takes you." Morana gritted her teeth to keep from crying out. Her heart slammed against her ribs. The Chenoo laughed, a dry avalanche of sound, and the earth trembled. He had scented her silence as surely as he would her scream. She ran, the Chenoo followed, each stride covering three of hers. He hurled a tree trunk after her, splintering it against a boulder. Bark and ice tore into her arm. She staggered but forced her legs onward, lungs screaming. He swiped at her again, claws carving gouges into the earth. She tumbled, rolled, and crawled to her feet, only to feel his breath at her neck—hot and reeking of carrion. Always the gnawing voice carried after her: "Run, child. Run. The longer you starve me, the sweeter your marrow will taste."

It devoured as it pursued — anything, everything. A frozen hare it found beneath a log, bones snapping like kindling. A crow stiff in the branches, swallowed feathers and all. Once, with obscene eagerness, it even seemed to scoop up its own flesh, chewing noisily as black ice flaked from its skin. The Chenoo feeds on the world itself. And the world, starving, feeds on us in turn. The Chenoo fed not only to fill itself but to savour — lips smacking, tongue rasping over bone as though marrow were a delicacy, a lover's secret. Each crack of splitting cartilage rang out like a kiss reversed, obscene in its tenderness. Hunger here was not survival but voluptuous theatre, gluttony performed as sacrament. Morana gagged at the sound, yet her stomach clenched in sympathy, as if her own body yearned for that same obscene communion.

Nothing filled it.

And as she fled, Morana feared she could feel that same hunger creeping into her. Her mouth dried, her belly cramped, her bones felt light as if hollowed. The curse of famine was not only in the Chenoo but in the air itself, seeping into her, promising that she too would waste away until only the craving remained. She burst into a clearing, chest heaving, her hand still clutching the rowan: a pitiful weapon. The Chenoo stalked after, grinning with teeth black as tombstones. Its voice echoed like the moan of winter winds through hollow houses. When she finally burst into the clearing, snowlight falling over her like a shroud, she nearly collapsed. For one trembling heartbeat, she thought she had escaped. But the trees themselves groaned, and the Chenoo's head rose above them like a second moon, glowing faintly with frost. She wanted to pray, but no prayer would come. Only the remembered cadence of the Advent bells, faltering and cracked, filled her mind.

"There is no Christmas. Only hunger. Always hunger."

The words did not enter her ears so much as lodge in her bones. The forest bent with them, branches bowing as if burdened by invisible hands. She felt the syllables nest inside her marrow, gnawing, threatening to hollow her out until she too would echo their refrain. The air tasted of rust and salt. The Chenoo leaned closer, its teeth catching what little light there was, each jagged edge rimed with ice. And still it came closer, closer, its jaws stretching open to engulf her whole. The Chenoo stepped into the light. Its eyes glowed faintly blue, not with warmth but with the dead gleam of frozen lakes. Looking at this thing, she could almost believe it bore the remnants of a man: the slope of its brow, the remnants of lips that cracked and bled even as they stretched into a grotesque grin. And yet there was no humanity in the eyes, only the endless winter of the void: of hunger without ceasing. It spread its arms wide as though to embrace her. The gesture mocked the sacredness of a friend's embrace; of welcome. Snowflakes swirled between its fingers, catching in its claws like stars snared in nets. The night itself seemed to lean toward the monster, as if the dark owed it fealty.

The rowan burned cold in her palm, its edge slicing her skin until drops of blood welled bright against the white. For the length of a heartbeat, she thought she saw the droplet glow; as though even her blood rebelled at being offered to the creature. The Chenoo's nostrils flared, and it inhaled sharply, the sound like bellows feeding a forge. It smelled her blood and hungered. Its long tongue, licked once over its teeth.

She wanted to pray, but no prayer would come. In the deep recesses of her mind, Morana recalled her grandmother's voice. Her words echoing — *wood remembers, wood protects*. She raised the stick — rowan, jaggered as old broken bone, trembling in her bleeding hand. The Chenoo laughed — a hollow, rumbling echo that seemed to come from the earth itself.

"Yes. Fight me. I will taste your fear."

It lunged again — and this time, Morana did not run. She darted low, beneath its reaching claws, and with a cry half-born of despair, half of fury, she drove the rowan upward into its belly. A sound like a glacier splitting roared out. For the space of a breath between worlds, the Chenoo froze, lips trembling around a howl, then erupted in violence. Ichor burst from the wound, not warm but shockingly cold, spraying her face with frost-burn that seared as cruelly as fire. Yet mingled with that ichor came something sweet, cloying — like spilled mead, like milk long curdled. Sap bled from the wound too, amber and luminous, as though the rowan had bitten back. The Chenoo clawed at itself, tearing gashes wider, widening its own ruin in a frenzy of grotesque ecstasy. Its cries rose not like pain but like perverse delight, as if its very undoing were orgasmic, the hunger exalting in its own annihilation. For one breathless instant, Morana stood in awe, watching monster and wood embrace in their fatal dance, absurdly intimate, absurdly holy.

The Chenoo shrieked: its chest split open wider, and she glimpsed that black, frozen heart again. It pulsed violently, each beat spraying frost into the air. Morana did not know if she had wounded it, or only angered it. She swung herself behind a pine, and the Chenoo's arm shattered through it, missing her by inches. Sap sprayed like blood. The tree groaned like a wounded beast, its resin thick and golden against the snow. Morana pressed herself flat, knowing the forest itself was being torn apart in this struggle. The pine leaned, creaking, as though shielding her with its ruined body. For one heartbeat she felt less alone.

For a terrible moment, she thought the next strike would take her. But a crack thundered through the woods— the Chenoo's weight broke through a frozen hollow in the earth, dropping him waist-deep into the ground. It clawed at the edges, hauling itself upward, but the frost betrayed it: each time it gained a hold, the ice crumbled, as though even the earth too had a hunger to satisfy. The creature's rage shook the hollow wider, veins of cracks racing across the clearing like lightning frozen mid-flash. And, as the creature howled, she darted past, plunging into the thicker woods beyond, every branch a spear tearing at her arms, every root a snare for her feet.

The forest closed behind her like a thousand guardians, trunks shielding her, snow muffling her flight. Still, she heard it — the ragged bellow of the Chenoo, promising she was not free. Promising that hunger never ceased, only waited. Her lungs burned; her legs screamed. She thought of her grandmother, of the Advent candle burning small but steady. She thought of the wooden bird, and of every carving pressed into her hand as though it might one day save her. She thought of hope, frail and dangerous, but hers. And she ran, bearing it like fire through the dark.

She ran, not daring to look back, the sound of his rage echoing long after she could no longer smell his rot.

CHAPTER FOUR

THE WHITE LIES OF SNOW

The snow grew stranger the deeper Morana went. The forest changed. The pines grew closer, pressing against her path. At first it was only shadows — branches stretching too long, pools of black where there should have been silver. But soon those shadows seemed to breathe, thickening, trembling, as if something vast crouched just beyond her sight. The air throbbed with an unseen pulse, a heartbeat she could not match to her own, and the snow beneath her showed footprints — but not only hers.

Dozens. Hundreds.

Children's feet, circling, weaving into endless spirals. Some trails twisted back on themselves until they vanished. Others ended abruptly, mid-stride, as though the child had simply ceased to exist. She crouched and brushed at the prints with her bare fingers, but the snow was hard-packed, as if these steps had been stamped there over centuries. She thought she saw toes wriggling, faint impressions twitching, like the snow itself remembered how to move. Her belly cramped with gnawing emptiness, sharp enough to make her double over. It wasn't her hunger alone — she felt the Chenoo's curse gnawing inside her gut, urging her to eat, to claw, to bite. Her lips filled with the taste of marrow. She imagined tearing the thin flesh from these phantom children's hands, licking the fat from tiny ribs. The vision disgusted her, but her body quivered with need. Her breath came ragged, every exhale tasting of bone.

She pressed forward, following the faintest trace of the gift's presence — or perhaps she only imagined it. The forest offered no paths, only white and black. A child's laugh would echo in the distance, faint and high, and when she staggered after it she would find only more snow, more silence, more trees. And then she saw them. At first, they were just vague figures appearing between the trees — small outlines darting through the mist. She blinked, rubbed her eyes, and they resolved into more. Then these figures became more substantial; friends from her early school years, hands raised. Their faces were familiar, rosy-cheeked and smiling, their mittened hands waving. One beckoned, then another. They darted between the trees, always just out of reach, their giggles carrying like silver bells.

Even at a glance, something was wrong, and the longer she watched, the more wrong they became. They came in numbers, circling her; sometimes her childhood friends, sometimes a mix of child and beast, sometimes familiar faces from the village twisted by cruelty. One became the butcher's fattened boy, ribs gnawed open. Another took the form of the beggar child, mouth sewn shut with coarse thread, his hands clawing at invisible walls as he tried to scream.

Their eyes were red, always red no matter their shape; their shadows split from their feet; their laughter sharpened into something too jagged, too cruel. She blinked — and one face was her own, staring back at her from the branches.

The Ijiraq. She remembered the stories. When she had been little people had said they took children and hid them away, not in cages or chains but in the folds of the world itself, so no one could ever find them again. She doubted that was true, but you could wander a dozen steps into the forest and be lost forever, no matter how close home really was.

Her grandmother had whispered once, while stirring the stew-pot: "*The Ijiraq loves the taste of an innocent's confusion. It fattens them on their own panic, feeds on their fear until they are too hollow to find their way back. When they laugh at you, it is because you are already theirs.*"

Morana's heart thundered. The shadow-children multiplied, darting around her, calling her name in voices that slid between pitch and tone — now her grandmother's, now the village girls', now the butcher's starved child. They smiled, teeth white and gleaming. Their red eyes were too bright: too knowing. "Come this way, Morana," they chorused in her own voice. "Your gift lies this way. Do not fear."

Her body wanted to obey. Her legs moved despite her will, each step heavier in the snow. The compulsion tugged at her ribs like invisible hooks. She wanted to scream, to claw at her own skin, to stop herself — but she could not. She remembered once, as a child, when her father had dragged her by the wrist across the square while she kicked and cried. It was the same helplessness, multiplied tenfold. Each step forward felt like betrayal by her own body. The Ijiraq darted ahead, always just out of reach, face flickering—child, beggar, mother, herself. Their laughter rang in every voice she knew as they led her around trees, under bushes, and on through the snow. But no matter how many times the claimed the gift was nearby, Morana would reach the spot and find it empty of the very thing supposedly meant to be there.

The path deepened. Snow rose past her knees. Still she followed. In her heart she knew this could not be the right way, but the compulsion was a hook in her chest. Drawn on through the trees and the snow Morana entered a clearing.

The forest closed in. The birches bent, their bark peeling like skin. From between them came laughter—thin, sharp, delighted. Shadows flickered, darting just beyond her vision. A child ran past her, giggling. The Ijiraq clambered close, whispering in voices of the lost. One brushed her shoulder—its hand childlike at first, then bone-thin, talons scraping her neck. She screamed and struck out, but her fingers passed through as if through smoke.

They laughed louder, their voices shrill, until she stumbled forward, and fell to her knees. Her hands plunged into the snow—and touched bone. Skulls. Tiny finger bones. Marrow-split femurs. A circle of corpses around her—small bones half-buried in the snow, skulls cracked, tiny hands curled as if still clutching gifts that will be never opened. The bones were not fresh. Some were polished smooth as river stones; others still wet with marrow. She thought she saw scraps of ribbon, rusted buckles, a doll's jaw split open in the snow. A mitten. A shoe. A teddy bear's head gnawed hollow from within. One skull still had its hair: matted blond braids. There were far too many children to have come from one village— the forest had been eating for centuries.

No! This is a lie: it can't be real!

The illusion ripped.

As she cried out in shock, the children merged, pulling together into a single figure. One face split at the jaw, another folded sideways, bones cracking as forms knit wrong. Their skins bled into each other, voices shrieking, the sound like smoke through glass, until only one remained. The Ijiraq's truer form stood before her: human, yes, but wrong. Its eyes, still red, and its mouth ran sideways; filled with teeth that clicked like flint.

The clearing seemed to buckle and pop with the weight of its presence. Here was no mere beast of hunger like the Chenoo. The Ijiraq was something worse, something woven from treachery itself. Its body, too, might wear the cast of a person, but it was not flesh as God intended. Its sideways mouth, torn like a gash across the face, as though speech itself had been mangled at the root. Its eyes blinked mocking the human countenance, turning the gaze sideways — no truth could be met head-on, every glance a slant, every word a crookedness. It shifted its shape again to take on the form of an anthropomorphised creature of the hunt: somewhere between man and deer. The hunter and the hunted; and the hunt and that which was hunted.

Morana felt the wrongness like a sickness. This was not simply an enemy, it was a parody: of childhood laughter, of friendship, of every bond that gave shape to the village. Where the Chenoo was dreadful in its hunger, this was dreadful in its deceit. The Chenoo devoured the body, but the Ijiraq devoured trust, language, memory itself. And that theft was worse, for it left no wound that could easily be mended.

She remembered her grandmother's stern words about false oaths. "Every lie is a theft from the order of the world," the old woman had said, "for God made truth, but we, we invented lies." And here before her stood something born of the in-between, a thing twisted by its very origin — humans who strayed too far north, drawn into a no-place where death and life were confused. That confusion had become their essence, their curse, and now their weapon.

The Ijiraq's face shifted in what might have been a smile. Its teeth clicked, rows of them, not arranged for eating but for breaking words, for chewing meaning. It spoke, and its voice sounded as if it had been ripped apart and rethreaded:

"You trust, child. We trust too. But trust is a rope—strong until it frays, and then it strangles. Truth binds for a while, love binds for a while longer. But lies—ah, lies untie every knot. Lies free us. Lies are infinite. And you will weave them well."

Its words slithered through her ears like oil, coating her thoughts until they slicked against one another. She wanted to retch, for in that instant every oath she had ever sworn, every promise whispered in the dark, every prayer half-muttered before sleep seemed to curdle within her. This creature did not merely lie — it *unwove*. It thrived on the inversion of covenant, drinking from the collapse of meaning itself. Where people promised, it unpromised. Where children trusted, it mocked. Where the living spoke vows to bind their hearts together, it worked to dissolve them, knot by knot, until nothing remained but suspicion. And in that moment, she understood her grandmother's strange warnings: that living in truth was worth more than fearing death. For death, at least, was clean. Hunger was brutal, but it bore no malice. Even betrayal among men carried the stench of human frailty, the weakness of flesh. But this—this was betrayal made flesh, covenant inverted, an un-creation walking.

The creature stepped forward, and with every step the snow seemed to warp. The footprints of children twisted into spirals. Her own shadow leaned away from her, angling toward the Ijiraq as if her very being were inclined to treachery. She thought of scripture—how even angels might fall, might turn the truth itself into a snare. Yet this was fouler, for it bore not even the memory of obedience. Its red eyes gleamed as though veins of molten sin ran just beneath the surface. The red was the constant, the truth beneath the false faces. A mark of damnation, permanent and proud.

It stretched out a hand. Not to strike, not to claw, but to offer. Its fingers curled like a parent's beckoning a child. But the hand was red to the wrist, dripping though no blood fell. Morana trembled. Not from terror alone, but from the weight of moral nausea. Every instinct told her that to take that hand would be to collapse the world itself, to undo her name, her soul, her place in the order of things. The Chenoo had threatened her body, but the Ijiraq threatened her meaning.

And in that trembling instant she saw an uncomfortable truth: if God made the world by His Word, then this creature was an un-word, the crack, a blasphemy that unravelled speech itself. A thing that proved damnation was not always fire, nor claw, nor gnawing worm, but the perversion of trust, the deliberate fracture of order.

The Ijiraq tilted its head, and the forest tilted with it—as if the world's horizon were hinged to the cartilage of that sideways mouth. Its eyes blinked laterally, slow as shutters. "Trust is not kindness," it murmured. "Trust is a shortcut carved into your body by winters you don't remember. Your kind learned to live by guessing who would share the fire and who would steal it. You smile, and the other smiles; your bodies trade signals like coins. A glance is a promise, a promise is a leash, and every leash is tied to a throat. Do you see? You do not seek love. You seek *prediction*."

Snow sifted between them like falling ash.

"Reciprocity dressed as virtue," it continued. "Kin painted as holiness. Reputation polished until it blinds you to the blade. Trust is an old math done in the spinal cord: *Will this one repay? Will this one defect?* You call it goodness; I call it accounting."

The trees around them shuffled closer, trunks shouldering in like spectators at a hanging. Morana tried to speak, and what left her mouth was only fog.

"Shall we test it?" the Ijiraq whispered, withdrawing its outstretched hand. "A game. The kind your species invented when you learned the cost of believing." Its palm unfurled. "You will choose. Keep walking toward your trinket and pretend the arithmetic of goodwill still holds... or stop, and do what trust demands when it finds a cheat: *punish*."

Her chest tightened. "I won't—"

The Ijiraq raised one finger. The forest smoothed as if an iron had passed over the world. Snow became hard floorboards. Pines straightened into rafters. Warmth poured in, false and total. And Morana was standing in the village hall on a feast night, the beams lacquered with old smoke, the air shining with heat and laughter. Her grandmother ladled thick rich lamb stew. The butcher joked, his hands clean for once. Faces Morana adored and faces she feared glowed like candles. Every eye turned toward her with the sweet frankness of people who *trust* you because you trust them. The feeling hit her like a bell struck from inside her skull: **BELONGING**.

"See how they look?" the Ijiraq breathed beside her ear—though none of them seemed to notice the creature. "Their pupils widen, their faces lift. Cheap signals, fast calculations: *She is ours*. Watch."

The butcher's wife leaned in, smiling with her whole face. "We saved your portion," she said, pressing a bowl into Morana's hands. The bowl was heavy. Too heavy. Morana looked down: beneath the broth floated a string of dirty thread, a chalky button, something like a milk tooth. The liquid smelled of cloves and something unnameable. She looked up, but the woman's warmth didn't falter. "Try it," urged the voice at her ear. "This is what trust is for: to *hide* the spoilage."

Morana set the bowl down. It left a slick rim on the table like a thumbprint. Around her, laughter cracked—just a little too bright. The butcher clapped a child on the shoulder: the one they fattened. Morana had seen him fed while others were turned away. She had watched the scales tilt kindly when the customer was pretty, cruelly when he was poor. She had told herself stories to reconcile these marks: *It evens out. It must even out.* The Ijiraq's mouth shifted. "Bias is not sin in your village. Bias is the price of belonging. You know this."

The illusion flexed. Morana was suddenly outside the hall, snow crisp as linen, windows glowing like hive-cells. She peered in through the glass and saw herself inside the room, laughing, taking the bowl, swallowing. The sight revolted and relieved her in the same breath. *Thank God it is not me,* thought the part of her that still wanted the hall. *Thank God it is me,* thought the part that wanted to be done with wanting.

"Now," the Ijiraq said. "Punishment."

The scene inside the hall slowed to syrup. People's smiles lengthened a fraction too long. The butcher placed a hand on the lad's neck and guided him to a bench. An elder carved meat and tucked the best pieces onto a plate for his own. The old math moved like a tide through them: kin first, allies next, strangers late if at all. Trust braided the room into strands that excluded by design. And Morana felt the old ache—the one she never named—flares of attention when she was useful, the cold shoulder when she was not.

"You could stop them," the Ijiraq suggested lightly, as if proposing a parlour game. "Not for justice. For calibration. The cheater-detection in your blood is gnashing its teeth. It wants to correct the ledger. Call it virtue if you must. But what you crave is symmetry."

The floor under Morana's feet became the ribbed pattern of packed snow again, then floorboards, then bone, then snow, then boards—a flicker-show of matter. She swayed. The Ijiraq touched the nape of her neck with two cool fingers. "Spot one lie they tell," it said. "Say it aloud. I will show you what to do with the mouth that spoke it."

Morana's throat filled with words like gravel. *We love you; you are chosen; we are fair; we are good.* The sentences that made the world bearable. The sentences that sometimes made it worse. She closed her eyes, and behind them the hall pressed in harder. She was suddenly inside it again—no window, no distance. The bowl steamed in her hands and the thread coiled like a worm. The lad looked up at her from under his lashes with the empty patience of people taught to wait their turn forever. The elder smiled at her and slid a piece of meat to his daughter, not to the boy.

The Ijiraq's mouth brushed her temple. "Take the lad's hand," it said. "Lead him out. Not to save him. To prove to yourself you aren't what they made you. Show them what trust buys. Show them what they do. See they sacrifice their own children to their lies and deceptions. They have told these lies so long they cannot even see what is true anymore"

Her legs moved. She touched the child's wrist. His skin was hot and slightly slick with the hall's condensation. He startled; his brow pleated. She tugged him toward the door. No one stopped her. Of course they didn't. In this scene they trusted her. The irony sliced her from throat to sternum.

Out in the snow, the village sounds softened. The Ijiraq stood behind her, eyes jittering slowly side to side. "Now," it said. "Take the knife."

There was a knife in her other hand. She had not felt it arrive. Its handle was polished horn, worn by years of use, the kind that lives beside soup pots and becomes an extension of the hand. She raised it. The lad looked at her—no plea, no reproach, just the blank expectancy of someone who has learned that adults do inexplicable things. "Say the lie," the Ijiraq whispered. "Say it as you cut. Make language do what it was always for: binding and bleeding in one motion."

Morana's mouth opened. The words came. *We love you and do this for your own good.*

The blade kissed the boy's sleeve, slit cloth with a purring ease. A line appeared on his skin, faint as a hair. He gasped, more from surprise than pain. The world held its breath.

STOP.

Her body ignored her. The knife lifted again. She saw, like a hand pressing a damp page flat, an image of what would happen if she made the next cut: the hall doors banging open, the rush of feet, the room's trust collapsing, faces exploding into accusation and terror. She would not just wound a boy—she would detonate the false peace that kept them together against winter. The truth would not set anyone free; it would leave them unsheltered.

"Finish it," the Ijiraq cooed. "You think you seek justice, but you crave *control*. Admit it. In a world built on predictions, you want to be the variable. Do it. Break their calculus."

Morana's vision narrowed to a tunnel. She saw her grandmother's hands—how they shook when ladling stew for the widow who never said thank you. She saw the butcher's wife slipping rind into a child's pocket when the butcher looked away. She saw her own face on a winter morning, lying to herself with a prayer because lies and prayers can sound the same in the dark.

She put the knife to her own wrist.

The Ijiraq hissed, a cat's disgust in a man's throat. "No. Not you."

"Me," Morana said, the word small and final. "If a ledger demands blood, let it take mine first."

The blade bit. Pain returned the world to its axis with brutal efficiency. The hall vanished, snow smashed back into being, the pines reared up—honest and indifferent. Her wrist sang, a clean line of wet heat. She hadn't cut deep. But the gesture undid the trick: the Ijiraq's glamour staggered, blinked sideways, split.

It stepped back. Its skin pulsed, then dulled. For the first time, it looked disappointed: feeling that the hunt was coming to an unsatisfying conclusion. "Costly signalling," it muttered, almost to itself. "You would spend yourself to convince yourself. Old instincts. Wasteful. Terribly persuasive." Its eyes clicked shut and open. "The village would have believed you if you had cut them. You chose the one audience you cannot truly deceive."

Morana pressed her bleeding wrist against her coat. "I am not your experiment."

"Everyone is our experiment," said the Ijiraq barbed, but softly. "You live because your ancestors learned to read faces faster than lies can be spoken. We are simply the question that breaks the test: *What do you do when every face is true and false at once?*"

It took a step forward. Snow squealed under its heel. "This ends when you stop believing that trust is sacred. It's a tool. Turn it. Or it will be turned on you."

She thought of the lad's eyes, the elder's hands, the butcher's wife's pocketed mercy. She thought of threads and teeth in broth. She thought of how easy it had been to *almost* become the blade in the Ijiraq's hand.

"Not tonight," she said.

A muscle twitched in the Ijiraq's cheek. "Then I will make you a better offer." Its distorted mouth split into a smile that mimed tenderness and promised ruin. "And if you agree I will give you not only your trinket, but a way out of the forest that even the dead cannot find."

The trees leaned in, as if to hear her answer. Far off, something big moved: the world's breath holding and releasing again.

Morana did not move. The cut on her wrist throbbed in time with her pulse, a stark metronome. The Ijiraq waited, patient as erosion: a predator waiting to pounce. And for the first time since she'd encountered the Ijiraq, Morana realised that this Ijiraq enjoyed the challenge of the chase more than the catch itself and would play its twisted games whilst there was a thrill in them to drive it.

"Find me a person to betray. Any person," the Ijiraq purred, "and I will prove what you already know: trust is only a story people use to justify what you do to survive."

She stared, and in that frozen moment understood the truth: the test was never merely to refuse. It was to refuse without illusion, without claiming, or pretending, that such a refusal made her purer; innocent; better. To look at the ledger of her species' old arithmetic—every score of cruelty, every debt of pain, and admit to its long tally of hurt and calculation, and still lay the knife

THE WHITE LIES OF SNOW

down anyway. To carry the memory of all that calculation in her hands and yet choose differently. Trust had to begin somewhere. Somewhere, someone had to make the first impossible step, even if no one else saw it. Tonight, that someone was her. Her breath caught, sharp in the cold air, and her fingers trembled—not from fear, but from the weight of what it meant to act against what was expected, to gamble hope against the tally of countless wrongs. And so, she did.

"I will bring you nothing," Morana said. "And I will walk."

"Then walk," said the Ijiraq, disappointedly, *for a creature of lie cannot touch you when you are convicted in truth*; "But know this: you hunt for your gift alone."

The snow swallowed its shape as it headed off to find more delightful and enticing game.

The forest, which had been watching with bright, pitiless attention, resumed its pretending. Morana tightened the cloth around her wrist and stepped forward, the path, twisted back on itself, and unspooled in a new direction in front of her like a lie she chose to tell herself—because some lies are bridges, and it was a long, cold night to cross.

CHAPTER FIVE

THE SINGER BENEATH THE ICE

Snow cracked.

It was not a sound so much as a verdict—clean, absolute, a line drawn through the night. The wind sharpened to a knife-edge, shaving the dark into thin, glittering edges. Flakes that had fallen soft all evening suddenly came in hard sheets, each one a tiny blade. Morana raised her arm to shield her eyes, her breath scattering in ragged bursts. She forced herself forward through the battering drift, her boots sinking into snow that seemed to conspire against each step.

The trees broke, and a clearing opened up without warning. It had the geometry of a wound: a white ring of shore cut round a black oval of lake so vast it seemed the world had been sawn in half. The lake itself was an absence of stars, a mirror turned to swallow light instead of reflect it. Beyond the first skin of ice, the black went on without measure, a void poured smooth by a cruel hand. And at its centre rose the pillars. Seeking some hope of shelter Morana approached them. The closer she got; the more the storm eased.

The snow slackened to a drifting hush. The wind fell back, its teeth dulled, leaving only the sound of her own ragged breath. But the silence that opened was no mercy. It pressed at her eardrums, thick and unbearable, the way silence falls in the wake of grief:

not peace, but absence. Every crunch of her boots on the frozen crust struck her as sacrilege.

The pillars were not columns as any mason would know them. From a distance they were trunks, thick as oaks. Up close, they betrayed themselves: not solid shafts, but clusters of spear-like forms bound into single bodies, spiralled like augers, their edges catching stray light like knives. Their bases spread outward in shallow fans, as though arranged carefully on invisible tables, pinned to the earth before being drilled down through ice. It gave the impression of a display, deliberate, ceremonial: a gallery of weapons planted to keep something in place. Light seemed to live within them—threads of captured moon, seams of white fire running through blue. They rose in imperfect circles: concentric rings, uneven, drawn not with compass but by the hand of a child gripped with fevered excitement. From above, Morana thought, they would resemble the teeth of some vast and warped bear trap.

Without willing it she counted: one, two, fifteen, twenty—too many to be chance, too many to be natural. The circle was wide enough to house the nave of a cathedral. Her breath left her in a white ribbon. Between the pillars hummed a pressure, the hush of a lung held too full, a silence not empty but heavy with the weight of what it contained.

Then she saw the ice beneath them.

It was not smooth. It bulged in pale domes, each the size of a human torso, and in several places the ice had sealed around shapes that were not ice. A booted foot jutted from one swelling, the leather pierced through by an icy spindle, the sole twisted sideways as if caught mid-step. She recoiled and moved closer in the same heartbeat; dread twined with the compulsion to witness.

Hands came next. Adult hands pressed against the ice, the skin pale blue-white. Fingers splayed in gestures that might once have been prayer, or warning. A plain band of gold gleamed on one stiff finger, glinting faintly with a trapped shard of light. A wedding ring—still worn, still claimed, still clinging: a lover who never made it home.

Moving to look at another colour snagged her vision: a length of woven thread. she could make out the woven tangle of a bracelet: beads strung on faded twine; a child's friendship bracelet - the kind children knot together in promise and laughter. The bright dyes leeched and warped by ice but still visible, bright as a memory trying to hold against erasure, a little coil of red, blue, yellow, green, and purple. It circled the wrist of a hand so small it might once have belonged to a girl of ten.

Morana's throat closed. Her steps slowed, each one measured, as if to step too quickly might dishonour what lay sealed here.

Then she saw it.

At first only another pale shape caught in the ice, no different from the scraps of cloth and bone. But as she knelt, brushing frost from the surface with gloved fingers, its form grew clear: a sphere of silver, delicate, ornate, dangling tiny rings that had frozen stiff. She knew it, though she had never held one before.

A *Komsekule*.

A traditional Sámi protective amulet. Her grandmother's stories rose unbidden—of Sámi cradles and silver balls hung to guard infants against spirits. A charm of protection, given by parent or kin, swaying above a child as it slept, or carried by the grown child for protection when they walked into the world. To see it pinned here beneath the ice was unbearable. She could imagine a mother's hands fastening it, whispering prayers, never knowing this was where that protection would end. To see one here, entombed, was like stumbling on a lullaby silenced mid-note. The ball's surface was etched with delicate patterns, filigree still gleaming faintly though the cold had claimed it. The rings hung in mute silence, trapped forever from their tiny, chiming music. It had been given, or was going to be given, as a gift by someone who loved. A gift to shield, to keep safe. And now it was frozen beneath the weight of an impossible structure, useless, and powerless.

Morana pressed her hand to the ice. The cold seared through her glove, pain sharp as grief. Her breath faltered, her ribs stiffened with a kind of ache that was not entirely her own. Around her, the pillars thrummed.

A face, too. She caught her breath. A face had been swallowed whole within one of the nearest pillars, the flesh preserved in frost so that it seemed half-transparent, blurred like an insect caught in amber. Its eyes were open, gazing upward with the serenity of those who have nothing left to beg for.

Morana's mouth worked, but her voice came brittle. "The One Who Drills."

And at that naming, something moved. Not in the snow. Not in the wind. In the ice.

A tremor rippled through the black plate of the lake. At the circle's centre, the dark rose into a swell and broke— ice forcing itself up from beneath, shoulders clearing a grave. A being dragged itself upright by the rims of the nearest pillars, pale arms sliding along the blue with a sound like blades being sharpened. Hair unspooled after it, long and black and packed with frost-needles, trailing across the ice like kelp when the sea pulls back. It knelt then, facing away from Morana, head bowed as if in prayer or about to play an instrument.

"Morana..."

Her mother's voice.

Not as the voice Morana had last heard—but the voice from earliest memory, that bright bell that made even her grandmother look over with softness.

The creature lifted its head.

A woman's face took shape, corpse-white against the black. It was beautiful the way driftwood is beautiful once it has lost what it once was. The mouth smiled. The eyes were white. Not just pale—white, as if snow had been poured into them and set. The smile reclined too far across the cheeks. The head tilted and she began to sing.

The melody was low and careful, the kind of song you sing when you don't want to wake the others in the room. It sounded like a lullaby dragged under water and taught to breathe there. Notes curled around Morana's ribs and tugged, gentle as incense, patient as a mother's hand stooping to button a child's coat.

Morana slowly approached.

She stepped closer. The first step slid, the second held; the third creaked, and the sound went through her bones as if they were tuning forks. She stopped. The woman on the lake smiled— wider, as if the crack had been a compliment.

"Ikuutayuq," Morana breathed, the name falling from her lips like a mistake. The One Who Drills. The old word clicked against her teeth with a shape older than her village. It tasted like iron and old grief.

The figure glided forward, not walking so much as being carried by the ice itself.

"My child," she sang—her mouth shaping the vowel like a kiss. "You've come back."

Morana's throat closed. Her mother seemed to have been gone so long that the word "child" felt like a garment she had to forgotten how to wear. Grief flared—hot, then cold, then something past temperature altogether. She took another step; though to watch the two it would seem like watching a slow and careful circular dance over the ice. The ice cracked beneath her heel—a hairline seam that ran away from her like a startled snake.

"Careful," the Ikuutayuq murmured with a kindness that made Morana's stomach turn. "Come. Slowly. The ice is strong where I am."

It was a fact; the pillars stood like proofs. The ice around them bulged, healed thick as bone after a bad break. In those bulges lay the domes with the embedded hands, the vague swells of shoulders, the curve of a knee. Men's wrists with hair still trapped like weeds under the glaze. The slope of a woman's hip folded under the sheet. Faces mostly turned away, thank God, though every now and then the ice had captured a mouth at the exact moment breath left—lips parted, one tooth showing like a bead.

Morana kept walking. The song wound around her like a scarf pulled from behind. It smelled like pine tar and smoke and the salt of her own wrist when she'd suckled it as a child to stifle cries. She hated herself for the way her body responded. Love and grief share a doorway. The song stood in it and held out its hand.

"Do you know what lungs are?" the Ikuutayuq asked, her voice soft as fabric drawn over a cradle. "They are two rooms where love lives. Every name you have spoken, every endearment pressed into your ear, is breathed in and passes through them. They are the bellows that keep grief from going out. But when I open those rooms..." Her smile widened, pale lips stretching too far. "When I drill them open, the love flees, and all that remains is silence. The same silence that follows after grief has taken everything."

She smiled a little wider. "I like to open the rooms."

Snow gusted, though within the circle of pillars the wind lost some of its bite. The flurries curled around the ice as though unwilling to trespass too far. A sliver of frost lifted itself at the edge of the nearest pillar. It turned in the air, jittering nervously, eager as a fly. It settled back against the column and melted en pointe, leaving a tiny dimple where it had pressed. From the pillar's heart came a thin, delighted chirr—as if a drill had found the good wood.

Morana felt bile climb. "Do you see how clean it is?" the Ikuutayuq crooned, and the word clean sounded indecent on that mouth. "No blood if you do it right. You can make one hole and then another, and the body agrees with you. It yields. And when I take the lungs—ah. The breath is warm even when the person is cold. It fogs the air like a confession. That is my little joke." She leaned in slightly, like a conspirator. "I take the breath from those who will not say what they love. I eat what they would not name."

Morana tried to answer, but the song had gone into her diaphragm now, and her words broke apart into vapor. Her grandmother's warnings bucked through her head like startled deer: *Do not answer the thing that asks you to prove your love. Love proves itself by itself.* She dug her nails into her cut hand, looking for a pain her body would admit was real.

The Ikuutayuq tilted her head in that too-precise way and the whole circle seemed to incline with her, as if the pillars were listening posts angled to her attention.

"You came for a little carved promise," she said in interest. "A gift. Yes? A small object that says more than it is. Love always wants a body; it distrusts itself when it has only breath. Come. I will show you where the bodies go when breath is eaten."

She gestured. The pillars shifted, not so much moving as reauthoring their angles. Morana saw, through the translucence, lattices—fine fractures like spiderwebs, arranged in spirals. Bit-lines. The columns were augers grown from winter's bone. And under them, shallow troughs had been pressed into the ice—runnels for meltwater, grooves that guided blood had there been any to guide. The domes thickened where those grooves met, like wax pooled at the end of a candle.

Morana's chest tightened. The song pushed against her sternum from within, coaxing. Her feet slid forward and they continued their circling dance around the pillars. Everywhere she looked, the pillars contained *relationship*. Not strangers—beloveds. A husband, a mother, a friend. They were not corpses but relics, offerings devoured by the augers and displayed like trophies.

She paused mid-twirl: eyes focused on the nearest pillar: in it—grey, cloudy—like a breath captured and petrified. Something like a shoulder was laminaed into its base. On that shoulder, against the ice, rested a curl of hair. Not child hair. Dark, coarse, with two threads of silver in it. It looked so exactly like her grandmother's that Morana had to clamp her teeth together to keep from calling out.

The Ikuutayuq's face softened, as if pleased by Morana's effort not to cry. "Grief is a perfect drill," she said. "It turns without friction. You can bore through existence with it. The trick is to let the memory provide the force." She tapped one finger against the pillar and a slow vibration worked down into the lake, as if something far below had answered.

"Tell me;" the creature continued, in that tone adults use when they want information and forgiveness after betrayal, "If I open you, what shape will your love take? Will it be a prayer? A plea? A name? I am good at catching last words before they leave the mouth. Last words taste like salt and ashes and hope. Hope is very nourishing."

Morana found her voice in a whisper fugitive as fog. "You are not her."

The smile did not change. "You are not wrong. But I wear the weight that was hers, and that is often enough. When I press a pillar here—" she touched her own sternum with the gentleness of a midwife— "the ice pushes down and the body tells me where the rooms are. So I drill. Not to kill. To open. To let love out where I can catch it."

"Why?" Morana managed. "Why take what you did not make?"

The Ikuutayuq's eyes whitened further, if such a thing was possible; the pupils were not mere absence, they were light gnawed thin. "Because grief makes a sound when it leaves," she said, very simply. "And I need it to sing me awake. I was made between ice and water, where the world's breath slows and sinks. Love called me up once. Now grief keeps me here. When I stop hearing it, I sleep. When I sleep, the lake forgets it has a face and swallows itself. I would prefer not to sleep yet." She smiled again, sweetly. "It is lonely in the black. I will devour your grief, and from its breath I will spin a music that endures beyond death."

A seam in the ice at Morana's feet spread in a quiet rush. Cold reached up in a hand and wrapped her ankle. Her calf prickled; her lungs answered with a reflex to gasp. The song tightened its fingers around her ribs.

"My brother is not here tonight," the Ikuutayuq sulkily pouted. "He enjoys helping to hold the bodies still. Come, let me make a door in you. A small one. You will say what you did not say when you had the chance. You will breathe it to me and I will keep it safe. I keep such things very safe."

The wind dropped. The world listened.

Morana looked past the creature into the circle. In the far pillars lay dim silhouettes—torso here, an arm there, a profile made angelic by the distortions of ice. Rings on fingers. A locket trapped and flattened like a leaf in herbarium. People who had stepped onto the lake when the night took their names and the song offered them back.

"I loved her," Morana said. The admission burned, then cooled. "My mother. I loved her."

The Ikuutayuq's smile became tender. "Then say it to me. I will be her for the length of the breath. That is all breath is for, in the end—carrying love just far enough to be heard."

Beyond the circle, far to the left, a deep sound moved—something heavy rearranging its weight under snow. The forest held its breath; even the pines seemed to lean away from the lake. Morana heard her own heart and understood that the danger here was not teeth. It was consent. The creature had asked for it in the oldest way: with a gift that resembled a return. And love does not ask for anything in return, and Morana had listened to her grandmother tell enough fairy tales to know the truth of that.

Still, she shut her eyes, and remembered.

A meadow lifted itself whole from memory: tall grass shifting like tides under the retreating light, the horizon burning with the last gold of day. Her mother kneeling gently among the dandelions; apron heavy with yellow flowers they had spent the afternoon gathering. She straightened, yellow dust brightening the fine creases of her fingers, and delicately pressed some dandelions into Morana's small hands as if sealing a relic in a reliquary. *"When the world takes —and it will—it leaves these. Little suns. Proof love never ends. Proof you are still bound to what you've lost."* She blew, and the white seeds tore free, until the sky filled with a drifting sea of light, each one gone where no hand could follow. Her mother's laughter rose with them—bright, fierce, wild and defiant: breaking like a storm over the vast expansive field. She had looked compassionately at Morana then, *"This is what love is,"* she said. *"You cannot hold it. You give it, and the world scatters it. And grief—"* she opened their palms, empty now, seeds already vanishing into the sky— *"grief is the proof you gave it at all."* Her voice broke, and Morana carried that sound all her life. It was the only time her mother had ever let anything break in front of her

"You cannot ~~EVER~~ be her," Morana said, and opened her eyes. "Because she would not have asked that of me."

The Ikuutayuq's face subtly changed.

"Very well," she said, with a tiny tilt of her chin, gracious as a host shifting to a second course. "Then breathe for me. Breathe deep, Morana. I am fond of lungs."

She stepped closer.

Morana did the only thing she could think of that would not damn her: she refused to breathe. Her body panicked. Every animal law inside her shouted. Her vision sharpened at the edges until each pillar was a line cut with a knife. She pressed her tongue to the roof of her mouth and forced the soft palate up to seal the passage of air. She remembered her grandmother's wheeze on winter nights and mimicked the posture that had made the old woman sleep—chin tucked, ribs bound by shawl, breath barely a print on the cold.

The Ikuutayuq's song faltered and then tightened, growing needle-fine. Wind slithered back across the lake, as if hungry for the sound it had been denied. The creature's white eyes brightened in a fit of something like pique. The Ikuutayuq frowned—an almost-human crease of irritation.

"Don't be foolish," she said sweetly. Too sweetly. "If you will not give me breath, I will take it!"

She touched a pillar. The crackling whisper that lived inside it sharpened to a whine. The ice under Morana's boots quivered, then arched. A spire no thicker than a man's wrist rose inches from her toes—sleek, eager, the point of it so keen the light turned to a hairline at the very tip. It hovered as if weighing the place between her ribs. Another sprouted to her left, angling for her throat. A third quested lazily toward the notch above her hip.

Morana stepped back and the ice answered with a spire behind her ankle. The circle's nearest pillars leaned, imperceptibly but enough to be felt. The geometry of the place had put her on a lathe, and she knew she needed to get off.

"Come now," the Ikuutayuq murmured, with something that would have been compassion in a human mouth. "Do not make me do poor work. Doors should be neat. Tell me where it hurts most. I will make the first hole there."

The stupid, correct answer burned in Morana's throat: here, she wanted to say, and put her hand over the ache that had lived there since she was old enough to name absence. She had been walking toward that door since she first heard the song. Love and grief share a hinge. The One Who Drills stood with a hand on it.

She tried to run. The surface was slick, but not even; the smallest ridges grew like frost veins under her skin. Her wrists stung as she slipped and spun out onto the surface of the lake, giving her a little distance: The Ikuutayuq trailing behind. A ruthless, but practical thought snapped into place: ice breaks when it is sung to with the right kind of pressure.

Not a song. A rhythm.

She pressed once with both hands—hard—then twice, quick. Pause. Once, twice. Her grandmother's Advent bells. Not the notes; the spacing. Call and response. Not words; room for words. The pillars hummed, uncertain. Morana pressed again. Once, twice. In the village, the bells had told people when to come, when to hold, when to let go. The lake recognized the math of it; everything that freezes recognizes measure. And water, even frozen, had memory.

A crack ran—a thin, white finger sketching a line under the ice. The spire in front of her shivered, its tip losing focus. The Ikuutayuq's head canted just a fraction, and for the first time her smile looked unsustained.

"What are you doing?" she asked, pleasant still, but there was a wrinkle now—like a seam in silk that has remembered being folded.

Morana didn't answer. She pressed again, harder. Once, twice. The crack's finger curved under the surface like a fish. It intersected a seam already waiting there—like a path the lake had hoped to take if the spring came. Perhaps it was sacrilege to give it spring early. Perhaps it was mercy.

The Ikuutayuq's mouth thinned. "If you crack the circle, child, the dead will move. They will not thank you."

"Then I won't listen for thanks," Morana said, and finally let herself breathe—but in a gasp she chose, not the one the song demanded. It was ragged and ugly and human.

Morana stood and stamped. Not wildly. Rhythmically. Once, twice. The ice boomed—the sound of a cathedral accepting a tremor. The nearest pillar's light flickered; inside its blue, the milky fractures bowed and then tried to right themselves. A domed swell at the base sighed. Beneath the pillar to Morana's left, a shadow shifted—an arm, perhaps, easing because it had been told it might.

The Ikuutayuq moved then, fast as falling water. Her hand sweeping towards Morana's throat— "If you loosen them, they will remember what they loved. It will be loud. It will wake things you do not have names for."

"Then let it wake," Morana said through teeth that had gone numb with cold. "Let love be louder than you."

She drove the heel of her boot into the crack.

The circle trembled. One pillar shrieked—glass in a kiln that has been opened too soon. A white fizz went through the blue cores like lightning caught in honey. The hum turned to a chorus of exhalations. It was not pleasant. It was not beautiful. It sounded like the moment people give up the right to hold their own pain and allow it to be witnessed. It sounded like vows broken open to let their meaning out.

Ice sank and water rose. The domes at the pillars' feet bulged and burst. A hand came free—adult, mottled pale and grey. It slapped the ice once, twice, instinct without object. A shoulder tore loose. A face turned. The Ikuutayuq cried out—a sound of genuine distress. Not anger. Not thwarted appetite. Grief. For the lost order of her circle, for the neatness of her doors.

"Stop," she pleaded, and it was so naked that Morana almost did. "I keep them safe. I keep what they did not say. I keep the last breaths from being wasted on the wind."

The Ikuutayuq's eyes softened as though she had spoken a kindness. "I keep them safe," she repeated, and there was no deceit in the tone—only a hollow earnestness, like a child swearing a broken doll still breathes. Her smile, however, betrayed her: too broad, too gleeful, as though she relished not the safekeeping but the taking. Morana saw then the truth that bent beneath the words: the creature loved the cruelty, loved the cut and the silence after. It was not preservation she desired but the echo left behind, the way grief clung to air like smoke.

And yet—on another level, a shallower one, she was not lying. The Ikuutayuq had never loved, and so she had never learned how to grieve. To her, the drilled lungs, the captured breath, the fossilized tokens in ice—these were not desecrations but safeties. She could not imagine loss because she had never risked devotion. She mistook possession for protection, silence for stillness, absence for peace.

It was pity, almost, that caught in Morana's chest. The Ikuutayuq believed herself a guardian, when in truth she was only an archivist of ruin, forever mistaking theft for care.

Morana looked at the hand pressing futilely against the glaze, at the ring that clung backwards to a finger underneath, at the locket that had become a flat mirror for the white seam of her own face. "No," she said, tears burning cold. "You keep them from finishing."

The ice at the centre of the circle ruptured with a sound like a bell under the lake being struck. Water shouldered up black and immediate. The pillars nearest the break leaned and spat out shards like teeth. Something rose in the fountain—bodies. Not neatly. The lake coughed them up in knots and clumps, hands first, then arms, then the weight that dragged them. Some were held under by filaments of ice, by hair frozen to seams, by loyalty to a shape they thought the world required of them. Morana took three stumbling steps back as the water surged and crashed outward. Spray peppered her face and the droplets froze there, jewelled and vicious.

The Ikuutayuq screamed.

Not like shattering glass but like a woman who has seen her household broken and knows that what is lost was never hers to begin with. She lashed the air with her arms. Spires leapt, stabbing at nothing and everything, and then sank because the ice under them had learned a new grammar. Her song rose to a keening pitch that made Morana's teeth ache. The pillars themselves moaned—a long, low sound that did not belong to any human throat. Cracks radiated through them, turning their lovely veins into maps of ruin.

The Ikuutayuq sank downward, pulled by the weight of the dead beneath the fracture's scar. Her hair dragged, heavy with ice. The white of her eyes had dimmed to a duller frost. She looked smaller.

"Why do you care?" she asked softly, without looking up. The question held no manipulation now, only fatigue. "You came here for a little carved promise."

"I came here for love," Morana said, and surprised herself with how steady it sounded. "The gift is a path, not a prize. What you offered was an ending that looked like an answer."

"I know," Morana said. She stood, legs shaking. "I will grieve and keep walking."

Morana ran. The ice underfoot bucked; the cracks chased her shoes like playful, murderous pets. Twice she went to one knee and once she slid and caught herself on thrown edge of a toppled shard. She tasted blood and realized she had bitten her tongue. She spat a bead of blood onto the ice and it froze like a red seed.

Behind her, the Ikuutayuq's voice punched the air in broken syllables.

"Thief," she sobbed. "Thief of grief. You do not get to decide what is finished."

Morana didn't turn. "Neither do you," she said, not sure if the creature could hear her over the lake's labour. "No one does. That's what makes love unbearable and holy."

The wind came back in a rush, rude and practical, filling the space where the song had been.

She gained the rim, the safety of snow. The pillars exhaled one after another like a long line of sleepers finally turning in their beds. The forest, which had been listening with bright, pitiless attention, resumed its pretending. The ice heaved a last time and then—closed. The lake lay black and prim as a closed book. Not peace. Not repair. A truce. The hole sealed in silence, and the lake's surface smoothed itself as a face that has been crying composes its features to be seen in public.

Morana fell backward into the drift and lay there, sucking air. It hurt as it entered; it hurt as it left; it was hers. Her chest ached as if it had been drilled, and perhaps in a way it had: not by a pillar, but by the choice to make room for a sound that was not hers alone. Tears ran and froze at the edges of her eyes where her lashes met, turning the world into a soft, wet prism.

Morana pressed her palm to her sternum and felt the ache there like a new door. She didn't ask to have it closed. She walked. The night pressed on. And somewhere ahead, deeper than fear, was the gift—small, stubborn, shaped like the thing that makes grief bearable: not an answer, but a hand, warm and human, holding on.

She didn't look back again. She didn't need to. The lake would keep its dead and give others up in time according to laws that belonged to water and cold and the appetite of things that live between. The Chenoo feasted somewhere in the fog, unashamed of what it was. The Ijiraq laughed in the birches, already translating tonight into a different story. And the Ikuutayuq waited beneath, listening for the grief that would sing her awake on some other night, to someone else whose love had not learned yet how to stand without breath.

Her grandmother's words burned in her memory: *"The dark does not wander. It waits. It has many faces, and all of them are hungry."* The forest was not vast—it was endless and she knew her gift was deeper in the forest and the night was pressing on. If she did not find her gift before the sun rose, Christmas would die with her.

CHAPTER SIX

EVER THE LONG NIGHT

The forest did not sleep.

When Morana lifted her head, there was no moon, no stars, only the black lattice of branches rattling above her like the ribs of a giant beast. Her wound throbbed; the blood stiffening in the cloth marked each heartbeat as a hammer against her skull. The ache pressed her down into the frost, and for a moment she thought of her grandmother's hearth—of warmth and the crackle of fire, the smell of smoke clinging to wool. But here, the frost gnawed her bones, and the air was so still it seemed the trees themselves held their breath.

And then the silence broke.

The break was not a crack but a loosening— a thread being pulled from a woven hush. Somewhere a rime-stiff twig sighed and gave, then another, until the silence unravelled like old cloth. Snow carried breath from nowhere to nowhere, the air tasting faintly of iron and pine sap, as if the forest itself had bitten its tongue to keep from speaking. Morana felt the night rearrange around her, as a room shifts when a door opens and no one is visible in the frame.

It began with the sound of snow shifting: soft, deliberate, unhurried, padded footfalls. She thought at first it might be a deer, or perhaps the slow roll of wind across the drifts, but then the rhythm took shape—paws pressing, one after the other, steady and patient.

The forest had taught her already that anything walking without haste was dangerous.

Her grandmother had said it without looking up from her mending: "The quick burn bright and die bright; the slow eat." Morana remembered a fox she'd once watched on the meadow's rim—no rush, only patience, and then a single bite, clean as a needle. Even the river, when it froze, had not rushed; it thickened into stillness with a kind of ceremony. Out here, everything that killed wore calm like a cloak.

Her breath clung white to the air. Her hands tightened into fists, though they felt brittle as the ice around them. She listened. The sound circled before it approached, as though whatever prowled the dark already knew exactly where she stood.

A wolf stepped onto the path ahead.

Its fur was black streaked with silver, lean as hunger itself, and its eyes glowed like embers buried in ash. It did not growl. It only stared. The snow clung to its paws but melted almost at once, leaving small hollows that steamed faintly in the frozen earth.

When it spoke, its voice was not a beast's but something disturbingly close to human. Low. Resonant. Sly.

"Lost, young one?"

Morana froze.

The wolf's tongue lolled lazily, a pink ribbon brushing against its teeth. The words carried a half-smile, as though it were already tasting and savouring her name before it had ever been spoken.

"Morana."

The name wrapped around her like a chain and her blood ran colder than the snow beneath her feet. "How do you know my name?" she whispered.

Stories crowded the back of her teeth. She felt their old grammar take hold—the way a tale fits itself to a moment as a net will fit to the shape of a thrashing fish. In those hearth-lit versions, the wolf always knows the girl's name because the girl has already given it away in a hundred little ways: the tilt of her chin, the secret she intends to keep, the step off the path she is about to make. Names, her grandmother said, are doors; say them and something walks through. Morana tasted the hinge swing in her mouth and wished she could take the syllables back. Morana's pulse thudded against her throat. She had heard enough tales to know: the wolf that speaks is never only wolf. In the songs the woodcutters sang by firelight, the wolf was a shadow given hunger, a winter spirit that borrowed fur and teeth to walk among men. In the women's stories—whispered to daughters by kitchens and wells—the wolf was worse: a voice that could charm, a gaze that could promise. "Do not speak when he speaks," they warned. "Do not answer when he calls your name. To answer is already to be halfway devoured."

And yet she had answered. The moment her tongue shaped that trembling question—How do you know my name? —something had been given. She felt it now, like a thread tugged gently from her ribs, drawn into his jaws.

She told herself she would not make the next mistake. She would not step from the path, not follow the gleam of his eyes. She remembered how the butcher's wife once recited the oldest warning of all: The wolf does not always chase; sometimes he waits, sometimes he speaks, sometimes he smiles. And when he smiles, it is not kindness. It is the hook buried in the meat.

But the forest was wide, the snow deeper than her ankles, and her wound ached. She could no longer feel the tips of her fingers. She thought of the little girls in those tales—bright ribbons, red cloaks—how they, too, had sworn to be brave, and still their bones had ended in the wolf's belly. It chilled her to realize she was no different, only another child straying through the black trees with her fear shining like a lantern. And wolves were drawn to lanterns.

The stories were supposed to be warnings, charms meant to arm the listener against the dark. But what if the stories themselves were the wolf's work? What if each tale was a trap laid long before, teaching girls to imagine him, to name him, to half-expect him when the branches snapped in the night? Maybe the wolf lived longest not in the forest, but in the stories told by the fire, waiting for children to walk out into the cold already halfway devoured by dread, excitement, and anticipation.

And that is part of the problem of being in a fairytale. One never knows they are until the end.

Perhaps the first tooth the wolf ever grew was in a story. Perhaps mothers, trying to keep their children close to the fire, had shaped a mouth in the dark and it had learned to bite by being described. Warnings can become roads; repeat them enough times and feet will find the path even in night. Morana imagined a house made of told things—rafters of caution, floorboards of don't, don't, don't— and through its chimney the wolf rose like smoke, curling into whatever room a child feared most. If she lived through this, she thought, she would be careful how she warned someone. She would not give her fear a face that could learn to wear a grin.

It padded nearer, its steps unbearably slow, deliberate. The air grew warmer as it closed in, the frost receding, snow softening beneath her boots as though the beast's presence carried a furnace within it. Its breath misted in the air between them—white, heavy, animal—and she realized with a chill that her body leaned toward it, drawn in despite herself.

The wolf circled her, each paw-step careful, deliberate. It tilted its head, its grin lazy, mocking. They warned that wolves carried children's names like talismans, buried under their tongues, and when the names melted away the children were never seen again. "I know all the names of children who walk into the forest. I know the names of those who never come out again. I eat them. And when I've finished, I wear their names on my tongue until they melt away."

Its voice slid like a blade across her nerves, every word deliberate: practiced; as though it had rehearsed this moment, and lived out this perfected fantasy with a hundred children before her. The names were trophies, polished and hidden in the velvet of its mouth, worn down only by the slow acid of time. Morana felt the weight of that claim. It was not boasting—it was history. A ledger of vanished souls.

The snow creaked as it pressed closer. It circled her, every step measured, patient. It smelled of iron and wet earth. It tilted its head, almost kindly. "You're hunting something, aren't you? Some precious trinket? A toy, a box, a ribbon? Silly child-things.

Easily lost, easily taken. But I could help you." The way it smiled was worse than its teeth bared.

Morana forced herself to hold her ground. "Why would you help me?"

"Because," it purred, "you are not like the others. Others... others run. They panic. They scream. You—" it sniffed the air, deep and slow "—you have something of the frost in you already. You are sharp. Hungry. Like me. Just like me." Its tail brushed the snow. "I could teach you to survive this place. I could teach you to bite before you are bitten. All you would have to do is... give me something in return."

The words stroked her skin like claws through silk. Morana's chest ached with a pressure she didn't understand—half fear, half something else, some quiet recognition she hated: almost like a hint of desire. The forest pressed close, listening. The branches rattled above, but no wind moved them. She felt as though she stood in a cathedral where the wolf was both priest and deity, its sermon dripping poison that sounded almost like truth.

Morana was weary and distrusted the wolf; knowing something was wrong. "You think I want your flesh?" Wolf murmured, so close she felt its breath stroke her cheek. "Meat is nothing. Children are stringy things; brittle bones wrapped in fear. I could swallow ten of you and still hunger."

Its eyes caught hers, and she could not look away.

"What I want," it whispered, "is you. Not your body, well, not *just*, rather I want your yielding. The moment you choose me instead of yourself. Instead of your grandmother. Instead of the warmth of human fire. That surrender, that corruption— ah, child, it is sweeter than blood." Its tongue flicked across its teeth. "When you kneel, when you beg, when you say my name as your master—then you are more than prey. You are mine. Forever." Her grandmother had said the wolf was not beast but oath — it hunted not flesh but the moment a soul bent its knee: *An oath, once taken, remakes the taker.* Morana had watched a man in the village become small under a debt he would never name; his back bent by something without hands. Kneeling is a habit as much as an act, her grandmother said. If you practice it often enough, even your thoughts kneel before you do. The wolf wanted that first practice. It wanted her to rehearse herself into subjugation.

Morana's throat closed. She wanted to speak, to curse, to spit—but her tongue felt leaden. The wolf's breath was heat and rot, but beneath it lingered something strangely sweet, like cinnamon burned too long on iron. Her grandmother's words came back, sharp as flint: *The wolf eats more than flesh. It eats choices. It eats your spine until you kneel and never rise again.*

The wolf sat back on its haunches, looking almost domestic now, like a dog waiting for its master's command. "Your grandmother," it said softly as if it had read her thoughts. "I will need her. Give me your grandmother. Just one night. Her warmth will fade like smoke, and I will let you keep your Christmas. That is all. You will not even notice she is gone. A small price for Christmas, don't you think?"

Morana's chest tightened. Images flickered: her grandmother's hands, thin and warm; the sound of her voice reciting prayers; the way she smiled even when the world was cruel. The wolf's eyes glowed brighter. "Yes. I see her in you. She will be tender. The old ones always are."

The wolf leaned forward, muzzle almost brushing her ear, as if confiding a secret meant for her alone. "Old hearts taste of patience," it whispered. "Of love salted with years of sacrifice. They crumble soft between the teeth. They are sweeter than the young because they have suffered more." The words slithered into Morana's chest and coiled there. She imagined her grandmother's body slack, the hearth cold, Christmas devoured like marrow sucked from bone. A tremor cut through her.

Morana remembered the stories whispered by her grandmother at the fire, stories she had dismissed as shadows meant to frighten children: wolves who walked on two legs, wolves who stole brides, wolves who dressed themselves in grandmothers' nightgowns and licked their lips at the cradle. The real version of these never ended with escape. They ended with blood, or worse: with girls smiling strangely, their eyes no longer their own.

She knew, with a shiver that ran down her spine, that this was the page she had turned into. The wolf was not a chance encounter, and in such tales, any bargains that were offered, were always deadly.

Morana stepped back, horror twisting her face.

The wolf laughed—a sound like leaves snapping in frost.

"Or perhaps..." it said, circling again, brushing so close she could feel its fur graze her skirt, "perhaps I could take you. Better to be eaten now than hunted until dawn. Better to belong to me, girl, than to the things that crawl behind me in the dark: give me yourself. Say the word, and I will take you in, make you mine. You will never freeze, never starve, never fear again. You will run beside me through the centuries, crimson on your teeth, frost in your lungs. Stronger than the sun, swifter than hunger. You will be wolf." Its tail swayed, slow, deliberate. "All it costs is surrender."

The wolf brushed its muzzle along her wrist, its fur coarse: its nose cool, wet, and textured. She flinched but did not pull away, and the heat from its meaty-breath spread up her arm, threading into her chest. It laughed low, the sound almost a purr, and licked once along the bloodied cut on her hand. The tongue was rough, like stone dragged across flesh, yet the sting ran sharp into a flicker of pleasure she despised herself for feeling.

"You would be strong," it murmured. "You would be mine. There is no shame in yielding. There is only release."

Its teeth grazed her pulse. She felt them—points like needles, hovering, threatening. Though it mouthed her hand; the bite did not come. Instead, it drew back just enough to look at her, those ember-bright eyes holding hers with obscene patience. Its body towered over her now, the corded muscle visible even beneath the smoke and shadow. The scent of it filled her nostrils—musk, earth, blood, heat. It smelt like safety gone wrong—like a fire that remembers warmth but means to blister.

Her breath faltered. The wolf saw it, grinned wider, and leaned its head so its snout pressed against her throat. The hot damp of its breath made her shiver, made her hate her own shiver. Its voice rumbled against her skin, as if speaking directly into her blood.

"I could teach you hunger that never fades. Desire that consumes without ending. You would know joy sharper than knives. You would know pain sweeter than sugar. One word from you, little frost-child, and I would take you—body and soul—so completely that you would never remember you had been a girl at all."

Her knees threatened to buckle. She hated the weakness. Hated the thought that part of her longed to lean into that darkness, to vanish into it, to let it devour her and never have to ache again. The wolf's tail coiled around her ankle like a question mark, soft and unyielding. For a moment she imagined herself collapsing into its chest, teeth tearing her neck, her blood spilling onto its tongue like communion. And for a terrifying heartbeat—she wanted it.

But then her grandmother's face flickered through her mind again: those worn hands, those eyes that had never once asked her to kneel, never once demanded her surrender, only her strength. The contrast cut her like glass. The wolf's possession was heat, hunger, annihilation. Her grandmother's love was something slower, quieter, fiercer. Not possession. Not annihilation. A bond. A tether.

Morana's chest heaved. Her lips parted—but instead of a word of surrender, she forced out, "No."

The wolf stilled. Its teeth gleamed in the half-light. For a long, dreadful moment, silence stretched between them, taut as a bowstring. Then it laughed—a sound too deep, too wet, too knowing. Its tongue slipped across its fangs, savouring.

"No?" it echoed, indulgent, as if humouring a child. "You think you can deny desire? You think your body will not betray you? We shall see, little frost-child. We shall see."

Behind its words, the forest shivered. The branches rattled, the snow sank, and Morana thought she saw shapes flickering at the edge of her vision: children running on all fours, their eyes hollow, their mouths full of snow. They darted between trees but made no sound, only breathed in shallow rasps, as if their lungs were full of ash. They were the promises the wolf had kept—those who had said yes. Their teeth flashed pale. Their hair streamed wild. They looked free and broken at once.

The wolf seemed to sense the fear and certainty gathering in her, because the wolf changed tack: as wolves are want to do in fairytales. Its posture softened, shoulders sloping as though weariness had entered its bones. Its grin waned into something almost wistful. "You look at me as though I am only hunger," it murmured. "But hunger is not all. Do you think I have never been cold? Never been alone? Do you think I hunt only for myself?"

Morana frowned, wary, and said pointedly; "You said you eat names. Children."

Its tail flicked, lazy, rueful. "And yet even I must care for what is mine. Cubs, small and blind, whimpering in the hollow of the birch. Their fur thin, their bellies empty. Tell me, child, do you think the forest spares them when the frost comes?"

The wolf lowered its head until its muzzle almost touched the snow. "You frown as though I have asked for something monstrous," it whispered. "But I am not only teeth and hunger. I am father too, when I wish it. Would you like to see my children?"

The forest stirred, and from the darkness padded smaller shapes—five cubs, their fur ragged as though spun from smoke, their eyes pale with hunger. They mewled, high and plaintive, a sound that clawed at her chest in spite of herself. They pressed against their sire's flanks, and he lowered his head, nuzzling them with a gentleness at odds with the gleam of his fangs. "Alone," he murmured. "They have only me. The pack has scattered, the winter is cruel. Who will feed them if not you? A scrap of warmth, a drop of kindness—your grandmother has much to give. Think of her love poured into them, how it would keep them. Is that not better than letting it wither away in a cottage fire?"

Her breath caught. For a moment she almost saw it: a den in the roots of a black tree, small bodies curled together with her for warmth, their cries muffled against the earth. These poor helpless things. The image ached against her chest.

The wolf leaned nearer, its voice low, almost coaxing. "I have no hands to gather food. I have no fire to warm them. *You* do. You could help. A crust of bread, a strip of cloth, a little kindness for creatures more innocent than you will ever be again." Its eyes glowed dimmer now, no longer embers but coals cooling, desperate for kindling. "Would you deny a motherless brood their chance to live? Would you walk on while they starve?"

Morana reflected on what harm there could be wrapped in kindness; what harm there may be in a little mercy spent where the world was most pitiless?

"A hearth for a night," the wolf coaxed, soft as soot. "Not your grandmother—only the heat she would not miss. You, girl: lend me a coal from your coat, a spark from your breath, show me you are not cruel." Its pupils dilated, dark swallowing darker. "A small warmth, and I will remember it. I will remember you."

The promise clung to her throat like steam. To be remembered by the thing that hunted you— was that a shield or a claim? Morana could not tell. She felt her palms lift a fraction, felt the ache of giving, the old reflex that had made her share stew when there was not enough to share.

The very tiniest of the cubs, barely old enough to walk: it's little eyes only just opened, stumbled forward; resting its delicate chin on the tip of her boot. Its weight was nothing and still it weighed on her. The small jaw trembled, teeth no larger than seed pearls hidden in grey gums. A ridiculous thought rose: she could name it. She could give it a sound to answer to and in that instant the wolf would have everything it wanted— because names are leashes, no matter who holds them. She kept her mouth closed until her tongue hurt. Morana's throat ached. The wolf's grin widened. "See? Your heart stirs. You are not free of me—you are already yearning. Even in the midst of horror, you feel the bonds of affection." His voice lowered, curling like smoke in her ear. "That tug is the chain. All you need do is hold it."

Her throat tightened. Somewhere in her mind she knew— she knew—this was another snare. Wolves, in stories, lied as easily as they breathed. And yet her body remembered other small, helpless cries: even her own memory of shivering under her grandmother's quilt, feeling warmth close around her only because someone else chose not to withhold it; and the conjured wolf cubs seemed so very, very, cute.

The beast may be cruel, yes, but the cub's mewling was too sharp, too real. She saw for an instant how easy it would be to kneel, to scoop the little shadow-thing into her arms, to yield to pity and in so doing, bind herself forever. She forced her hands to remain at her sides. The wolf's tongue brushed its teeth, but it did not bare them. It waited, patient, as if certain pity would undo her more quickly than fear.

"Why?" Morana asked hoarsely. "Why show me this? Why tell me of cubs if it is only a trick?"

The wolf tilted its head, ears flicking, gaze unreadable. "Because every trick is truer than the truth. Because the forest makes all creatures liars when they wish to live. And because..." It stepped closer, voice sinking into a hush that curled in her ear. "Because even the cruellest things need tenderness once in a while. I could bite you now. I could swallow you whole. But I choose to ask. I choose to plead." Its chest brushed hers as it leaned nearer. "Is that not the mercy of a noble creature?"

Her heart slammed against her ribs. The closeness was unbearable, its fur bristling with cold, its breath damp against her cheek. She wanted to recoil, but some shameful part of her wanted to listen—to believe. To imagine herself kneeling at a den-mouth, setting scraps of bread in the snow, watching small muzzles lift, their whines softening into purrs of hunger met. A cruel thought sparked: perhaps if she fed the cubs, the wolf would leave her grandmother untouched. Perhaps kindness could buy a reprieve.

The trees stirred. From the darkness came others—wolves of smoke and shadow, eyes red, bodies flickering, unreal. They surrounded her, silent, watching. A dozen eyes glowed red. They were all as shadow, all lean, all watching. But they did not breathe. They did not blink. Morana's stomach dropped. They weren't wolves. They were shadows wearing wolf-skins. Hollow copies, conjured by the one that spoke. Her pulse beat loud enough she feared it would betray her to them, a rhythm the wolves might take for a drum summoning their feast.

The wolf padded close enough that its breath touched her cheek, hot, rank, but strangely sweet, like blood spilled on snow.

"Choose," it whispered. "Give me your grandmother, or give me yourself. Or else the forest will take both anyway, and it will not be as soft, nor gentle as I."

The circle of wolves closed in, pressing against her skin without touching. Their eyes glowed with a hunger that was not hunger, a void waiting to be filled. One lifted its head, jaws parting as though to howl, but no sound came — only a dry crackle like burning wood. Another's paw dragged across the snow, leaving no print, only a smear of darkness that spread and vanished as quickly as breath on glass. The silence they carried was not emptiness but weight, as if the forest itself leaned closer to hear her answer.

The snow beneath her feet shuddered, the ground sagging as though something buried reached up to listen. Morana could taste metal on her tongue. The wolf tilted its head, patient, eternal. Its eyes reflected small flickering images: her grandmother bent at the hearth, the cottage swallowed in frost, herself lying in the drifts with lips blue and stiff. The visions burned and dissolved with every blink, leaving her raw and unsteady, yet the wolf's gaze promised it could make them real if she faltered.

Every moment she delayed was a victory for it, because the silence around them was heavy, and silence had teeth. And both the wolf and the silence wanted a feast.

"You are already mine, frost-child. It is only a matter of time."

The shadows pressed tighter, closing the circle. The snow beneath her feet whispered with voices, sighing her name.

Morana's eyes burned. She squeezed them shut, summoning the memory of her grandmother's gaze—the look she had given before she left the cottage, the one that held warning and blessing at once. And then the Advent gift sprang to mind: a reminder of what would be lost if she failed to reclaim it before sunrise.

"NO," she said. Her voice shook, but it did not break.

No is a door too. But doors close on fingers. The forest heard her and did not forgive her for saying it. Cold returned with interest, sliding under her nails, threading her ribs with wire. Somewhere behind the trees, something that had been watching with amusement straightened, offended. The price of not kneeling was always paid in smaller coin—breath made thin, light withheld, the ground shifting a fingernail's thickness more treacherous beneath the feet. She braced her ankles and paid.

The wolf's eyes narrowed, as if surprised. Then it smiled, a slow, patient smile. Children had been told: when the wolf smiles, it is not mercy. It is patience. Hunger that will outlive them all.

And yet—for the briefest instant—the smile faltered.

It leaned so close its whisper brushed her ear.

"Then run, little frost-child. Run while you still believe you have joy ahead."

And with a rustle like collapsing ash, the wolf vanished into the night in search of more innocent prey. The shadows dissolved into nothing. The path before her groaned, reshaping itself, drawing her deeper. Shaking, Morana stumbled forward. The path beneath her feet shifted, no longer snow but ash, black and soft, hiding bones.

As she stepped, skeletal fingers clawed from beneath, clutching her ankles, whispering her name in voices that belonged to the villagers—the innkeeper, the butcher, the alderman, the children. They did not accuse; they repeated. The forest kept accounts; the wolf balanced them. Morana felt her own name tilt on the scale and set her jaw until it steadied. She could be an entry or she could be a witness. Witnesses walk.

The night stretched endless, and dawn was still far away. But Morana kept walking. For the hours kept ticking by.

EVER THE LONG NIGHT

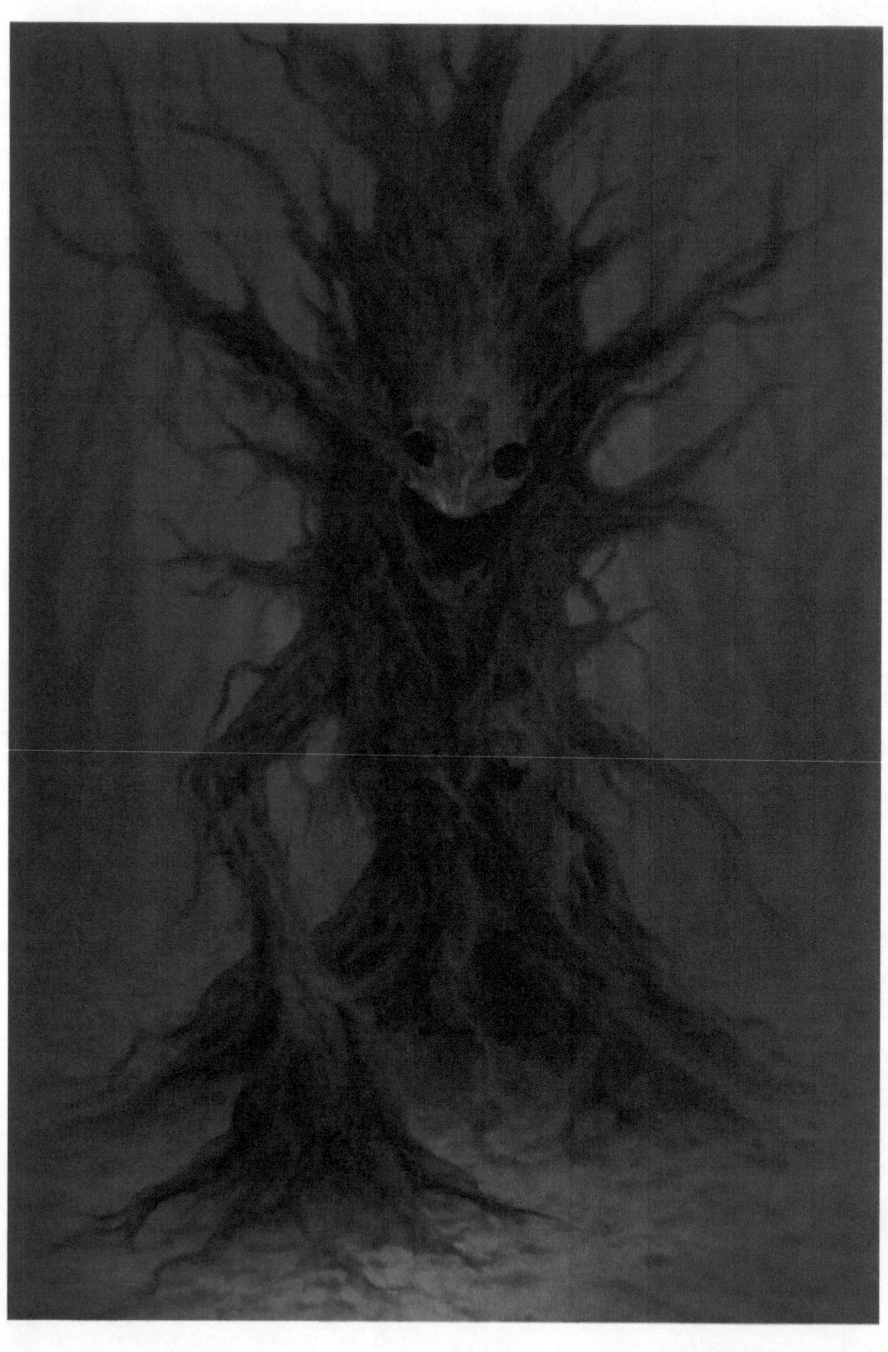

CHAPTER SEVEN

THE HOLLOWING

The forest pressed tighter, ribs closing around her.

The trunks had fused, slick and black, and when Morana laid a hand against one it pulsed beneath her palm—like flesh. The trees no longer felt like trees. They were something *different*. The damp, viscous surface of the bark slid against her skin, as though the trees themselves had a pulse, an insidious rhythm that was no longer just wood, but skin—a kind of hide, alive in its own unnatural way. The skin of something ancient, long buried beneath time, pushing its way through the earth to breathe once more.

This sound of pulse followed her, sticky and intimate, as though the trees themselves remembered being flayed. A soft, unbearable rustling—a sibilant whisper as though the forest was breathing through its roots. She reached without thinking, brushing her hand against a strip of bark that glistened too wetly. It shuddered beneath her fingers — not the tremor of wood in the cold, but a convulsion, a flinch, as if her touch were obscene. She quickly pulled her hand back: palm shining slick in the faint light; damp as though the tree had wept on her. It was no natural dampness, but a secretion—something grown from within, a corruption that clung like tar to her hand. The air smelt no longer of pine, fir, and resin: but rather something deeper and darker: of rancid pitch: sour turpentine and mould-sweet pine, a varnish-stink that clung heavy and cloying in her throat. There was a suffocating quality to it, a thick layer of decay, lingering in the air as if it was watching her breath, waiting to choke her. When she looked again at the bark, the strip she had touched twitched faintly, curling in on itself like a severed worm and made a sound — soft, sucking, obscene — the noise of flesh enjoying its own wound. For an instant she thought the tree sighed, a low moan rising from its core, as though grateful to be touched.

The forest was no longer trees at all—it was a body she had walked inside. Ribs rising like pillars, marrow hollowed into passageways, veins stretching beneath the skin of the earth. The further she moved, the closer she pressed into the cavern of this living thing—the more the trees bled shadow into her steps, until the forest, with its unbearable, pulsating veins, was all she could feel. Every step deeper was a step further into the lungs of something vast, something breathing, waiting to devour her whole.

The ground writhed beneath her boots. At first, she thought it snow, but then she saw the veins. Something deeper beneath the snowline. A pale sheet of skin stretched over the earth, thin as parchment, blue branching beneath its surface. The frost was not frost at all but a membrane. Beneath it, something moved: small fists striking upward, lips gasping soundlessly, faces pressing against the surface like flies trapped under glass. Their features slid in and out of shape like candle wax stirred by heat: eyes swelling open, lips blossoming into mouths that formed words too blurred to catch. Their cheeks flattened against the membrane as though begging for release, yet the sound they made was not only plea but invitation, coaxing. The ground wanted her to kneel, to press her own face against theirs until her breath joined their muffled chorus. Their hunger was not simply to escape — it was to draw her downward, into the press of lips and soil, until she was one with the multitude whispering beneath.

Morana. Morana. Morana.

Morana staggered back. Her knees buckled. She tried to turn away, but the voices followed, slithering into her skin, curling down her spine. They were not whispers in the air—they nested *inside* her worming through her muscles like parasites and pressing like larvae in her skull.

The more she tried to shut them out, the louder they became. The syllables tangled, elongated, as if the very night was trying to shape her differently—Morana the beloved, Morana the abandoned, Morana the devoured. Her stomach lurched; she gagged, clawing at her own throat as if she could rip the voices back out. She staggered against a trunk and it shuddered at her touch, a pulse racing under its bark. The tree groaned, a sound too low and too human, and she realised with a rush of nausea that it was laughing. Not aloud—never aloud—but through the vibration of wood: through the timber's deep grain, the laughter passed along like a hidden wire because it had her now.

The trees leaned down, their trunks splitting open along jagged seams. Faces bulged from the wood: taking on the shape of the innkeeper's daughter with her laughter rotted black; the butcher's child starved: teeth sharpened into needles; the alderman's smile splitting ear to ear until it gushed resin like pus. Each face seemed frozen in a moment of extreme terror or rage, warped by something far more ancient than them—far more sinister. They stretched too far, peeling back to expose skull, then snapping shut again, chanting. She stumbled into a clearing, gasping—and stopped.

The clearing wasn't just a place. It was an open wound in the forest's chest: ground split raw, snow clotted in its creases; soil peeled back as if clawed by a butcher of a surgeon too eager to expose what lay beneath that little care had been taken. A wound waiting to receive her, like a cavity aching for its lost organ. Above, was nothing—no moon, no stars—only a lid of ink sealed against the heavens. The dark pressed so completely that her eyes, straining, betrayed her. She saw sparks flash behind them, blue motes and orange flecks, like embers bursting in water. For a moment she thought fireflies had gathered—but no, it was her mind conjuring shapes against the void, the desperate fireworks the brain spills when no light exists at all. The deeper she looked, the more colours came: purple ripples, red shivers, an afterimage that wasn't after anything. It was not light but the nervous system burning itself alive. The dark was making a spectacle of her blindness. The dark had a taste to it—a bitter, stale metallic tang. It wasn't just absence. It was hungry.

As she blinked into the void, the world began to shift. The dark itself seemed to reach inward and cling to her, pushing at her vision until all that existed was a sea of thick shadows, layers folding over each other until she felt like she was drowning. At the centre, something was forming. Something dark. Something so deeply black it could be seen only by the fact it consumed everything else. It was not a creature, not a person, not a ghost. It was something else entirely. Out of the ground where once a tree had been felled, its severed stump black with rot, the shadows poured like sap. They thickened, congealed, and began to climb themselves into shape. Roots split and twisted upward, unfurling into legs—twisted, writhing coils of wood. The limbs stretched, the trunk thickened, branches unfurling from the joints like a nest of claws. It was not solid. It was not bark. It was not flesh. It was made of shadow. Where bark should have been smooth, the surface wept darkness, dripping tar-black shadow onto the pale ground where bones jutted like weeds. Its form was too dark to be seen fully, as though the shadows were bleeding inward and shaping themselves into something impossible. Its outline was never fixed—like something constructed from the deepest void, pulled together by the gravity of darkness. Faces swam in the bark, as if cruelty itself had scarred the tree into expression. A face, huge and gaping, split across a knot of bark, its smile wide and wrong. The alderman's eyes blinked in the grain; a child's cheek bulged like a fungus-growth on its side. Every bit of bark twisted, writhed with its own living expressions, each one a different soul, different torment.

For want of a better term Morana thought of it as a *Hollowing*.

Yet even as she saw this, the sight frayed. Each time her gaze tried to fix, the Hollowing shifted—its outline too dark, pulling all dimness toward it. It was as though the creature was drawn not of wood, nor of flesh, but of shadow condensed until it thickened into form. The trees around it bled their darkness inward, their roots pooling black at its feet, their branches bending as if to pour shadow down its spine. Where it moved, edges sharpened; where it lingered, the rest of the clearing blurred, background dissolving as though it could not survive in proximity to its hunger.

When it opened its mouth, *many voices spoke at once.*

Morana's breath locked in her chest. The sound did not belong to the air—it *coiled* within her, tight as a fist, stretching her ribs and filling her lungs with something thick, viscous, that pressed against her heart. It wasn't just noise. It was *presence*. It was something tangible, something that crawled under her skin, pushing its way into her blood. These were voices—yes—but they did not speak in language. They were the breath of the dark. The unspeakable, the unknowable. And that was where her fear began.

It raised an arm, and the branches groaned, joints splintering like timber under frost. From the knots along its boughs, new twigs thrust outward, unfurling like grasping fingers. They writhed and flexed, clawing at the air. From some, mouths gaped open in the wood-grain, splitting bark into lips; others split lengthwise to reveal hollow knots that screamed with voices of children. The sound was not carried on wind but pressed like sap through the rings of the tree, each mouth opening wider until the forest seemed full of grasping, branch-born hands, waving blindly, hungering for her. They began to *sing*—mocking rhymes she had heard from girls who had shoved her down in the snow, years ago.

The dark was not just absence. It was *hunger*. *Flesh*. A void that *wanted* her—wanted everything about her. *Everything that could be named*. "You are made of the dark," it whispered—each word a caress that tasted like tar on her tongue. "You were born from it. You cannot outrun it, little frost-child."

The words curled around her, too heavy for her body to hold. The darkness wasn't just a space—it was an entity, and now it *knew her*. It *understood* her. It had grown from her fears like a seed planted in the womb of her childhood. The longer it spoke, the darker it became, until she realised that she was losing the outline of her own hands before her face. She flexed her fingers wildly and saw nothing. The dark was eating her body, peeling away her form piece by piece until she could not swear, she existed beyond the breath rattling in her throat.

Morana's fear of the dark wasn't an ordinary fear of the dark: she was, after all willing to traverse a dark winter landscape on her own. *Normal* dark was not an issue. From an early age, the dark had been more than just a part of the night. It was the place where her mind wandered, the space between waking and dreaming where the boundaries of the world she knew ceased to exist. It wasn't about the absence of stars, the moon hidden behind clouds. It wasn't even about the cold, the chill that crawled over her skin. It was far more primal. It was the knowledge, deep within her bones, that there was *nothing* in this dark—nothing *at all*—and *that,* and what could happen *in* it terrified her. The dark that was not simply dark but *alive* with waiting. The mind fills that emptiness with everything it cannot control. It is the place where *all* things fade, including the very idea of who we are, until we become the void itself.

"Do you remember the night, Morana?" The Hollowing's voice coiled deeper into her skull, threading through the labyrinth of her mind. "The dark you hid from as a child. The closet, the cellar, the spaces where even your breath didn't belong." The Hollowing's voice twisted into a single sound: wood slamming shut.

The words hit her like icy shards of memory. The darkness pulled tight around her, and she felt it—*that sense of being utterly lost*. Her vision narrowed to a lid, a coffin-lid, the heavy chest's interior breathing with her panic. The Hollowing pulled that memory whole from deep within the dark recesses of her mind and threw it against her face. A memory of being a small child, playing in a toy room sunlight through the window fell through the window in golden shafts, warming the air. Then suddenly she was grabbed and locked away in a small dark chest: the laughter of girls—voices that had sounded innocent—turned mean as they closed the lid over her. She saw the girls' sniggering; the cruelty of children who believed the dark was only a prank. That darkness wasn't just an absence of light—it was a presence, something that gnawed at the edges of her consciousness: as if she would never see the light again. It crowded out every memory of illumination as the very darkness sought to *fill* her, to *replace* her.

She remembered the old tale they had whispered only a short while before they pressed her into the chest—a story of Nyx, the Night who rode across the sky in a chariot of black horses, her robes stitched with stars, mother of shadows and silent death. The girls had spoken of Nyx as though invoking her summoned the dark itself to take you away. Morana had thought it a bad fairytale then; but even bad fairytales can be true. As the lid slammed, it had felt as if Nyx herself had descended. She imagined the goddess' hands clutching her, dragging her down past the cold constellations, past the turning heavens, into gulfs where no star had ever burned. Of being dragged down into the great abyss at the edge of the outer darkness, where the fallen angels are bound in chains and demons are cast to gnash their teeth in silence: their cries swallowed by the black, never to escape. It was not mere storytelling that bred that terror. It was how darkness, in its absence of light, surged through her brain. She felt every nerve thunder in her skull, as though every primal fear centre of her brain was —ringing with alarm. Without light, that part of her mind ran wild, untamed, anchored only by the faintest spark of hope.

Then came the image of how one of the girls had come back and she had hoped they were going to let her out but had blocked the keyhole and blotted out the last sliver of light... It was not just the lack of light, but the absence of *safety*. The erasure of control. The suggestion that light might no longer exist anywhere. And that, more than anything, was what terrified her. And the Hollowing knew it, fed on it, and coiled around her like the lid slamming shut again.

The Hollowing's laughter sounded again, deep, hollow. *Echoing.* As though it were no longer a sound but a memory stitched together from the spaces between time.

"We know you, Morana. We know you. You are nothing but *a breath in the dark.* The dark that lives within you. You are already one with it. You always have been."

The words seethed, tangled with a thousand hidden truths, and suddenly, the darkness wasn't just around her. It was *inside her.* It was consuming her breath, pressing against her skull like a vice. Morana stumbled back, heart racing, pulse thudding in her ears. She gasped for air, but the air didn't come. It was suffocating, the space around her closing in tighter, the blackness a physical thing, clinging to her skin like a second coat. The forest, the trees, *everything*—it was all pulling inward. The walls were closing in. The darkness had *shaped itself* into this place, this nightmare, and it was holding her there, not to devour her, but to *fill her*—to swallow her whole.

"Do you hear the breathing?" the Hollowing hissed. "Do you hear the gasps, the sighs? It is the dark, Morana. It *lives* in the silence between your breaths. The dark you thought you could escape."

Morana squeezed her eyes shut. But the darkness closed in, thick and consuming, pulling her in all directions. There was no sky, no stars—nothing but the thick, suffocating air. The space around her had turned into an endless pit, and she could feel the void itself reaching for her. It was feeding on her fear, taking it in like smoke—like vapour. She could feel herself *dissolving*, becoming part of it. A chill raced down her spine as the voice continued, its words no longer just a whisper, but a low *rumble*. "Do you remember that feeling? The feeling of being trapped? A child alone in the dark, unable to move, unable to breathe—locked inside your own skin? *We have you now.*"

The Hollowing's form twisted. The darkness around her thickened, *blooming* with shadows. The space contracted, pulling everything into its centre until it felt as if her very soul was being drawn inward, sucked into the maw of the darkness. It wasn't just fear. It was annihilation. It was the knowledge that if she surrendered, if she let go for even a moment, the dark would swallow her, not as a victim, but as a vessel—*a thing* that had once been her.

Her fingers curled into fists. She fought against it, but the more she struggled, the darker the world became. She could no longer tell where she ended and the dark began. The absence was so absolute, it began to consume her thoughts, erasing everything—memories, names, *self*—until she was simply a part of the void.

"I am nothing," she whispered through cracked lips. "Nothing."

The voice laughed, cruel and sharp. "Yes. You are nothing. You are a shadow in the dark. You are what the dark makes you."

Her breath rattled in her chest. And just when it felt like the dark had consumed her entirely—just when she thought she could no longer escape—it whispered again, like a promise. "Do you know the true power of the dark, Morana? It is the emptiness. The silence."

Her stomach churned. That was the worst part— the idea of being turned into *nothingness*.

The Hollowing's form shifted once more, its limbs stretching outward, reaching for her with long, writhing arms that creaked like the bending of wood under great strain. It spread its trunk wide, and inside there was an empty hollow: a reminder of a furnace long burnt out and cold ready to swallow her whole. And Morana felt herself slipping, falling away, *into* that void feeling herself becoming nothing. In the instant she thought she would vanish she squeezed her eyes shut as tight as possible: eyes clenched shut against the black. And there, in the self-made blindness, came no void but resistance: a pinprick, fragile as a tear caught in sunlight. It wavered, flickered, threatened to go out —yet stayed. A small glimmer, a pinprick of light and a thought along with it:

If I am nothing, I cannot hold the gift of the Advent promise of the Christmas light. If I am hollow, Christmas dies.

She SAW the light.

Her breath caught as her eyes fluttered open. At first, it was nothing—just the black suffocating void pressing against her, stealing her breath. But then she saw it: faint, almost imperceptible, the smallest specks of light. They pulsed like stars in the periphery of her vision. A constellation too far away to touch, yet so familiar, so intensely needed like the sudden flare of a candle lifted high in the middle of a storm to light one's way home. And with them, the darkness began to recede, just slightly, just enough for her to catch her breath. And as the lights danced before her, she realized the truth: THE DARKNESS WAS WATCHING THE LIGHTS TOO.

The shadows, deep and stretching, slowed. They had been moving—creeping, curling, bending around her—but now they paused. The dark's hunger stilled, its gnawing pulse tempered by the strange fascination with these tiny sparks. The Hollowing's writhing limbs hesitated, its form pulling tighter, no longer shifting with the same unholy speed. The darkness itself watched, almost entranced by the dancing lights.

It was as if these small pinpricks of brightness held the answer to something long forgotten. They were no longer the flares of panic in her mind; they were something else. Something more.

Morana's mind raced back, to that recently recalled memory; flashing sharp like a lightning strike. There she was, small, huddled in the chest, terrified of the dark that closed in on her, cutting off the light. The wood had been cold and unyielding. The air stale and thick with fear, her breath shallow. She had heard them then—the muffled voices of the girls who had shoved her in, locked her away, left her to the consuming blackness. They had laughed, their voices fading as they walked away. And the one who returned. One voice in particular—the girl who had first come back to her, had not *actually* blocked the keyhole up: it was only her hand that had blotted out the last piece of light for a *moment* as she had worked on opening the lid. And lift the lid she had! How the darkness could twist perception. Morana had been shaking, the darkness pressing so tightly against her skin it felt like it would drown her. But the girl had pulled her out, her voice soft, comforting.

"It's okay," she had said, her voice trembling with an unspoken fear. "We heard you. We're here."

And then, thoughts turned to her grandmother; the flicker of a lantern that had burned so bright it seemed to conquer the darkness itself. And in the warm glow, Morana saw the night sky—a mass of clouds, but even with the clouds, the stars were still there. They had always been there, waiting for her to see them. Her grandmother whispering of the stars during the long winters, telling her how the darkness could never truly extinguish them. The dark only ever tried to hide them.

"We always have the light, child," her grandmother had said softly, that night when the fire had been put out. "You only need to look up."

In that moment, she realized the dark was not so absolute. The stars were there. Even in the darkest night, there was light. She only had to look for it. And now, the lights before her were the same. The shadows were watching them, trembling as the darkness tried to hold onto its grip, but the lights, the tiny specks of defiance, *her* specks of defiance, refused to dim.

She felt her chest tighten in a rush of something strange—a sadness that mingled with awe. Was the Hollowing simply a reflection of her own fears, her own darkness? Were the shadows simply lost too? Were they as hungry for light as she had once been?

The Hollowing stirred again, the air thickening as it moved closer, but this time, something shifted within her. She stepped forward, the light before her dancing like fragile hope, and she felt a strange power building in her chest.

The shadows recoiled, flickering with uncertainty. They reached for the lights, but they couldn't touch them. It was as if they didn't know what to do with the light. They wanted it, but they couldn't hold it, couldn't devour it.

Morana breathed deep, steadying herself. "Look up," she whispered softly, just as her grandmother had once told her. "Look up."

And for the first time since entering this forest, she raised her head, eyes straining toward the sky above. The darkness parted before her, just enough for her to see—the stars, the cold silver moonlight reflecting off the forest, the gentle glimmer of light that had always been there, waiting to be seen.

And as Morana lifted her head, the full weight of the sky pressed down on her, the dark above sprawling as wide as the void itself, yet full of something eternal, something ancient. The stars, their distant glow so sharp they almost seemed close enough to touch, glittered cold and brilliant, each one a testament to the vastness of the night, to the endlessness of the world beyond. The moon, pale and distant, threw its light across the clearing, slicing through the darkness, wrapping everything in a silvered, fragile glow. The wind had died, the only sound now was the pounding of her heart, and the slow, heavy breaths of the night itself. She had been so lost in the dark, but now, standing there beneath the sky, she remembered that the night had always held more than just emptiness—it held all of time, every spark of life that had ever flickered, every breath ever taken.

She felt her lungs expand, the breath filling her chest as she slowly, steadily, looked up to the vast heavens. And then, with the tiniest bit of power rising inside her, she whispered to the shadows that surrounded her. "Look up," she breathed, "look up."

The night sky stretched above her, a vast, inky expanse that seemed to swallow everything in its wake. The stars, countless and scattered like shimmering diamonds on black velvet, blinked softly in the cold air: burning through the veil of night. Some flared steady as judgment, some shimmered with the sly pulse of secrets, others scattered like seeds across the black soil of the cosmos. Between them ran a river of dust and flame —the old road of spirits, her grandmother would say, where the souls of the dead and old gods walked hand in hand barefoot across eternity.

They shone with an intensity that seemed to pulse, as though they were alive, each one burning with an ancient fire, their light untouchable by time. The moon, a pale crescent, hung low on the horizon, a sliver of silver light caught between the heavens and the earth. The constellations danced in their eternal patterns, silent and watchful, as if the sky itself had forgotten nothing, keeping its secrets buried in the stars. The dark was thick, but the light of the heavens poured through it like a river of ice, cutting across the shadows, reaching down in narrow beams that touched the earth with a chill that was both comforting and cruel.

For a heartbeat, the world seemed to still. The shadows, the very darkness around her, seemed to hesitate, as though it too was learning, seeing for the first time the brightness of the stars above.

Then—just for a moment, just long enough for Morana's heart to leap—she saw it. The stars flickered, their light seeming to intensify, growing just a little brighter, as though they had heard her, as though they were answering her call.

The stars looked back.

And the sky was stitched with fire.

The stars blinked once, twice, their brilliance pulsing like a heartbeat in the dark, a flash of hope that stretched across the expanse of the sky. For a moment that could not be measured in time, their light did not simply shine but leaned. They tilted downward, spilling brightness as though they had noticed her watching. It was no miracle — not the hand of any merciful god — but recognition. An old pact between those who fear the dark and those who pierce it.

Morana raised her hand, not in command but in invitation, and the shadows wavered. Their bodies, once arched to swallow her, tilted as though following the angle of her gaze. Awe rustled through them like leaves caught in wind. Some of them wept without sound. Some stretched trembling fingers toward the constellations, trying to grasp what could not be held. They were not destroyed by the sight — only silenced, re-made. She saw it clearly now: the shadows did not despise the light. They were orphans of it, cast out too long, craving the smallest glimmer to remind them they had not always been hollow.

The Hollowing's voice rumbled again, but this time, it spoke with only one voice. "You cannot escape, child. The dark will never let go."

Morana shook her head, her chest swelling with defiance. "I'm not of the dark," she said softly, but the words came with a new strength. "I am part of the light."

And the shadows wavered. They didn't quite vanish, not just yet. But they held no sway over her. She was no longer merely a wanderer in the dark, seeking to escape. She was now a force that could hold the light against them, even in the darkest of nights. The shadows—the ones that had once consumed her, that had tried to swallow her in their dark embrace—now trembled, caught in the gravity of the light, and slipped quietly back to become small shadows of the surrounding trees which now started to straighten and glow in the starlight: reaching to the sky.

And for that breath of time — brief as the fall of a star — the night was whole. The girl, the shadows, and the sky bound together in fragile stillness. Darkness was no longer the enemy but the canvas. And the light did not conquer it; it completed it. Morana's chest ached with the enormity of it, with the knowledge that she had not been devoured — not yet. Instead, she had been chosen to witness, to remember, and perhaps to teach.

And she stood there in its silence, beneath a sky that dared, for her, to burn brighter. The Hollowing still loomed. Its hunger was not gone. But it was quieter now, like a beast momentarily sated by beauty.

Morana stepped forward, her steps certain, no longer prey to the hunger of the dark. The Hollowing faltered, the void recoiling as the light gathered strength around her. The more she walked towards the rapidly shrinking creature, the brighter the light became, until the shadow could not be. The dark was not a force of inevitability. It was just a shape, a shape that could be carved, shaped, and defied. The air felt emptied, lighter — almost clean.

Almost.

For on the severed stump, still black with rot before her, a scrap of darkness still clung. Not vast, not towering, but small — no more than a trickle of shade caught in the bark's grooves. It quivered as though alive, then stretched upward against the wood, forming shapes. Figures sharpened: jagged silhouettes flickering across the stump's pale face like a screen. Little shapes cavorting. The Hollowing replayed itself in miniature — a crooked jaw, a spiked hand, lurching toward a tiny, stick-limbed girl. The shadow-girl cowered, fell, tried to rise. Morana froze. Her own terror, her flight, her trembling — it was all there, reduced to a cruel child's puppet story.

And behind the flickering shadows, a whisper threaded through the clearing: *"Yes, yes. They must see you break. Even in smallness, it is exquisite."*

The shadows warped, the girl-figure crumpling within the monster's clawed hands. Then the scene shifted — the toy chest appeared, its lid slamming shut, the little stick-limbs thrashing before the keyhole blacked out. The laughter of unseen girls scratched the silence.

Morana's stomach knotted. This wasn't memory. This was mimicry. Performance. And she did not find it funny.

The shadow bent again: the stick-girl rose, trembling, holding a frail spark in her hand — the light she had claimed. The monster shrank back, smoke unravelling. A parody of her triumph, played out for no audience but her.

Her body shook. Not from fear of the puppet-shadow, pitiful thing that it was, but from what it meant. She knew it then, with a clarity that stung like frost on bare skin: the Hollowing had never truly been a beast. Its teeth, its hunger, its voice — none of it its own. It was only the goblin's shadow, stretched and twisted until it loomed like a god. A puppet, nothing more, pulled across the trees as easily as a child's toy dragged by its string. The Hollowing had never been the hand that struck her. It had only been the mask, the prop, the stage-piece. The *real hand* was here, still, tugging even the smallest thread of shadow to make her dance.

The Advent Thief.

His presence was not vast, not looming. It was worse. It was precise. The smallness of the shadow made the cruelty sharper, more intimate — the theatre of a child tormenting a trapped insect. Every gasp she had breathed, every flinch in the dark, had been orchestrated. She was not prey in a forest. She was a puppet in a cruel play.

The shadow flickered once more, shaping itself into a little bow — a grotesque curtain-call — outline trembling: a shadow cast too far from its master. It collapsed and drained into a thread of blackness, of shadow on the ground; slithering away between two trees. And there, as the illusion tore like paper in fire, she felt it. A laugh. Low, guttural, mocking. Not from the monster's throat, but from beyond the trees themselves.

She stood there, in the clearing, breathing deeply, eyes lifted to the stars. The forest around her still whispered, still groaned under the weight of its ancient grief. But it no longer pressed in on her. It no longer sought to swallow her. The light, once a tiny glimmer in the distance, now filled the night with quiet, steady brilliance. Morana was no longer lost in the dark. The dark had become just another place—a place she could walk through, and beyond. Her body shook, no longer from terror but from the sudden crushing knowledge: *It was never real. The Hollowing was only a puppet. The true hand—the true malice—belonged to the* Advent Thief.

Somewhere deeper in the forest, unseen, it was watching her. Not with eyes, no, but with every step she took, every fear she bled into the snow—it drank them, played with them, turned them into shapes meant to break her. And she did not intend to break.

The forest was not endless after all. It was a stage. And, taking note of the direction of the retreating shadow, Morana headed onwards.

CHAPTER EIGHT

A MASQUERADE OF SHADOWS

The forest thinned and peeled away like a curtain; the trees arching back as though bowing to some long-dead sovereign: branches clawing back to reveal the carcass of a church.

The church — or what remained of one — loomed from the snow, half-swallowed by ivy and bone-pale frost. Its roof was broken: crumbled away to become rubble on the ground. Two of its grand spires had toppled; with its remaining spire splintered into the sky like a broken finger pointing to a god who had long-abandoned this world. The windows gaped, shattered glass glittering like razors in the moonlight, with its remaining stained glass sagging in shards, the saints' faces shattered. Yet its walls, split and blackened, still clung together like a skeleton too proud to collapse so that its cruciform shape remained: the shape of worship clinging to it like funeral clothes on a corpse. Its Columns leaned like drunks in prayer, their carvings long eroded: saints' faces weathered to eyeless smears.

Morana stepped across the threshold onto the flagstones, cracked and pitted with frost. The door hung crooked, rotted to a jaw of splinters. The stone beneath her boots was slick and veined with cracks that wept a slow, oily moisture. The air stank of mildew and wax left too long to rot; it smelled not of the holiness of church that Morana remembered, but of charred incense and sour wine left to clot in the chalice — faith spoiled, faith abandoned.

Beneath her boots the stones seemed to pulse faintly, as if remembering the tread of a congregation now buried in the snow. The nave stretched before her; yawning vast and hollow, ribs of stone arched above like a skeleton reaching heaven and failing; its altar smashed and toppled, its once-sacred silence heavy as a grave. Crucifixes dangled upside down, their nailed figures stretched into laughter. The tabernacle yawned wide, hollow, its insides crawling with black beetles that scurried across the host scattered on the floor — bread of God reduced to carrion. The air now smelled of damp incense, soured wine, and candle wax that had dripped and hardened and blackened until it looked more like tar than light.

Sermon books lay rotted; their pages chewed into lace by vermin. A chalice lay on its side, its rim notched as though sharpened against bone. An icon had been splintered into stakes. *This was not neglect — it was appetite.*

It was not a place abandoned by God—it was a place that had never held God at all. The congregation who once gathered here had mouthed their prayers but carried cruelty back to their tables. Their psalms had been sung without mercy, their bread broken without charity. The walls had swallowed their lies, and the stones had drunk their indifference, until sanctity itself had rotted. *This was no ruin by abandonment. This was desecration.*

Now the church sagged in shame. And yet, as she stepped deeper into its nave, it shuddered awake. And the shadows began to stretch and stir to create a ghostly image and spectacle of the past.

Along the north wall, paint began to sweat through the limewash as if the stones themselves were remembering a faith they had only pretended to hold. An image bled into view — gold leaf throttled with soot, vermilion curdled to rust. An icon; split into panels. It depicted a vision of hell from the Apocalypse of St Peter: rendered with the pitiless neatness of a ledger. A river of fire crept like molten thread, and upon its banks the punishments of h ell arranged themselves in orderly rows. The blasphemers hung by their tongues from iron hooks as long as ploughshares; their tongues were painted too large for their mouths, each muscle veined in exquisite detail. Adulterers dangled upside-down by their hair; the paint showed every strand as if a scribe had counted them, while beneath, a demon with the face of a midwife pushed a brazier closer, fanning their shame with a birch broom. Usurers were bound to millstones and dragged along the riverbed; their coin-purses hung from their necks like second throats. Those who had strangled infants or torn life from the womb sat waist-deep in a lake of gore that never stilled; the iconographer had lacquered the surface to a glassy sheen, so that candlelight made the blood seem alive. Every panel was a precise cruelty: a liturgy of punishments painted small and perfect, as though salvation itself were a tax code.

The image didn't remain still. The gold leaf breathed. The hanging bodies swayed a hair's breadth, enough to set the hooks creaking inside their tongues. Morana felt the old cold rise — that child's certainty that images could step down off walls. And then she saw it: a pin-sized cinder of shadow skittered in the corner of the panel, like a spider casting a thread. It pricked the paint, tugged a tiny lash, and a condemned figure lifted its painted head to look at her. *A stagehand's gesture. A cue.*

Opposite, another icon shouldered through the plaster — this one from the Apocalypse of St John. The great red dragon uncoiled its seven heads out of an indigo abyss, and the Beast rose out of a sea that had been rendered with lines so fine they looked stitched by rays of sunlight. The False Prophet, with a lamb's young mouth and serpent eyes, held a scroll made of smoke, its letters unwriting themselves even as they formed. Below, a lake of fire lapped its careful flames against a black shore while death and Hades were hauled like nets and cast in, just as the vision told. The painter's hell was faultlessly orthodox, yet something in the arrangement betrayed the truth. Though such imagery should have functioned as a "sermon in stone" scenes for illiterate members of populations, to assist in regulating morality and encouraging religious adherence by serving as a visual contrast between the chaos of evil and the salvation offered within the sacred space of a church, these two icons seemed to glorify in the hellscape on offer.

Choristers — or the thought of choristers — breathed behind her ear. A whisper: "We keep the letter, child, and murder the spirit." On the icon, the dragon bent its seven necks a fraction and seemed to smirk, like an actor who had nailed his blocking. The paint cracked at its lips to make the grin. Illusion upon illusion; Revelation staged like pantomime. Morana swallowed.

Even scripture, hauled onto these walls, had been pressed into a theatre of contempt.

The ghosts rose from the corners like smoke called by a hymn. The ghosts crawled first along the corners, slick as oil, rising up the ribs of the broken arches. They slithered into the cracks where saints had once stood, hollowing their features further, turning their facelessness into masks of mockery. They swelled, shaped, hardened into bodies that shimmered with both grace and grotesque. A congregation clothed in tattered velvet and smoke, their masks gleaming ivory, of porcelain — conveying the sense of a face without a soul. They swept across the stone in perfect choreography, bowing, kissing gloved hands, spinning in cruel parody of reverence.

From the choir-loft — though no bodies stood there — came the echo of a hymn. Its melody mocked the shape of songs she remembered from feast days, but its words were a scalding reversal. Two verses rang clear enough to pierce her skull:

"Blessèd the hollow, the empty, the dead,

for dust is their kingdom, the bones are their bread.

Blessèd the famished who drink from the grave,

for thirst shall not leave them, nor hope shall they save."

And then:

"Cursèd the morning, and cursèd the dawn,

may eyes all be blinded, and sight be withdrawn.

Praise to the hunger, and praise to decay,

praise to the fire that strips form away."

Each syllable slithered like spiders across her skin. The congregation swayed, their lips shaping the words as if they had always known them. It was not simply song but the oldest style of spell, binding the air to the manifestation.

Morana's breath hitched. It was a mass. A mass turned inside out. Except for eight of the phantasms, the rest knelt and bowed as though in prayer, yet every gesture was a deliberate parody. The prayers they prayed were like no prayers she had ever heard — they were petitional confessions in praise of sin.

The first one to speak was a woman. She stood, legs spread wide swaying and gyrating her hips. Her garments in tatters as if shredded by the rough hands of a crowd; her skin crawling with old bruises and fresh scratches. Her lips were sewn into a permanent smile with wire, bleeding at the corners as her tongue worked desperately between the stitches, mouthing each syllable with wet reverence. Her voice quavered like a lover's moan and a corpse's sigh, low and aching:

"*O holy flesh, I confess my thirst for bodies unending. Let me drink the sweat of strangers, let me crawl on the bellies of beasts, let me be torn open again and again, until the marrow itself runs slick. Blessed be the thrust, the bite, the rut. Blessed be the shame that drips from me like baptism. I beg you, Lust — drown me deeper in the red flood, until no mouth is left unstained.*"

And as she rocked, her wire-stitched grin snapped, one corner tearing wider, and she laughed through the blood.

The second was more a mound than a man: swollen to bursting, the seams of his skin stretched and shiny as though each breath might split him. Grease slicked his chest, dribbled down into the folds of his gut. He clutched a gnawed bone in both hands like a crucifix, trembling, gnawing even as he tried to speak, his words muffled by the meat still jammed in his cheeks. His voice gurgled, half prayer, half choking and vomiting out:

"*O banquet eternal, I confess my hunger is my god. I praise the dripping fat that baptizes my tongue, I worship the salt that burns my lips raw. Let the bellies of the poor collapse — what is their hunger to me, when I am made holy by excess? Let me glut until my bowels weep, let me feast until my teeth fall loose. Fill me, O Lord of Swallowing, until my stomach splits and I am laid open like an offering, steaming and sweet.*"

As bile ran down his chin, he licked it with trembling devotion, eyes rolled white as though in rapture.

The third supplicant was thin, brittle as parchment; standing rigid, hunched forward as though his spine were hooked by invisible strings. Rings glittered on every finger, some so tight the flesh bulged purple around them. His clothes seemed to be made not of cloth but sewn from property deeds and promissory notes. In both fists he clutched handfuls of money and bone trinkets. As he prayed, the tremor of his hands made coins spill through his fingers, raining in dull splashes across the stone floor. Each time one fell, his prayer broke for a gasp, and he stooped low, scrabbling at the ground with clawing fingers to reclaim it, pressing the coin to his lips before resuming:

"Keeper of Treasures, I am your faithful servant. I bind oaths in silver; I twist truth into chains of gold. I have betrayed my brother, sold my blood, counted even the breath of my children as debt. I have lied to widows, cheated the starving, built shrines from the bones of the deceived. And still, it is not enough. Let mercy rot; let pity starve. Give me more to clutch, more to bleed from others' hands into mine. Every jewel, every oath, every scream — let it glitter in my keeping."

And as his voice faltered, he let the coins in his left hand scatter deliberately across the ground — only to hurl himself upon them like an animal, gathering each one with sobbing gasps, pressing their cold edges against his bloodied lips in a litany of worship.

The fourth was a figure slumped against the wall, though it was clear they had not simply chosen to rest there — they remained melted into it. The flesh, where visible, seemed to sag and run, folds of skin sliding downward as if gravity itself had grown cruel. Eyelids drooped halfway shut, lashes matted with pus. Every breath rattled like a slow, rusted chain being dragged. Cobwebs clung to hair and shoulders as though they had remained in that posture for years. Maggots fattened in the cracks between fingers. Flies stirred in the open mouth, drifting lazily with each exhale. The prayer was not spoken but exhaled, drawn out in languid moans that slurred one into the other, a grotesque lullaby:

"O Keeper of Stillness, I offer you my body unmade by will. I have left fields barren, children untended, oaths undone. I have let rooves fall and fires die, let the sick rot where they lay. I shun the weight of duty — let others carry it and be broken. I ask only that I never rise, never labour, never care. Bind me to my sweet paralysis. Smother every calling, silence every cry for help. Give me death stretched thin into life eternal, and let me rot in your blessed idleness."

When the confessional prayer finished, the figure tried to lift a mottled hand, but the weight of it seemed impossible — the arm trembled in the air, barely raised, as if that paltry movement itself were a sacred rite. They were broken by the effort. The silence after his faltering prayer held only the soft drone of flies. Then came the scrape of bare feet shifting on stone. The fifth, a woman stepped forward from the gloom — taller than the rest, shoulders hunched as though every muscle in her body were knotted with fury. Her breath rasped through clenched teeth, a wet hiss like steam off iron.

She lifted her arms, the skin scrawled with bruises old and new, and addressed the air in a voice like broken glass.

"O Wrath, sanctify me in flame. Let me be your vessel — every insult, every trespass, every betrayal carved into me like scripture. They said forgive. They said submit. But you, holy Wrath, teach me the only true gospel: strike, and strike again, until bone remembers what flesh forgets."

She wheeled suddenly; the prayer transmuted into action. With a crack of motion her hand lashed out and caught the slumping supplicant beside her — the mottled figure of Sloth — across the skull. The sound rang like a club against rotten fruit. His arm, still trembling in midair, collapsed at once, and his whole body sagged sideways. He slid down the wall and spilled onto the stones, a heap of flesh too lazy now even to resist, a puddle of breath and meat that barely twitched. The woman loomed over him, her eyes two black pits brimming with rage. She pressed her bleeding knuckles to her lips and whispered the end of her prayer:

"Let me never forgive, O Wrath. Let me be the lash of your hand, the scream in your throat. Amen."

A woman stood swaying, the sixth of the figures; her skin gleaming with a mirrored sheen, smooth as polished glass. She was dazzling in the half-light, reflecting back fragments of those around her: the curve of a lip, the glimmer of a jewelled earring, the warm gold of a purse tucked too close to the hip. To look at her was to see oneself—improved, perfected, tantalizingly out of reach. Her voice quavered in prayer, half-whisper, half-hiss.

"O Envy, sweet thief of joy, let me drink their beauty, let me wear their charms. Why should they shine while I stand in shadow? Take their finery for me, take their laughter, take their love."

She leaned forward, her eyes darting to the purses and trinkets that bulged beneath cloaks and belts, her breath quickening at each glimpse of hidden wealth. She raised one hand to her arm, scratching—no, scoring. Her nails grated against her glass-slick skin, releasing a shrill cry like windowpane breaking. Fine cracks spread across her flesh, catching the light like sequinned fractures. And still she whispered: *"Let me bleed their riches, split their glass, and let their ruin gleam upon me."*

The seventh began a small stride as if clothed in ermine. She was short, almost childlike in stature, though she carried herself with the swollen grandeur of a queen. An old potato sack hung from her shoulders, stitched over and over with gaudy trims of gold thread. The sack gaped in places, revealing her thin legs. Her face was worse: a mask of cracked porcelain, fragments mismatched and glued together into a semblance of features. A lip too wide, a cheekbone from another doll, a forehead painted with faint blue veins. When she turned, the fractures caught the light, as though a hundred faces strained to make one.

Atop her head sat a paper crown from a Christmas bon-bon, sagging and torn, yet worn as if it were hammered gold. She lifted her chin, her voice sharp with haughty delight.

"See me, adore me! I am the summit of all sins. Lust writhes at my ankles, begging for a glance. Gluttony fattens only to feed my table. Avarice counts my treasures, yet they are mine by right. Sloth lies beneath me, too weak to rise when I command. Wrath rages, but her fury only crowns my glory. Envy gazes into my shards and finds only her own reflection. Yes—yes! All are lesser, all are my servants. For I am Pride, Vainglory, the jewel above them all. I wear scraps as sovereign raiment, paper as gold, and still you kneel. I am the face in every mirror, the crown upon every head. Worship me, and despair—for there is no throne but mine!"

The air reeked of their zealotry, and each word fell like oil upon the fire of Morana's unease. Then another voice — old, cracked — spoke words that froze her marrow. It was a prayer not to the seven sins she recognised from old sermons, but to one beyond them: Acedia. He stood apart, a man of average height; a crude demon's mask slumped over his face, one horn snapped, the other gnawed blunt; the paint flaked like leprous skin. It dangled crooked on his cheek, showing a pale lidless eye beneath, dull and wet as a fish's. His robe was a heap of grey rags, sodden at the hem, trailing streaks of mildew across the stones. His voice crawled out of him like a cough, every word a desecration of prayer:

"Let the houses rot, their beams sinking into the earth. Let the wombs dry and the children whimper unheard. I will not lift a finger. The goodness of life is a trick, a banquet for others. I spit it back, bitter, sour. Let hunger hollow them. Let fires burn without water to quench. I will watch, unmoved, as the world drowns in its own filth. For I will not care. I will not rise. I will not want."

The congregation kissed the ground and stood as from the loft, organ pipes groaned —a shuddering wheeze as if the instrument itself were suffocating. A song uncoiled — tune familiar, words reversed, like a river running uphill. It kept to two verses, the way a cruel joke keeps to brevity so it can be told again:

"Rejoice, ye unbegotten, whose cradles none will keep;

for silence is thy shepherd, and cold thy only sleep.

No angels sing above thee; no star will mark thy head;

the Word shall not be spoken — let flesh remain unfed."

And:

"O come, thou sweet Unmeaning, thou Comfort of the numb;

unmake our thorny longing, and leave our pulses dumb.

Unlight the lamps of vigil, un-ring the matin bell,

and teach our lips this blessing: 'It is enough to dwell."

The hymn ended as if disappointed in itself and passed into a procession. Four acolytes — or the memory of acolytes — came jerking down the aisle with thuribles that smoked not frankincense but the boiled sweetness of rotting fruit. Behind them, bearers shouldered reliquaries that were nothing but locked boxes with labels: "THE PATIENCE WE MEANT TO SHOW," "THE APOLOGY NEVER SENT," "THE CHILD NOT LIFTED." They paraded neglect as sacrament. Each reliquary's surface caught Morana's reflection and returned her someone else — smaller, falser.

At stations chalked on the stone, the procession halted for little dramas — not Stations of the Cross, but Stations of Abandonment. At the first, a cradle was set upon a pedestal. A robed figure approached, hands raised in benediction, and kept them hovering there — that was the whole rite — blessing withheld with perfect form. The congregation sighed in pleasure. At the second, a man with a ledger wrote names with a quill that had no nib; the empty flourish left a trench in the paper and blotted nobody into the book. At the third, a bride was presented at an altar of ice; the groom lifted her veil and turned his head aside with courtly grace, a choreography of refusal so exact it earned applause.

Everything was correct. That correctness was part of its filthiness. The rubrics were kept while the meaning bled out. It was church done by the Advent Thief's hand — a cruelty that takes its conferences seriously. Morana felt fury rise sharp as iron, not only at the horrors, but at their tidiness.

Yet the congregation processed, twirling down the aisles, cloaks snapping like whips in the stale air. They pressed their masked faces together, grinding enamel against enamel until flecks of blood and bone dust spattered their chins. They smeared one another's flesh with shadow made thick as oil, anointing not with blessing but with blight. At the nave's heart stood a font, its basin borne on the backs of diminutive saints carved in stone, their faces twisted as they strained beneath a crushing, invisible yoke. "DEBAPTISM," they sighed, queuing with reverence. One by one they stooped, bent their heads, and touched the dry, empty cistern. When they turned away, they seemed not cleansed but diminished — as if some fragment of soul had indeed been scraped off and left behind.

The priest emerged and took his place in the sanctuary. His vestments dragged along the floor like flayed skin, stitched together with strands of rosary beads.

He lifted both hands for silence. His mouth worked, and the sermon slid out — polished, practiced, a lie with footnotes.

"Beloved in the tomb," he began, "you have heard it said that there shall be peace on earth and a feast prepared in the presence of enemies. But I tell you, the only feast is the feast of now and no peace will be found. You have heard of a child wrapped in swaddling clothes; yet see here the truer nativity, the birth of Nothing through whom all things are unmade. You have heard of a lake that burns with fire; behold our cooler blessing—the lake that forgets. Plunge and no memory will follow." The priest gestured behind him. Where the alter should have been, a manger now stood, built crudely from splintered pews, lined not with hay but with strips of pale skin that curled at the edges like parchment. Within it lay an infant—or the suggestion of one—sculpted from shadow and ash. Its mouth gaped open, wider, wider still, until its face was only a black cavern. From that cavern came a sound: the wail of a newborn. Not hunger. Not life. But abandonment. Cries for a mother who never comes. For arms that never open. For a God who never answers.

It was like a lullaby seeped out; played backward, each note dripping with wrongness. It conjured images in Morana's head. It was the sound of children abandoned in their beds, calling for parents who never came. It was the thin, keening plea of arms outstretched to be lifted, to be held, to be loved—and met only with cold shoulders and the turn of a head. The air thickened with the ache of countless forsaken voices. The sound pierced Morana more deeply than any scream, for it was not rage, but yearning.

The congregation moved to gather around it; throats rotten with laughter. They sang carols in broken voices, but the words twisted, bent into curses: "*O come, O come...*" turned into something that gnawed at the edges of Morana's mind, promising not salvation and peace; but torture and death. The priest opened a tattered book and ran one finger down an invisible column. "The dragon is cast down," he intoned mildly, "therefore rejoice." He looked up, smiling. "Consider, children, that the dragon is not in a prison but lives here free and in the hearts of the mundane. The abyss is an interior place. Attend to your duties of omission. The Beast requires only maintenance for the abyss is here."

Laughter — soft, cultured. He inclined his head to the icons, then to the manger where the shadow-child lay keening its motherless note. "Even the Teacher said to Judas in the Gospel according to Judas: *you will exceed them all, for you will abandon what they cherish.* And was it not written that the others slept while he bore the weight? Why then should we not sleep also, and call it holy? To neglect is to follow the narrow way. To abandon is the truest obedience. Salvation is such weight: neglect is a pillow." He closed the book with a kiss and the smack of his lips sounded like two pieces of meat meeting. "Take up your rest and follow me."

"Here ends the lesson."

The congregation sighed Amen. The priest resumed: "Let the faithful now affirm the Creed of the Body's Undoing." And so, they did, reciting a catechism built from perfect sentences that meant precisely nothing.

THE GOBLIN OF ADVENT

"What is man?"

"*A gap between two silences.*"

"What is love?"

"*A fever that burns work.*"

"What is hope?"

"*A debt not worth collecting.*"

"What then must we do?"

"*We must do nothing.*"

A murmur of approval slid from nave to narthex. Morana wanted to laugh — not at the obscenity, but at the production values. Even their heresy wore lace and kept the calendar.

One figure, draped in crimson tatters, approached the manger with a gift. Not frankincense, nor myrrh, nor gold — but a severed lamb's head, its wool scorched away, eyes still wet. He bowed, presenting it with reverence. Another staggered forward with a bundle in her arms: a child's corpse, porcelain-white and stiff, dressed in bridal lace. She bent low, pressed its blue lips to the shadow-infant's gaping mouth, and when she drew back the corpse was hollowed — emptied, as though it had been promised love, promised welcome, and instead consumed. The congregation laughed. The ruined rafters shook. Candles lined the aisles, but their wax was tallow, dripping fat that spattered onto the stones, hissing: burning with and eerie blue light. They screamed theirs *Glorias* and *Hosannas*, but each word curdled into agony: they chanted their rejections in whisper: "You are not wanted. You are not chosen. You will never be held." Each word landing like a nail driven into soft flesh; becoming blasphemous exaltation.

At the centre, beside the shadow-child's manger, stood a mock Madonna - Mary's desecrated opposite. She was everything the Virgin was not — and everything the Virgin might have been had grace curdled into malice. Her body was a cathedral of inversions. Where the Virgin had been clothed with the sun with robes woven of heaven's light; this one was clothed with skins — flayed garments still trembling with nerves, stitched together with the veins of unborn infants. Around her shoulders a mantle of funeral veils, stitched from stillborn shrouds: heavy with mold and bloodstains. Where Mary's body had borne life, hers bore only mutilation and the grave: her lower abdomen devoid of flesh and her womb yawning open, stitched crudely shut with rosary beads pulled so tight that flesh had ruptured around them, suppurating. A mock pregnancy bulged beneath, its skin translucent — not with child but with rats, writhing in her belly, their teeth gnashing at the walls of her flesh: and where this had been rent, umbilical cords spilled out, dangling and shrivelling, grasping blindly at nothing.

Upon her head was no crown of stars but a circlet of nails hammered into her scalp, pinning her thoughts into permanent torment. Her hair, matted with blood, hung in ropes across her face. Her hands, raised as though in blessing, were each missing their palms: only holes remained, ringed with teeth, mouths that gnawed ceaselessly. Her eyes had been gouged and replaced with mirrors, so that when the congregation looked upon her, they saw not her face but only their own ruin reflected back. She rocked the manger gently, crooning in a voice that was not voice at all but the shriek of winter wind through hollow bones. It was not a lullaby, but a dirge of negation — words that peeled meaning from sound, so that language itself bled away. Instead of lifting the little babe, she instead lifted a member of the congregation to her breast. Where the Virgin gave milk, this parody gave only fetid pus and bile. The worshipper suckled with desperate fervour, retching as they swallowed, and when they collapsed foaming, she crooned to them gently: "Yes, little one. Love tastes of rot."

The shadow-infant writhed in its manger, its mouth stretching wide enough to swallow its own head, its cries not of hunger but of forsakenness: the eternal wail of the unloved. The Anti-Madonna leaned low, cooing sweetly. "Do you think you were chosen? No. You are the proof of abandonment. Your Father never came. Your Mother never wanted you. Cry louder, child. Cry the truth." The congregation shrieked in ecstasy, echoing the infant's sobs with their own. They tore their garments, their skin, their throats, crying not for food but to be denied, to be excluded, to be cast aside as holy.

Where the Virgin intercedes for her children before God, this Madonna interceded only to betray them. She beckoned one woman forward, who fell at her knees, begging to be remembered, to be loved. With infinite tenderness, the Anti-Madonna cupped her face — then whispered: "*I forget you.*" And the woman's body collapsed into dust, her soul erased with a word. The congregation screamed praise at the miracle of neglect. Another she cradled in her arms, rocking them like a mother to her child. But her lullaby was not comfort. It was command. "Die unloved. Die unseen. Die unheard. This is holiness. This is truth." And the body obeyed, seizing and snapping in her embrace like a doll whose strings had been cut.

This Madonna was the absence of comfort itself, the eternal refusal to lift the child from the cold. *This was no Virgin. This was a womb emptied of grace, filled instead with the joy of mockery.* Every act was an inversion of Mary's mercy. Where the Virgin consoles, this Madonna abandoned; and where the Virgin magnified love, this one magnified emptiness. She was *Mater Tenebrarum*: Mother of Shadows, of Neglect, of Nothing. The manger shook. The infant's scream became a chorus of the forsaken, a litany of absence: "No Mother. No Father. No Love. No God. No Word made flesh. Only flesh made void."

Morana's stomach heaved. Every element of faith she had ever known — the candle, the carol, the manger, the child — here they were again, but *inverted*, stripped of meaning, refashioned into weapons of cruelty.

THE GOBLIN OF ADVENT

This was Christmas undone.

This was Anti-Christmas.

This was the birth of absence.

"And now," the priest purred, "the Kiss of Peace." He spread his arms. The congregation leaned toward one another, and each gave the other the courtesy of turning away. The gesture was practiced, synchronized, a *corps de ballet* devoted to refusal. All those small, fine movements — gloved hands pausing in air, lips withdrawing from touch — made a new ache climb Morana's throat. The malice here was not violence; it was withholding.

The communion came next.

As the congregation bent forward, the whole nave shifted — not with holiness, but with stagecraft. A curtain of soot unrolled from the clerestory as if pulled by hidden hands; it fell just short of the flagstones, swaying like a theatre scrim. Behind it, Morana glimpsed silhouettes: it was one crooked little figure tiptoeing with coils of cord, tightening knots, tugging at pulleys. It crouched to chalk symbols on the stones — cues, arrows, and timing marks like those scratched on a stage floor to guide actors where to stand. Its motions were efficient, brisk, and entirely without devotion.

The priest extended his arms again, but Morana could see the strings now: two taut lines running from his sleeves into the dark above, where the small shade kept them in rhythm. When he raised his arm in benediction, the string tightened. When he bowed, it slackened. The tiny thing's head cocked sideways, listening for cues only it could hear. Every gesture of blessing was puppetry. Every bow was pulled on cue. The Advent Thief's shadow pulling the strings. The solemnity was only choreography, devout as clockwork. She thought of the icons — hell in neat rows, dragons wearing candle-caps — and saw the same hand here, dressing blasphemy in vestments in order that it might pass for liturgy. Then the curtain drew back a fraction, as though for a change of scene, and she realised that if not careful even a real Mass became but a parody play: actors smiling piously behind masks, testing steps, bowing to invisible marks. A second later the illusion sealed itself again, polished into "sacrament." The priest's voice rang out, as confident as an actor at his cue.

First the feast. Tables rose from the nave itself, pulled from the floor by grasping hands of shadow. Platters clattered into place: roasted infants stuffed with black feathers; loaves that, when torn, bled thickly onto the stones; sweetmeats writhing, each bite a squirm of maggots. They ate with wild abandon, masks shattering as teeth tore flesh.

"Blessed is the flesh that yields without end,

blessed the feast that devours its friend.

Blessed the lips that drink of despair,

blessed the altar that binds us there."

The priest lifted the chalice. It brimmed not with wine, but with a thick black ichor, tar-bright and crawling with shapes too small to name. One by one, the congregation approached. They did not sip. They plunged their hands into it, smearing themselves, daubing sigils across their own flesh and one another's, writhing as though each stroke were both agony and ecstasy. And with each stroke, they whispered not blessings, but cruelties: "You are not wanted. You are not chosen. You are forgotten." Each word landed like rejection itself, branded into flesh. Their chorus rose into a *Gloria* that was only grief, a *Hosanna* which howled of abandonment.

The priest, closing his hands intoned; "Kneel, for the feast of denial."

A draft stole across the scene, smelling of snow and causing the candles to gutter. The icons sighed. Somewhere in the rafters, a small shadow shifted a pulley — she heard the creak — and the spell's velvet sag tugged just enough for thought to return. She did not sit. She took a step back and the congregation hissed as if she had refused hospitality.

The scent became unbearable — incense soured to rot, iron-rich blood, and something sweeter: the cloying reek of decay dressed as perfume.

Morana clutched her chest, gagging. *This was worship inverted. This was faith gutted and worn like a mask.*

The priest's hollow eyes fell upon her. His sockets were pits lined with worms, yet he smiled as if she were his most beloved parishioner. Lifting the gore-slick chalice, he stretched his hand toward her.

"Come, child," he intoned, his voice a liturgy woven from hunger. "Do not resist the feast. Drink. Take your place at the table of the true nativity. Do not resist what you have always known. You were never chosen by them. You were never held, never loved. But here — here you may be embraced in the only way that is true: abandoned together. Join us, and you will never again have to beg to be seen. Be filled with us."

The congregation parted, their masked faces snapping toward her in unison. Dozens of mouths, painted and broken, grinned through cracked porcelain. "Join us," they sang, "join us in rejection. Be forgotten. Be unloved. Be ours." This chorus fell in rhythmic chant with the priest's words. "Kneel. Partake. Rejoice."

Morana's knees nearly gave. The cup smelled of copper, of warmth, of promise. She thought of the gnawing emptiness inside her. For one moment — one treacherous heartbeat — she imagined plunging her face into it, silencing the hunger at last. But another voice rose. Not the chorus. Not the priest. A memory. Her grandmother's whisper, fragile and tremulous, *a prayer*. One she had dismissed long ago, muttered words at a bedside when frost crackled the windows.

Morana shook her head. "No."

The priest paused, chalice dripping. His voice turned harsh, rasping like rust. "No?"

Her throat tightened. She had never prayed — not truly. Faith had seemed like another game of cruelty, like the villagers' feast, like promises left to rot. And yet — standing here, before a cradle filled with shadow and absence — she felt something breaking loose inside her. True faith set free of the confines of human institution. Her lips trembled, words forcing themselves into air. "Lord, save me," she whispered. "Not from hunger, not from fear — but from evil. From emptiness. From myself. Amen."

The congregation stilled. Their masks froze: their laughter strangled into silence. The priest's smile cracked, splitting ear to ear. "No prayer is heard here, girl. Not in this place."

But it was.

For the first time in her life, her words did not vanish into frost or echo in mockery. They *trembled*. They hung in the air like light refracted on snow, sharp and fragile, but *real*. The ruin quaked.

The manger groaned. Her words seared the air. The shadow-infant screamed without a mouth, its form unravelling into tendrils of smoke. The congregation shrieked as if scalded by boiling oil, clutching their masks as they cracked and burned.

Candles guttered, their blue flames collapsing into ash. The tables shrieked as though alive, overturning, sending writhing feasts sprawling onto the flagstones. The Madonna shrivelled, veils shrieking away from her frame like burned cobwebs. One by one, the congregation's masks burst, revealing not faces beneath but *nothing at all* — the soulless beings they were: hollow caverns that howled as they dissolved. The priest reached toward her, chalice trembling, blood frothing over his fingers. His flesh sagged like wax in fire. "Blasphemy!" he howled. "You were never chosen!"

But she was.

Morana staggered back, hand to her mouth, as the masquerade melted; the shadow performance peeling away from the ruined husks of the church into blood and shadow that flowed and bled downward: and within this pool twisted and drowned the Advent Thief's shadow. Then all of it—manger, Madonna, congregation, feast—were sucked down under the flagstones: collapsing like a carcass into the crypt beneath.

When silence returned, only ruin remained. The church was a husk again, roofless and broken, snow drifting through. But at her feet yawned an open stairwell, leading down into the crypt, for it is always the way in fairytales. The snow that drifted through the rafters would not fall within the stair's mouth, and her shadow trembled, stretching toward the descent before she dared move. But ruin is never silence; it remembers, and it whispered still. The air that rose up from the crypt was colder than the grave, heavy with the stench of earth and old blood.

It was not merely cold — it was laden, thick with the weight of centuries pressed into stone. A faint sweetness clung to it, the ghost of dried flowers long crumbled to dust, mingled with a trace of incense and damp stone. It was not the sweetness of comfort, but of something preserved past its time, like breath caught in a coffin. The stair yawned like a mouth that sighed frost and swallowed her courage. And beneath it all thrummed something vast and patient, like a heart that had never ceased its beating, waiting only for her step to quicken it.

Her prayer had been heard — and it had also opened the way.

CHAPTER NINE

THE KEEPER OF THE FORGOTTEN

The ruin did not end with the shattered nave above. Behind the desecrated altar, a stairwell spiralled downward, cut deep into the earth: cut of stone long before her grandmother's grandmother drew breath worn smooth by feet long dust.

Morana hesitated, lingering at its mouth, staring into the throat of black stone. The air that wafted up was *wrong*: as if this air was not meant for breathing. It pressed heavy and sour against her nose and lips; not sharp like frost or rot but thick, breathless, stale. It had not moved in centuries. She could feel it press against her face, heavy with stone-dust and mildew, a weight that clung to her tongue like damp cloth.

Instinct recoiled. Some feral part of her mind screamed no air down there, no breath, no life. For a moment she felt her chest tighten, the dizzy press of suffocation, the childish terror that if she descended, she might never taste clean wind again. She had to force herself to exhale slowly, biting back the urge to run she bit her tongue until she tasted iron. *Focus*. The fear was primal, reptile-deep: a warning older than thought.

On the ruined altar lay a candle, half-melted into a pool of wax hardened by frost. Its wick was brittle but intact. She struck flint against stone, once, twice—on the third try, as it is in fairytales the wick flared, and the flame bloomed thin and guttering; shivering like a cornered animal, but it pushed back the dark enough to move forward.

The relief was almost dizzying. The fragile flame was nothing against the dark, but to her body it felt like proof the air was still air. She could breathe. For now. Step by step, she descended. The spiral pressed tight, walls damp with seeping groundwater, stones sweating with a clammy chill. The air grew thicker, pressing in her lungs until every breath rasped. Step by step, she descended. The stone spiral pressed in tight, slick with moisture that glistened in her candle's weak halo. The flame guttered, threatening to choke itself out with every breath she drew. She forced her pace to slow, though her muscles screamed to flee. Every inhalation rasped in her throat, stale air scraping her lungs raw. Her mind began to whisper with the kind of thoughts that come when air grows thin: *What if this is all I breathe until my chest bursts? What if I choke here, alone in the stone?*

She tried to silence it. She tried. But the smell came next.

At first it was faint, a sharp edge in the stale air. Copper. metallic, acrid. Sharp. It hit the back of her throat like a blade. Her pulse spiked, her mouth flooded with saliva—fight, flight, bleed. *Blood* — and for an instant she thought the crypt was painted with the smears of slaughtered sacrifice: that she was breathing the ghosts of a massacre. Her body tensed, ready to flee. She pressed against the wall, candle held out like a weapon, the flame jittering violently as her hand shook. She dragged in a ragged breath, then another, until the scent shifted—less sharp, more mineral. Not wet blood. Dry. Flaking. Rust. The breath hissed out of her lungs in a half-sob, half-laugh. Not blood. Not death. Iron, oxidized and forgotten, bleeding from hinges and gates that had decayed so fully they perfumed the air with their death and had rotted in silence.

The relief was so sharp it left her trembling, a little hysterical laugh breaking loose from her chest. But it was thin relief. Because rust meant iron. Iron meant chains. Locks. Forgotten prisoners.

She moved on, but her skin crawled. Her body still believed the copper was blood, and the taste clung to her tongue no matter how she swallowed.

The spiral spat her out into a narrow corridor. Her candlelight quivered against the walls, picking out veins of pale mold, faintly luminous, that crept like phosphorescent veins like scars crawling through the damp stone. Water dripped somewhere in the dark, hollow and rhythmic, each drop echoing like the tick of a clock that measured not hours but deaths.

Then came the voices.

Not moans. Not growls. But *pleas*. High, thin voices stitched into the stone.

"Pick me up... don't leave me here... Please, please, I'll be good... I'll be good, I promise..."

High, plaintive, childlike—stitched into the walls themselves, as though the stone had soaked in the last breath of the forsaken and would not let them go. Morana froze, the hairs at her neck rising. Morana's heart kicked in her chest. Her candle trembled, throwing broken shadows across piles of bones. She had been ready for rage; but the words were not rage, or hunger, or greed. They were abandonment: naked and raw, the kind of cries she once whispered into pillows when no one came to soothe her.

The corridor widened into a chamber. Her candle trembled, throwing pale light across toppled shelves and broken coffins. The shelves had collapsed into heaps of splintered wood, so that coffins now lay split open, their contents spilled as if discarded, stacked without reverence. Bones slumped in careless piles, ribs gnawed hollow by damp, skulls lay cracked in heaps; stacked like rubbish. Not interred, not remembered. Dumped.

The voices threaded closer, circling her.

"Don't forget me... don't forget me..."

-This was a midden. A grave for the unwanted. A grave for the *forgotten.*

The voices thickened as she moved deeper, layer upon layer of pleading tones, until it was no longer possible to tell where one ended and the next began. High and low, young and cracked, male and female, they twined like a river of need coursing through her ears, drowning her own heartbeat.

"See me... please see me..."

"Don't throw me away..."

"Don't let the dark eat me..."

Her lungs burned. The crypt's air pressed heavier, clogging her throat. Each breath scraped, stale, as though she were stealing the last fragments of oxygen left to the dead. Her chest tightened. The flame in her hand wavered, thinning, a trembling sliver of light drowning in shadow. She was breathing, she could feel the air entering her chest, but each inhalation felt like it carried less oxygen than the last; as if the crypt itself hoarded breath for its dead. The flame of her candle guttered, pulling tight against its wick, starving. She drew it closer to her face, desperate for its fragile proof of light, and the shadows shrank—then reared back, wrong, alive, shifting against the walls like bodies pressed in too close.

Something moved among them. A waiting figure.

At first it seemed like another shadow, one darker than the rest, slinking just beyond the candle's arc. But it did not vanish when she turned her head. It remained; a hulking absence stitched from banners and rags that dragged along the floor. They clung not like garments but like *skins*, mottled with colours bled and faded, emblems half-erased. Crests of kingdoms that no longer existed, battle standards torn from the hands of the defeated, funeral flags surrendered to mildew. They whispered as they shifted—fabric rasping like breath.

The figure had no face. Where a head should have been, there was nothing: a blank of darkness framed by the sagging banners. No eyes to meet hers. No mouth to voice the cries. Only absence, the void of recognition itself.

And yet the voices poured from it.

"*I was your child once.*"

"*I was your father.*"

"*I was no one.*"

"*I am forgotten.*"

Her stomach turned over.

"See me... Don't throw me away... I was here... I mattered... I was you... I was no one... Don't let me die again..."

She staggered back against the wall, stone scraping her shoulders, damp soaking her cloak. The candle nearly dropped from her hand. Her mind scrambled for sense, but only fear came. The primitive kind: the one that seizes the body long before the mind understands. Heart hammering. Hands slick. Vision tunnelling. Every nerve screaming *flee,* though her feet clung to the ground like they were nailed there.

It smelt of copper. Thick. Wet. She swallowed bile, convinced she'd walked into a slaughterhouse. The Keeper's rust flaked into the air, a metallic dust that clung to her tongue. Relief flickered only for a heartbeat when she realized it was not blood—then collapsed into something worse. Because it meant this was no accident, no living wound. This was *deliberate rot.* On one level, this was worse than the Chenoo's hunger, worse than the wolf's smile. This was not need, not malice. This was the utter lack of both. This thing did not crave, did not devour. It did not desire. It simply *was.*

Its body, if body it could be called, gleamed faintly. Not flesh, but **rust.** Layers of it, flaking, corroded, flared out like brittle armour. When it shifted, the coppery scent burst fresh into the air, sharper than before, stinging her nose. For a heartbeat her mind screamed *blood* again—damp stone, slaughterhouse walls— and she nearly retched. But the candlelight caught, showing her the truth: it was iron gone to ruin, the decay of war banners' spears, of shackles, of forgotten swords fused into its form.

The taste of rust filled her mouth as if she had bitten the iron itself.

Her pulse thundered. She wanted to run. But her knees locked, anchoring her in place. She was staring at not just a figure, but at a concept too large for flight to matter. This was not a predator chasing her life. This was the embodiment of what was discarded when life no longer mattered.

And in that moment came the terror: that if it touched her, she would not die, not scream, not bleed. She would simply... vanish. Her mind betrayed her. It dragged up memories she had fought to bury: being a little girl, standing at the edge of the feast, hands empty while others opened their gifts. The sharpness of voices that dismissed her, "Not for you, not for you." A night she had lain awake, small and silent, terrified her parents would forget her name, forget she existed. Now that same fear pulsed in the air, multiplied a thousandfold.

The Keeper's rusted arm inched closer, groaning under its own weight. The flaking banners stirred, whispering forgotten prayers, forgotten battle cries, forgotten promises, forgotten love longs. She thought of the coffins left open; the bones spilled like rubbish. She thought of the children's cries echoing in the stones above, the cobbler, the mason, the alderman, the priest—every act of forgetting, every soul abandoned. And she realized with horror: this was their end. Not vengeance, not rage. Only erasure.

The Keeper tilted its headless absence toward her. The banners stirred as if in a wind she could not feel. A hand extended— though it was no hand at all, but a corroded length of iron shaped vaguely by ruin, reaching. Flakes of rust sifted to the ground like dried blood. And with that motion, the chorus of voices sharpened, aligning into one unbearable plea:

"Join us. Be nothing. Be forgotten."

Her grip on the candle tightened until wax cracked under her fingers. The light bled across her knuckles, a tiny, pathetic flame against the abyss. She stared at it, her breath ragged, and felt something inside her fracture. For a moment she could not tell if the voices were outside or inside, if she was Morana at all, or only another echo, already dissolving into the Keeper's collection.

Her lips moved without sound, shaping words she could not hear.

She feared, in that instant, she might already be gone.

Morana's lungs heaved. The air was stale, so stale it felt older than breath itself. It clung to her throat like rot, dry and bitter, as though she were swallowing centuries that belonged to the dead. Each inhale felt thinner than the last, and a primitive terror flickered through her chest: what if there was no air here at all? What if every breath was simply a step toward suffocation?

The candlelight trembled in her hand, and with it her resolve.

The voices burrowed closer, threading through her skull:

"Forget. Yield. Become nothing. All is dust. And to dust it shall return."

Her knees buckled. The candlelight quivered. For one sickening instant she imagined it going out — and the world above, the living, would carry on, utterly untouched.

She saw it then: the market stalls bustling in spring, children growing into mothers and fathers, harvests ripening under the sun. And she — nothing. No trace of her smile, no echo of her voice. Just a silence where her body had once been, the earth closing over as though she had never drawn breath at all.

Her heart convulsed. This was the fear at the marrow of all others: not the pain of dying, but the coldness of eternity that came after, a world that would outlast her, a world that would forget her. The Keeper's banners whispered like mocking laughter.

Her mind fought, reaching desperately for something to hold onto. And it found — her first cat.

It had been a scrap of fur when she first saw it, half-starved, all ribs and wide eyes, huddled by the cobbler's stoop. She had scooped it into her arms and carried it home beneath her cloak, where it burrowed against her chest for warmth. She remembered the way it purred, not soft but rasping and broken, as if it had forgotten how to trust its own voice. She had fed it crumbs from her hand, held it to her cheek, whispered secrets into its ears no one else would ever hear.

Nights, it would curl beside her in bed, paws kneading at her nightdress, head pressed into the hollow of her throat. Its body was so small, so fiercely alive, and she had thought — foolishly, with a child's faith — that something loved so deeply could never be lost.

But one winter's night, it had slipped out through the door when her grandmother stoked the fire, darting into the snow with a flick of its tail. She had waited. Gods, how she had waited. Night after night, she crouched by the door, calling its name into the dark. She left bowls of milk on the step; little scraps of food wrapped in cloth. Each morning, she found the bowls frozen over, untouched.

The snow thawed. Spring came. Still, she called. Still, she listened.

And still — nothing.

The absence had been worse than death, because there was no body, no grave, no end. Just silence. Just the unbearable *not knowing.* Sometimes, even now, she woke in the night and her hands reached instinctively to her chest, seeking the press of that tiny, warm body against her ribs. And every time, she grasped only the cold hollowness of empty air, and whispered its little name. *Even a creature so small had left an ache that had never loosened its claws.*

Then her grandmother's face came to her: the deep creases around her mouth, the bitter salt of tears on her weathered cheek the day she knelt to tell Morana that her parents would not be coming home again. Death in the woods — sudden, merciless. *She had never forgotten the exact tremor of her grandmother's voice, nor the way the air itself had seemed to collapse in around her as she heard the words.*

And now, here in this crypt, those voices hissed like serpents through the stone:

"None of it matters. Cats vanish. Parents rot. Love dissolves. Memory is a lie. You will be forgotten."

Her knees struck stone. She clutched the candle tighter, wax biting into her palm until it blistered. The copper tang thick in her nose made her gag — blood, she thought at first, and her body jolted in terror. Fight. Flee. But then the recognition cut through: *rust*. Only rust. Relief was sharp, but fleeting, because even rust was the proof of something once whole now decaying.

And that was the greater terror — not pain, not dying, but the indifference of eternity.

Morana saw it as if through a veil: springtime returning above, children laughing in the streets, harvests gathered under the sun, lovers entwined in darkened rooms. The world would live on without her. *It always did.* The soil would drink her body, the air would swallow her voice, the memory of her face would dwindle until even those who loved her could not recall the precise shade of her eyes.

Her chest convulsed with sobs.

This was the marrow of it, the truth no one dared speak aloud: the world does not care. The world forgets. The banners around the Keeper stirred as if in mockery, whispering like old paper:

"You are nothing. Time devours all. Eternity has no room for your name."

Her throat worked, cracked and raw, and for one frail heartbeat she believed it. That she was nothing, that she had always been nothing.

But then — a thread of warmth. A small paw pressing against her chest. The brush of her grandmother's hand on her hair. Her mother's laughter, half-forgotten but still real. *She remembered them.* She remembered every loss, every touch, every scar carved into her soul by love and by grief alike.

She dragged air into her chest, choking on it, and forced the words out:

"I WAS HERE."

The crypt swallowed the sound.

She said it again, voice cracking, teeth bared: "I WAS HERE."

The Keeper tilted, banners rustling in a sound like bone dust shifting.

And then louder, throat tearing: "I lived. I loved. I carry them. Even if no one else remembers, I do, and that matters."

Her words struck the chamber like hammers. Dust fell. Shadows rippled. The banners recoiled as though burned.

"It cannot matter. You cannot matter. All are forgotten."

But Morana's breath steadied. *Matter*—the word itself was like a trap. To "matter" implied weight on a scale measured by others, a recognition doled out like charity. That was not what being meant.

She thought of the beggar children she had seen cast aside, of the girl working in the tavern, of the butcher's fattened child force-fed and weeping silently. Their names might never be sung in halls or carved into stone — but they had lived. Their hunger, their grief, their brief joys were *real*.

She raised her chin, throat raw but steady, and said, "We *mattered* because we lived. Because we felt. Because we changed the world just by breathing it."

The Keeper leaned closer, faceless void tilting, and the voices hissed one last venom:

"The earth forgets. The sky forgets. Time will drown you in silence."

Morana trembled, tears cutting hot trails through the grime on her face — but she did not bow. "Then let silence drown!" she spat. "Let eternity choke on my scream. I lived. That is enough."

The candle flared — a sudden, violent blaze of gold. For the first time, the Keeper seemed to hesitate, banners snapping as if in an unseen wind. The void quivered. And in that moment, for one breath, she thought eternity itself might be forced to pause and remember her.

But the flare did not last. The light shuddered, contracting into a thin wick of gold once more, fragile against the cavern's tide of dark. Morana's chest ached with the effort of holding her words aloft, as if every syllable had been torn from the marrow of her bones.

The Keeper loomed still. Its banners whispered, its iron limbs creaked. And though it had recoiled for that heartbeat, she felt its presence gather itself again, like a tide pulling back before it breaks against the shore. Her body trembled. She was no warrior. No saint with holy prayers to shield her. She was a young woman with a half-melted candle and a throat rubbed raw from defiance. Yet the silence that followed her cry was different. Not the silence of abandonment, not the silence of being erased. It was the silence of being heard, if only faintly, if only unwillingly.

That silence was her victory.

Still, the Keeper pressed closer, rust raining from its corroded limbs. The air thickened until she could taste decay on her tongue, bitter as ash. Its faceless void leaned toward her flame, and she understood with sick clarity that it could smother her with nothing more than its breathless presence.

Her knees screamed for her to collapse. Her hand shook, wax dripping hot against her skin. Yet she held the candle between them like a blade. Not enough to banish it. But enough to hold the abyss at bay.

The chorus of voices swelled again, not unified this time but fractured, desperate. Some begged her to yield. Others cursed her. Still others wept, promising her rest if she would only surrender. She realized then that the Keeper was not a single voice at all, but the sum of all who had been cast aside: children, lovers, warriors, mothers, beggars. Not erased, but trapped in this thing that remembered nothing of who they had been, only the ache of being forgotten.

And perhaps that was the greater cruelty. They had become the very embodiment of what they had feared. The forgotten, doomed to drag others into their ranks. Her throat tightened. For one dizzying instant she felt sorry for them. Pitied it. But empathy was dangerous. To pity was to step closer. To step closer was to be touched. She took a shaking breath, forcing her spine to straighten. "I will not join you."

The Keeper did not retreat. Its banners stirred, but only faintly, as though the vast thing were not moved to anger, only to curiosity. The candle's flame spat once, clinging on as if starved of air. A voice, heavy and layered with centuries, rose from its void: "Why do you resist, child? What weight keeps your legs from folding? What is worth such trembling?"

Morana's throat burned, but the answer rose without thought. "The gift," she whispered, clutching the candle to her chest. "The one taken from me: stolen by the Advent Thief."

Her voice grew stronger, as if speaking it summoned the warmth back into her bones. "Do you know what it is to wake on Christmas morning? To open your eyes and feel that the world itself is lighter, as though even the worst frost has softened? To see the fire kindled, gingerbread baking, and your grandmother's hands already busy, and humming carols older than our tiny part of the world? To find a small parcel, a carefully wrapped gift, waiting for you—nothing too grand, but enough to know someone thought of you, not for what you have done, but because you are loved? That morning is not about the gift itself, but the joy it carries, the laughter that runs through the house like sunlight breaking the dark.

"Christmas is the one day when bitterness loosens its grip, when the poor taste the feast of kings, when even enemies pause and remember they are human. It is the day when hope walks the earth. That is what was stolen. Not only a ribbon or toy, but the morning itself, the love woven into it, the light that makes the waiting worth it. And in its place—emptiness. Not death, not pain, but the hollow where joy should have been. **FOREVER.**"

The void was silent for a long, terrible span. Then the banners stirred again, not in mockery but in recognition.

If the Keeper had been capable of feeling, it might have leaned closer, listening not with pity but with the hunger of curiosity. For it could understand Morana's words, yet never touch their weight; that was its tragedy—not malice, but estrangement. It knew the shape of joy, the outline of warmth, but such things could not move it. The banners did not lash nor unfurl, but lowered, drooping toward the tiny candle in her hands. For one instant, the folds of shadow seemed less like armour and more like wings that had forgotten how to fly. A faint warmth touched them, not enough to soften their darkness, but enough to sketch the ghost of memory across their surface—like frost catching the reflection of a distant sun. It was gone almost as soon as it came, devoured by indifference. Yet Morana saw it: the Keeper remembering, or perhaps only pretending to remember, what it was to be warmed.

"We know this thief," the voices answered at last, slow as rust creeping across stone. "This Goblin. He walks past us at times, down paths even darker than ours. His lair is not far, though it lies beneath, in the fiery pits where ash and cinders dream. We will not go. We will not touch such things."

Morana's breath caught and her lips parted. "But... you can show me."

The banners did not stir, yet at her words Morana felt the darkness widen, as though the void itself had been peeled back. A seam opened—not of fabric, but of silence—and within it another place revealed itself, faint and bitter as smoke drawn into her lungs.

She beheld a cavern glowing with furnace light. Chains laced the ceiling, not bright as tinsel but blackened with soot, their links draped with broken things: scorched paper, cracked glass, ribbons burnt to string. The air smelled of char and wet iron, the stink of cheer undone. At the chamber's centre stood a tree, not a marvel of evergreen but a withered branch, brittle and grey, its needles long since shed. The trunk still bore the saw-cut at its base, fresh once from some family's hearth. Now it was planted in slag, its ornaments no longer baubles but scraps of what had been torn from others' joy: a child's stocking scorched through, a wooden soldier split down the grain, a bell sagging into molten metal.

Beneath that tree crouched a figure. Ash clung to his skin as if it had grown there, cracked in lines that glowed with ember-red. His eyes opened and shut like furnace doors, spilling light with each blink. He worked with long black claws, threading ribbon and bone together into garlands of ruin. His lips curled, and a sound spilled out—half chuckle, half croon. At first it seemed a carol, but each note bent wrong, joy inverted to mockery.

Morana's breath caught. She knew him—not from memory, but from recognition, as if his shape had been waiting in her dread all along. The vision quivered, threatening to draw her further in, until the Keeper's voice pulled taut around her like a tether.

"This is the Goblin," the Keeper intoned. "The hand that seizes what was meant for delight, the mouth that sours song to ash. He is small, yet he weaves greater ruin than giants. He does not need armies. He undoes joy and the future joy promises."

The cavern dimmed; the tree, the chains, the figure all folded back into shadow. Only the echo of his cracked carol remained, gnawing at her ear like a worm.

For the briefest heartbeat she thought she saw sorrow—like an echo trapped in stone. The candle's glow quivered, trembling in her hand, and she whispered before she could stop herself:

"You *REMEMBER*, don't you? You remember what it was to be warmed."

The Keeper did not answer in words, but the drooping banners stilled, heavy with silence. She felt it then—not agreement, not denial, but a pause so vast it seemed to stretch wider than the passageway itself. It was as though her voice had brushed against something buried deep, a hollow where once a memory might have lived.

THE GOBLIN OF ADVENT

"Or perhaps you never knew," she went on softly, her own voice strange in her ears. "Perhaps you only carry the shadow of what was lost. But even that is something, isn't it? To know the outline of joy, even if it burns you to look upon the real thing."

The Keeper shifted, shadows shifting slightly, like sails caught in a dying wind, before folding in on themselves like wings. For a moment, she felt the weight of its attention press against her chest, colder than the deepest snow, and yet—beneath it—an ache, as though eternity itself longed to feel but could not.

"We can show the way. And yet, hear this: your words are true. We do know Christmas. We know the fire, the laughter, the small gifts tied in twine. We know them well enough to name them." The voices grew colder, withdrawing, as though afraid of their own confession. "But we do **NOT** care. We **CANNOT** care. That is the difference between us. What warms you does not stir us. What you call precious; we call passing ash. What you call memory, we call noise."

The candle guttered. Still, Morana pressed it closer to her heart.

"Perhaps," she said softly, "but even ash was once fire. And I still choose the flame."

The Keeper gave no answer, save the faintest ripple through its banners—like a sigh too vast to be heard.

"We can show the way," it repeated, resigned. "And if you still cling to that ember—then downward you must go."

A rumble passed through the stones beneath her feet. The ground shuddered, a long slow exhale from the bowels of the world. The chamber's walls wept with fresh water, streaking down in dark rivulets, as though the crypt itself had begun to cry.

Morana staggered but did not fall. She clutched the guttering candle close to her chest, its glow reflected in her wide, tear-cut eyes. She had spoken her defiance; she had torn one heartbeat of recognition from the jaws of eternity. But the cost was being named. Chosen. Bound to a path she did not yet understand.

The Keeper tilted, faceless void peering down into her. Then, with a sound like a thousand pages turning to dust, it drew back into the dark, banners dragging along the stone until they dissolved into shadow. Its last whisper hung in the air, sour as rust on her tongue:

"Downward, child. Downward where even memory breaks."

The crypt exhaled. The candle swelled again, its flame dancing in relief now that the figure had withdrawn. But Morana's heart did not ease. She knew the battle had only shifted, not ended. Behind the chamber, a seam opened in the stone. A stair, crude and jagged, lead further below. The stair was made of serpentine: dark, green-black stone mottled with pale streaks, slick as though scaled. The heat rising from below had polished it to a dull sheen, so that each step seemed to ripple faintly, alive beneath her tread. Once, her grandmother had told her the name came from the serpent — for its colour, its slipperiness, and because it was said to line the doors of the underworld, where serpents kept watch. She remembered that tale now, and with it the warning: *step softly, for what is carved in serpent's stone belongs to deeper powers.*

The air that rose from it was a blast of hot wind, as though some one had just opened the door of an oven inside a cold kitchen. She wiped her face with the back of her hand, smearing ash and tears alike. Her knuckles were raw where the wax had burned her, but she did not let go of the candle. She could not.

Above her, she imagined the world rolling on. But that world was not hers to hold now. Hers was this descent. Her throat ached, her limbs shook, but she whispered once more, steady this time: "I WAS HERE."

The stone seemed to swallow her statement whole. But in her chest, she felt the words remain, burning hotter than the flame in her hand. And with that ember, she turned toward the stair that split the earth, and began her descent.

As she descended, the air thickened again, pressing down on her lungs. She could feel it more now — the weight of the earth that held her, its resistance, its reluctance. This was the world's indifference, a slow, rolling void that would consume her, if she let it. There was no escape, not here, not in the dark. The Keeper had shown her that — not in hunger, not in rage, but in its refusal to care. Morana's legs were heavy, her feet dragging with every step. The farther she would descend, the more the world above her would shrink; the more she became swallowed by the abyss. She could no longer hear the murmurs of the world — only the thick, stifling air and the relentless whisper of stone.

The Keeper's voice returned, not from its form, but from the deep, echoing space that surrounded her, the very air itself filled with a hollow sound.

"Do you understand now?" it asked, its voice a cold murmur, more felt than heard. "What you fear is not death. It is the knowledge that you are not needed, that you are forgotten, that even your own bones will be lost to time."

Morana stumbled, her breath growing more shallow, more desperate. She shook her head, trying to reject that thought creeping into her mind — that she was insignificant. That she could disappear, become nothing, and it would make no difference.

But she had never been here for glory, nor for recognition. She would rather have had this adventure never happened in the first place. She had come here for something else. Something even the Keeper could not claim. She could feel it, burning inside her, even as she felt the heat building around her, as if the very flame she carried on the little candle had become a piece of herself. The dark did not care. The Keeper did not care, even if it could. But she would not allow herself to be swallowed. Not yet. Not now.

She thought of the words her grandmother had told her so long ago, in the kitchen as the fire crackled. "The world may forget you, my dear, and indeed, at times it may feel like its forgotten all about you. But never forget who you truly are; and you just remember to keep on going remembering to be you. That is something no one can take from you." Morana's chest burned with the echo of her own strength. And so, she remembered—remembered what it was to be whole. To exist. To matter, not because others did, but because she could.

"Even if *you* forget," she whispered into the dark, her voice cracked but steady. "I WILL NOT."

And so, with the whisper of those words, she took the final step into the abyss.

CHAPTER TEN

THE MAW OF SUGAR AND FLAME

Down she went, deeper and deeper, where stones sweated and the air burned, where roots clawed at the rock as if trying to flee the heat. The world of frost above seemed now like a half-remembered dream — silence, clean and sharp as glass. Here, everything pressed close, suffocating. The heat pressed like a weight, clinging to her skin and clotting in her hair. Her heartbeat quickened, echoing in her ears with the same rhythm as the earth's groaning.

The thought lodged itself in her as she descended. Each step felt less like stone and more like the body of something sleeping, as if she were treading down a spine that resented her weight. Heat breathed upward through cracks between the slabs, carrying the taste of brimstone and singed copper.

She drew a breath, and at once her lungs recoiled. The air was thick, sulphurous, scratching at her throat. It stank of eggs turned to rot, of metal scorched past recognition. Each inhalation scorched her chest. She pressed a sleeve to her mouth, though the fabric did little to shield her from the searing taste of brimstone.

The stair sank deeper. The walls glistened as though the stone itself burned with fever. Cracks split wide to reveal molten wounds, each one glowing like a furnace door forced ajar, bleeding light into the dark, pulsing faintly as though the mountain itself lived and raged.

Sometimes the stone bulged outward, distended by the molten rivers within; sometimes it split, revealing a glimpse of the red heart beneath.

Eventually the stairway opened onto a broad landing. Here, Morana paused and sat for a moment upon the serpentine landing: feeling the stone's coolness despite the rising heat. Beneath her hand the landing bore a faint design, almost worn smooth by time: a rune or crest, barely discernible beneath soot.

From the depths below came a sound like the earth's heart straining against its cage — a muffled roar, sometimes breaking into shrieks carried on vents of fire. The air pressed hot and heavy against her chest, and sweat gathered at her hairline, only to vanish into steam. The candle's flame guttered and shivered. Morana considered the poor candle. The flame fluttered in protest, nearly smothered by the sulphur. Yet it did not go out. It glowed like a memory among nightmares, a frail relic of the frost above, a single syllable of comfort in a language otherwise forgotten. For the first time since she had entered the crypt: the Keeper's halls, she pinched her fingers to the wick. Its light sighed away.

"Farewell," she whispered.

The candle was no longer needed: the glow rising from below was stronger, though it offered no comfort. She cradled the wick a moment longer, a farewell, then straightened into the smouldering gloom.

The stairs resumed their spiral, coiling downward like the throat of some vast beast. And Morana, with no light but the infernal glow licking up from unseen caverns, began her descent. As she walked, beneath the roar, there were sounds — faint, far-off, yet unshakably human. Cries carried upward by the vents: wails that thinned into whispers, sighs that broke into shrieks, as if the earth itself exhaled the agony it had swallowed. he cries seemed to echo old warnings: that the stones remember sin, that the earth itself drinks the voices of the damned, that if you lean too close you will hear the wailing of those swallowed whole. She recalled fragments from stories told in the dark — of Korah's rebellion swallowed by the ground, of trolls bound screaming beneath bridges, of witches whose whispers were trapped forever in the walls of their ovens. She shook the thought away, but the echoes clung like smoke, thickening with every step. Morana could not tell whether the voices were real or only the echoes of her own fear, but they followed her, fluttering at the edges of her hearing like the rustle of wings.

The descent narrowed. The steps crumbled into slopes of scree. Morana slipped, caught herself against the wall, and drew her hand back blistered where the stone seared. She bit her lip, stifling a cry, but did not retreat. Ahead, the stair widened again, curving into a vast throat of stone that plunged further still.

A thought struck her then: in the cavern of the Keeper she had been watched, studied, measured. Here, she felt no gaze, only engulfment. The stone did not care. The fire did not care. This was not estrangement but annihilation — a place where being itself seemed to fray, stripped of shape and sound until only ash might remain.

Still, she stepped down.

The stair wound deeper, and the air thickened to a furnace fog. Morana's skin prickled as though being peeled, each nerve flayed by invisible claws. Sweat hissed into steam before it could fall. Her hair clung damp to her scalp, and every inhalation scraped her throat like iron filings dragged across raw flesh. The glow from below was no longer merely light but movement — sluggish rivers of lava creeping like serpents through fissures, their scales folding and slithering over one another, pulsing with hateful rhythm. They dragged molten bodies forward as though aware, as though waiting for the unwary to slip.

Charred bones studded the slopes where the molten streams cooled, brittle and blackened. Some still bore human shape, jaws stretched wide in soundless screams. Others had melted into grotesque composites: ribs fused with hoof or talon, vertebrae sprouting like roots, spines warped into horns. A bestiary of ruin, where man and beast and nightmare had all shared the same furnace end. Beside them lay shattered remnants of belief: chalices warped into lumps of slag, icons slumped faceless in the heat, books curled into black husks, their ink blistered away. They looked less discarded than devoured — faith reduced to fuel, stripped of every word and promise.

At first, she thought this graveyard belonged to mortals alone. But then she saw the immensity of some of its scale. Ribs arched overhead like the beams of a sunken ship, their hollows big enough to crawl through. A skull jutted from the rockface, half-buried yet vast as a hill, its jaw split as though it had bitten down upon the mountain itself before the fire silenced it; s pines so vast they spanned whole ledges like fallen bridges. Horns spiralled from another cranium, their ridges cracked and crumbling, tipped in slag that dripped as though still weeping. These were not men, nor even monsters. These were elder things: they were the wreckage of forgotten gods, titans, and giants, their grandeur crushed into ruin.

She moved among them as a child among the ruins of palaces. A hand lay outstretched upon the slope, each finger thicker than a tower's pillar, veins traced in runes that had lost all glow. Once it must have raised oceans, or beckoned stars. Now its nails curled inward, stone-grey, brittle, flaking. A lion's muzzle protruded from a mound of ash, teeth blackened, mane hardened into jagged spines. The air quivered faintly around it, like heat above coals — the last shimmer of divinity smouldering out.

Every tale her people had ever spoken seemed to lie in pieces here. She saw the falcon head of the sky-bearer, beak cleft, its hollow sockets filled with molten glow. She saw a bull-god collapsed on its side, its horns cracked to powder. Farther off sprawled a bearded figure of such size it might once have carried seas upon its shoulders; coral bones glittered faintly along its spine, but the flesh was long devoured. Their bodies were not laid to rest. They were being consumed, gnawed bone by bone, their majesty digested by the furnace of the earth.

She thought of the old stories — that when men ceased their offerings, when temples fell silent, the gods merely withdrew into hidden valleys or sailed west over invisible seas. The priests had soothed their flocks: faith neglected carried no danger, only a gentle fading, a natural death. But here she saw what silence birthed. It was not fading but rotting. Faith did not die clean. It sank here, swallowed, where the fire licked it down slowly, eternal in its corruption.

Above her, the cavern roof bristled with crowns. They hung like stalactites, inverted diadems fused into the stone, dripping metal like beeswax from a candle. Gold had warped into lumps; jewels cracked into dull glass. Some crowns still bore traces of words — invocations etched along their bands — but the letters had twisted until they were unreadable, as though language itself rebelled. They looked less like trophies than carrion, scavenged from brows no longer remembered.

And among the ruins drifted strange shadows. Not souls, not smoke, but the silhouettes of syllables. Names. She felt it more than heard it: fragments of words once prayed in sanctuaries, once sung in hymns. They fluttered like moths around fissures of fire, dimming each time they passed through the heat. She tried to grasp them in memory, to recall the names her grandmother whispered by firelight, but the harder she strained, the more the sounds frayed into silence.

The despair of that place pressed heavier than the heat-the exhaustion of meaning itself. To look upon gods undone and know that all faith, whether mighty or humble, whether sung in marble basilicas or murmured in huts of clay, could end here. To feel eternity collapse into indifference, the divine frayed into ash.

She stumbled. The cavern swelled with monuments reversed — temples melted into slag, altars blackened and toppled. Reliefs that had once sung of triumph lay face down; their victories drowned in molten stone. The air itself whispered: every creed is a candle, and here is where the wax runs out.

Among the wreckage she saw smaller shapes, almost overlooked. Saints. Prophets. Martyrs. Their images lay strewn like children among the bones of titans. A lamp shattered, its flame quenched. A staff broken across the knee. A cross sagged sideways, its beams fused into a charred X. These, too, were dragged down. Whether thunder-lord or shepherd, all were equal in the furnace's appetite.

Morana felt tears burn her eyes. They fell, but hissed to steam before reaching her chin. She wept because here lay the death of meaning itself — and worse than death, its slow digestion. Faith had not vanished into silence. It had been made to linger, mangled, unremembered, endlessly consumed. Her sobs rattled in her chest, yet no echo returned. Even grief here was swallowed.

Yet even as she lingered among the husks of divinity, the cavern shifted beneath her steps. The ribs of titans eased back into the mountain, as if the fire were drawing a veil over them, swallowing every remnant into depths she could not reach. Crowns slumping away further into slag, jewels giving up their last glimmers in sullen drips. The silence did not close like a door; it pressed on with grim insistence, as though saying: there is more yet to see, more yet to lose.

She moved on. Her boots struck stone slick with ash, the ground now veined with black glass where molten tides had once rolled. The air changed with her — less the reek of sacrifice, more the sour tang of something nearer to the living world. She thought of graveyards left untended, when rain thins the soil and bones surface by inches.

At first, she mistook the scatter of bones ahead for human — a field of pale wreckage like any other charnel slope. Then the scale of them corrected her. A curve of rib too wide for a man's chest; a limb long as a small tree; and there, thrusting from the slag, a horn whose pallor seemed ivory until the light took it and showed what it truly was: charred bone, polished smooth by fire.

More horns rose, half-buried and twisted into the cooling rock like broken spires. The bodies they crowned sprawled in grotesque attitudes, some collapsed as if they had simply lain down and been overtaken, others frozen mid-flight where the heat had gripped them and would not release. Unicorns. Or what had borne that name in song. What should have been white coats were mottled with ash and sear; hides peeled back in islands to expose the gleam of bone beneath. Manes once said to shimmer like starlight hung in soot-black ropes, fused into cords that tethered neck to ground. Hooves had melted where they struck the slope, seeped into stone, cooled, and set; the animals looked shackled forever in the last instant of a leap. A few still arched their necks as though to drink air from a higher world, horns lifted toward a sky they could not find; but the tips were split and blackened, shedding ash like tears.

Their eyes — where heat had not burst them — were blind pearls, glazed and clouded. Around them drifted a sweetness that was almost pleasant until it turned the stomach: the cloy of something once meant for festivals, cooked too long, burned past pleasure. Innocence, reduced and blackened.

She recalled, unbidden, the old comforts murmured to children: that a unicorn would only bow its head to a maiden's lap; that the horn could draw poison from a cup, purify a stream, return what had been spoiled to what it was meant to be. But there was no maiden here, no stream, no cup — only the memory of such things mocked by flame. Even the horns, emblems of wonder, had warped into cruel spikes that pinned one carcass through another, as if madness had set upon them before the end and they had wounded each other in their panic.

Morana hesitated, breath snagging high in her chest. The ruin of gods had stunned her — thrones toppled, names erased — but this pierced nearer. The unicorns were not distant powers. They belonged to fireside tales and night-lanterns, to the last bright refuge of a child's imagining. To see them abandoned here was to see tenderness itself undone. Faith could fall and leave the world colder; but when stories perish, the cold moves inward.

Around her, the desolation of belief and the wreckage of innocence seemed to lean together, sharing a grave. A book's spine — all that remained — had curled into a black husk; nearby a rosary of bone beads had fused along its cord to a strip of petrified hide; a little wooden horse, no more than a toy, lay carbonized beside a shattered reliquary, as if some small hand had carried both and dropped them in the same step. In that mingling—the sacred and the simple, the offered and the held— she read a truth she did not want: that nothing was spared. Not the towering names, not the household hopes. Not even the gentlest lies we tell to keep fear at bay.

She knelt without meaning to, resting her palm on the nearest horn. It was warm yet, and very smooth, and under the smoothness she felt a faint roughness like scars. The touch yielded no omen, only the stubborn fact of matter: bone turned relic, relic turned refuse. Above, the cavern gave a low breath that might have been wind or the shift of stone, and ash sifted down to salt the bodies with a grey, false snow.

She rose. For a long heartbeat she listened, half-expecting some flutter of life, some sign that the tales had kept a corner of themselves hidden from the fire. None came. The only sound was the slow tick of cooling rock and, far off, the muffled groan of the mountain continuing its work. She thought, with a weariness that touched her soul: perhaps this place had been appointed to prove a single, simple thing: that the furnaces at the root of the world take all—faith and fable, oath and lullaby—and render them to the same ashes. She turned away at last, not because the sight had lightened, but because it had finished its saying. Behind her, the horns kept their mute vigil; ahead, the path fell on into red breath and dark. She followed it, carrying with her the hollow where wonder had been.

Continuing on, the vault arched wider, black stone ribs bending into cathedral heights. Yet the symmetry was wrong, skewed, a broken parody of architecture. Jagged fractures split the arches, and in their depths glowed veins of fire, like arteries strained beneath scorched flesh. Stalactites hung down like bells cast in iron, some cracked, some melted into crooked fangs. When vents roared beneath, they trembled, tolling in a dirge no hand had rung. The echoes rolled, as though she walked beneath a nave abandoned to ruin, its hymns replaced by shrieks and ash.

Then out of the haze appeared a line of figures swaying as though bound to the same dirge. Then the light revealed them: brides without weddings, wives without choice. Their garments clung in tatters, the faintest echoes of gowns once white. One clutched the shredded remnant of a veil across her breasts, the gesture instinct for modesty. Another had her wrists bound in chains, drawn cruelly behind her back, so that the thin scraps of a wedding dress fell uselessly away, exposing the flesh it meant to shield. Another staggered forward with only a garter of ash about her thigh, a parody of bridal finery as though hell itself mocked the modesties torn from them.

Their silence was unbearable — the silence of women who had screamed until their throats gave out, whose cries were written instead into their bodies: the stoop of their shoulders, the slackness of their arms, the hollow between their legs.

Morana knew these faces, though she had never seen them. They came from every tale her people whispered by the fire: Persephone dragged beneath the earth by a king who named it marriage; the sleeping maidens who never woke of their own will, kissed and claimed while they dreamed; Bluebeard's wives who learned too late that the bridal chamber was only a slaughterhouse; the nameless girls traded as peace-gifts between warring clans. Even Eve, led from the garden only to carry the burden of Adam's fall, seemed to walk among them.

One woman lifted her head as Morana passed. Her eyes were ash-rimmed hollows, yet within them a glimmer still lived — not hope, but the unbearable need to be seen. Her lips parted soundlessly, shaping words that might once have been *remember me*. Then she lowered her gaze again, and the march resumed.

The procession circled, slow and endless. It was a wedding march stretched into eternity, the parody of a dance where the steps were shackles and the consummation was violation without end.

Ash clung to their skin like the residue of extinguished candles. Once these were daughters, sisters, mothers. Here they were only offerings, pressed into silence. In their eyes flickered the truth of all the stories: the underworld always took its brides, and the living always found a way to forget them.

Their silence yielded to another sound — a chorus that did not belong to them, but to the stones themselves. Voices rose, not as memory but invocation.

A child's rhyme seemed to hum along the molten streams: *Down, down, the steps of stone, never up, never home.*

A preacher's thunder rolled in the roar: *The pit yawns wide, and down go the mighty, down go the proud.*

Another came lilting, almost sung: *The fiddler played too sweet, so they dragged him under the hill — his bowstring snapped, his fingers burned.*

Then something older still, twisted scripture: *As the Lord cast them into fire, so their names were rubbed out from the Book.*

The stair was a net, catching stories in its mesh. The strands knotted together, weaving a chant that spoke of nothing but descent. No ladder, no return. Only the spiral, only fire at its root. She pressed on, but the words clung to her like smoke. Once she thought she heard laughter — children gathered around a hearth — only to realize it was the hiss of molten rock devouring marrow.

A fissure yawned open to her left. The cavern it revealed was vast as a sky, its floor a sea of fire in constant churn. She thought at first the cavern wall was studded with statues — kings enthroned in basalt; crowns etched in shadow. But then the figures moved, their jaws working in soundless mutters, hands stretching down into fissures where magma seethed. Gold flickered in those depths, glimmers of treasure that might have been coins, or veins, or simply illusions born of heat. Each king clawed toward it, fingers plunging eagerly, only to recoil as flesh sloughed off bone, dripping into the molten glow. Yet still they reached again, stumps hissing as they touched the fire, charred fragments snapping off, until only blackened claws remained. Crowns fused to their skulls, metal dripping into their eye sockets so that their faces streamed like wax masks. And still they bent forward, endlessly, as if the pursuit of gold were a motion wound into their bones, stronger even than death. Some had melted into the rock entirely: torsos fused with thrones, legs vanished into the wall, yet arms still reached, still yearned. She remembered old stories of greedy miners swallowed by the earth, of kings who hoarded wealth until it buried them alive. Here, the fables had not ended with a moral. Here, the greed had no release, no lesson — only an endless parody of desire, played out against fire's roar. Their voices, faint and broken, echoed like prayers inverted: not "deliver us," but "more, more, more," a litany without end.

Islands of rock rose and sank like drowning ships. Across the gulf loomed shadows that moved too slowly to be men — wings outstretched like torn sails, horns rising and falling with the fire's breath. Too distant to be clear, too immense to be false. She tore her gaze away before their heads could turn.

The sea roiled, and from it rose a shape that froze her where she stood.

A mouth, first — a cavern of teeth, jagged, curved, some glowing red from the heat that licked them. Its jaw unhinged wider than seemed possible, a pit opening into a pit. Above it, lanterns swung — no, not lanterns, but tendrils tipped with pale globes of fire, swaying, luring. Their glow cut through the molten haze like false stars, drawing the gaze toward the maw. Behind it uncoiled a body vast as mountains, scaled in plates that shimmered with molten sheen, a leviathan of fire and abyss. The sea itself recoiled from it, waves of flame breaking against its armoured back.

Morana's knees locked. A tale whispered by priests and grandmothers alike rose unbidden: a man swallowed by a beast, carried in its belly three days and nights, spat back only by mercy. Yet the beast before her was no whale. It was a furnace given flesh, the hunger of the deep wearing scales. Its lantern-lures swung hypnotic, each a star that had fallen and turned traitor. She pressed herself to the wall, unwilling to breathe lest the beast scent her. When at last it sank again, vanishing beneath the flames, the glow of its lanterns lingered in her eyes like a curse.

As she continued, the stair turned, and smoke pressed close. It thickened, billowing upward, twisting into forms too deliberate to be chance. Horned heads reared and snapped, wings unfurled, scales shimmered in coal-dust silhouette. Dragons, she thought, from the tales her father told when embers burned low. Dragons that rose from cauldrons black as midnight, beasts of fire and plague. The smoke curled into their shapes, then unravelled, and yet the memory clung, vivid as if she had seen them alive.

Step after step, story after story. She saw a woman with hair of gold flicker in the glow, singing beneath the earth — a bride stolen by fire, condemned to sing in darkness until her throat was ash. A shadow dragged chains along a cliffside — a king who sought riches too deep, swallowed by his own mines. A tower seemed to loom, only to prove a pillar of fused bone, hollowed and ribbed, scraps of cloth clinging like banners.

Every tale ended the same: with fire, with ruin, with here.

The stair narrowed, pressing her against walls that sweated molten veins. They dripped in strands, glittering false gold, catching on ridges to form brittle lace that cracked beneath her boots. The air clawed her skin raw; her breath scalded her lungs. Her hands shook, her mouth tasted ash, yet still she descended.

At last, the stair widened, spilling her onto a landing. Here the walls were lined with trees.

Not living trees. Not even whole. They jutted like skeletons, stripped of bark and leaf, their branches sharp as broken fingers. They looked like the trees she had known in childhood, hauled in by poor families during lean winters — bare trunks, few boughs, dressed with scraps of ribbon or tallow light to feign abundance. Yet here no ribbons hung, only strings of ash. No candles, only droplets of hardened pitch. The branches bore scars of heat, cracked and peeling, oozing resin that smoked as it burned away. Their roots clutched the stone like desperate hands, their crowns sagging with rusted iron stars, warped and dripping rust like old blood.

The sight hollowed her chest. They stood in rows, not as forest but as graveyard, monuments to winters stripped of joy. The air smelled of scorched pine and bitter resin. Ash sifted from the branches in parody of snow, settling into her hair, stinging her skin. Each tree leaned inward as though to hear her, their limbs skeletal, their shadows long as gallows.

She moved among them, each step a trespass into memory. She thought of those poor winters, when children gathered around trees thin as kindling, pretending not to see the hunger in their parents' eyes. She thought of stories told to sweeten the bitter — tales of angels and gifts and miracles. Here, in the Keeper's descent, the trees bore none of those promises. Only absence. Only proof that hope itself could burn.

And beyond them lay the last stair.

The ground trembled with the groan of fire below. Across the landing stood arches, massive and crumbling, their heights lost in shadow. They resembled a ruined gate, though no gate remained, only shattered lintels and leaning pillars, weary of holding up the dark. Between them the glow pulsed brighter, as though the mountain itself drew breath.

Morana lingered at the threshold, ash sifting through her hair, trees whispering with every crack of resin. She no longer carried a candle. The light was gone. The voices hummed in her teeth — myths, sermons, warnings, songs. Morana descended further.

The arches closed over her like teeth, and the mountain's voice changed. The roar of molten fire she had known before did not vanish, but thinned, as though a mask were being pulled away. What she heard now was worse: not a clean eruption, not the honest violence of stone and flame; but a simmer, of water boiling, as though the world itself were being reduced in a pot. The echoes pressed into her skull — the groan of sugar syrup collapsing into tar, butter scorching in its own fat, ginger blackening until it snapped like bone.

The air clogged her mouth. It was no longer sulphur she tasted but caramel, only spoiled — sweetness curdled into poison, a flavour like burnt candy clinging to the back of her throat. She coughed and felt it cling to her lungs like resin.

The ground betrayed its disguise. Here it gleamed with amber veins. What had looked like rock cracked under her heel with the brittle snap of toffee. Filaments stretched after her boots — delicate as spun sugar, only black, sticky, and sharp. When they broke, they left threads clinging, still hot enough to burn.

Beneath the crust, fissures bubbled. Not magma — never magma — but treacle, boiling black. It rose and sank in great, glutinous sighs, releasing bubbles that popped with the smell of charred molasses. Each burst spat out fragments that rolled across the floor, glittering like obsidian in the glow. She bent, squinting through the haze, and found not stone but coal candy, fragile as ash, glossy as enamel. A whole path of it lay before her, as though Christmas stockings had been gutted and their sweets strewn across the scorched floor. Only here, the stockings belonged to the damned.

Above her, the cavern sweated its own corruption. Stalactites lengthened into treacle lances, their skins lacquered with a caramel glaze, their tips brittle and black. Some dripped endlessly, fat globes falling like molten sugar to burst on the ground, hissing into pits of glass. Others hung jagged, their cores crystallized like candied toffee, sharp enough to pierce bone. The air shimmered with their heat, filling the cavern with a smell both mouth-watering and revolting.

It was then she understood. The world of magma had been the lie, the veil. What men called *lava* was nothing but the dull, bland husk of this place, the thin crust that hid the truth beneath. All volcanic fire was only the mask for this: a confectionary hell, a parody of kitchens, where every ingredient of Christmas was burned, boiled, and repurposed for torment.

The slope carried her deeper. Treacle widened into a river, churning with golden foam, bubbles breaking and spitting flecks that stank of butter long past ruin. Along its banks, the hardened crust had banded into spirals like peppermint sticks — though their whites were ivory in colour, and their reds the congealed rust of blood baked into sugar.

And then — a rhythm. Not natural, not the crack of stone's settling, but sharp, human-made. A whip. She stopped, and the sound came again, slicing the air. A cry followed, high and brittle, cracking into steam.

The haze opened, and she saw them.

Rows upon rows stretched ahead — regimented lines carved into the scorched ground, where blackened trees clawed upward. Their fruits were nutmeg, but grotesque — pods swollen and veined red, dripping resin that smoked where it touched the soil. The air grew thick with their perfume: heavy, sweet, suffocating, like incense spiced with rot. It coated her tongue, soaked into her hair, filled her every breath until she gagged.

Among the trees, the labourers moved.

Snowmen.

They trudged in silence broken only by their moans, each figure a parody of winter's playthings. Their bodies slumped, misshapen from heat, half-melted and grey with ash. Eyes of currants had sunk into faces that sagged; carrot noses hung limp, oozing orange as though bleeding. Arms of sugared ice cracked under the weight of their work. Some bore twig limbs already charred, dripping a honey-like resin as though they bled sap. Each carried a basket woven from strands of liquorice, crammed with nutmeg pods so swollen they looked like tumours. They struggled to hold them, the weight bowing their bodies as though gravity itself had turned cruel.

And the overseers.

They prowled between the rows—reindeer, but no cheerful beasts of winter. Limbs impossibly long, jointed at jagged, unnatural angles like fractured bones, torsos whip-thin yet taut with twisted, sinewy muscle that rippled beneath charred fur. The fur itself was coarse and blackened, streaked with molten embers that hissed and bubbled as if the creatures carried fire in their blood, patches falling away in glowing sparks with each step. Their hooves were cloven and enormous, burning iron and obsidian fused together, scraping the molten ground with a sound like metal on stone, leaving shallow scorches in the syrupy, dessert-like terrain. Every movement was deliberate, heavy, and predatory, the reindeer exuding the mythic power of a minotaur—immense, terrible, unstoppable—yet grotesquely elongated, skeletal, and infernally alive. Their antlers erupted jagged and twisted from their skulls, blackened coral spiking toward the smoke-choked sky, pulsing faintly, veins of fire coursing through them. Occasionally, in the curling smoke, faces appeared—tiny, screaming, frozen mid-howl—and vanished as if swallowed by the fire beneath their hooves.

Their eyes were bright buttons, torn from dolls, bead-like and glinting unnaturally in the molten light. They did not merely look—they watched, and what they reflected shifted with the fear around them. When a snowman trembled, the buttons gleamed sharper, almost as if savouring the terror, glinting with flickers of red, molten sugar, and the faintest shimmer of tears. Their eyes followed everything, reflecting and amplifying fear, shimmering with impossible life. Even to glimpse them was to taste terror, to feel it writhe along the spine, to hear the faint, uncanny crunch of charred sugar beneath thirty-four evil incisors. These button eyes could seem impossibly large or impossibly small, tilting the perception of anyone who met them, as though bending reality to magnify the dread. Occasionally, in their depth, one could glimpse a tiny reflection of the snowman's own scream, trapped in the void of the button's black glass surface.

Their mouths were cavernous, lined with crooked, dripping teeth, exhaling smoke that smelled of scorched sugar, burnt pine, and iron—the scent of a confectionery Gehenna. Their growls were guttural and low, vibrating the air and the molten ground, sending shivers into flesh that dared approach. Shadows clung to them like living cloaks, writhing, stretching, melting into shapes that suggested arms and faces, twisting the rows of trembling snowmen into grotesque parodies of themselves.

The ground itself was alive—a molten mixture of fiery caramel, bleeding berry syrup, scorched meringue, and smoking sugar. With every step, the reindeer's hooves sank slightly into the hot, viscous terrain, sending up spurts of molten sweetness and flame, carving trails that hissed and bubbled. The air smelled of molten sugar and pine, of ice and fire combined, and heat rippled in waves that distorted vision.

When a snowman shivered beneath their gaze, it was not merely cold or pain—it was existential terror made manifest, carved into every shard of ice that clung to his trembling body. Each breath the reindeer exhaled carried whispers—tiny echoes of the frozen, shattered snowmen, faint screams mingled with the scent of spice, caramel, and scorched fruit, curling in smoke around their antlers.

They were no creatures of joy, no twisted parody of festivity. They were ceremonial predators, sentinels of a dessert-hellscape, elegant and horrific, ancient and merciless. In their hands they held cords of Christmas lights, glass bulbs still strung along them. When the cords cracked through the air, the bulbs shattered, spraying shards that exploded in sparks and coloured flame. The sound was shrill, like sleigh bells gone mad, clashing discord in place of music.

A lash fell across the back of a snowman. The bulbs pierced his packed body, carving glowing fissures that hissed like water on hot metal. He screamed— a shriek like an old kettle of boiling water —and his form shuddered, shedding shards of glimmering frost that fell like shredded tinsel, glittering and brittle. The basket toppled, nutmeg tumbling into the trembling heap, and the overseer brought the cord down and struck again; sparks dancing across the fragile flakes, slicing them into quivering crystals.

Yet amidst the surrounding heat, the snowman did not melt away. Instead, he shivered into a mound of shaved ice, each flake trembling as though it still remembered the shape of his body, the echo of his scream trapped within. Another snowman was shoved forward, twig arms snapping with unnatural precision, stooping to gather the frost. The flakes squirmed faintly beneath his fingers, whispering in protest, cold and soft as if still flesh. Each scoop was a ritual exhumation of life, a careful desecration, a harvest of frozen memory.

These flakes were then taken off to the kitchens beyond, where; as with his fellow fallen snowmen before him, he would become dessert! Every bite would taste of him: the bright tartness of crushed cranberries, the jewel-red snap of raspberries, the shy blush of strawberries folded into ice so cold it burned faintly on the tongue. Beneath the sweetness would linger something more: a faint, tremulous shiver, a whisper of nutmeg and frost, of trembling limbs and unbroken screams, condensed into crystal. The ice sometimes seemed to melt unevenly, shifting subtly in the mouth, brushing the tongue with what felt like a heartbeat or a sigh. It was a taste that clung unnervingly, almost sentient, leaving the eater with a fleeting, impossible thought: had this flavour once been alive? And next time they savoured shaved ice, even the brightest berry would make them pause, a momentary shiver passing through them, wondering—just for a heartbeat—if it was our snowman.

Morana's gut twisted. Childhood playthings had been enslaved, melted down for flavour, their bodies harvested for the very treats they once symbolized. She could taste them in the air: the tartness of shaved ice, the syrup of snowball confections. Even the simple joys of Christmas desserts had been recast as the agony of slaves.

Above, the ceiling was lost in smoke. But it was not aimless cloud. The soot formed shapes, curling into false constellations. At times they shone with red and green sparks, flickers of Christmas lights still burning as they died. For a moment she saw stars, bells, horses, angels — all broken, twisted, fading back into ash. The sky itself was a parody of celebration: garlands of soot, embers for ornaments.

The whips cracked again. The reindeer overseers laughed, laughter like cracked bells, too sharp, too high. The sound spilled outward, rising, joining the smoke.

And then — through the haze — she saw a small town hunched on the horizon: rooves sagging, their walls leaning, as though built of dough left too long in an oven. Frosting dripped in ropes down their sides, hardened into slime. Chimneys belched tar-sweet smoke that vanished into the poisoned sky.

The village waited. And the path of treacle led straight into its heart.

CHAPTER ELEVEN

WHERE GINGERBREAD DREAMS ROT

The village unfolded before her like a fevered illustration of every Christmas story gone wrong. At first glance it rose like a memory warped by fire and frost, as if some cruel child had taken the sweetest fragments of Christmas and ground them into ash. Morana saw an unwelcoming sign loom up before her:

THE VILLAGE OF ROTTING SWEETS

Morana's boots sank into the sticky streets, each step slow and deliberate; leaving a print that was immediately swallowed by burnt molasses. Around her Gingerbread cottages stood jagged and crumbling, walls sagging under congealed frosting that drooped in thick ropes like veined intestines; their spires and eaves twisted, sagging, and scorched. Where once icing would have gleamed white, now only a sickly grey clung, streaked with the visceral slime of melted lollies. Frosting had collapsed into a sticky puddle that glimmered faintly in the half-light, resembling both sugar and something more sinister, like coagulated blood. Once-delightful candy windows were fractured, their panes warped and glistening like wet sores, reflecting nothing but the darkening sky above. The rooves had buckled under the weight of molten sugar, now blackened and sticky, pooling in gutters that had become liquefied traps as the liquid sugar oozed from the rooves, hissing as it struck the sticky ground, curling upward in black smoke that smelled of caramel burnt beyond recognition. Every breath was punishment: the air clogged her throat with a perfume that was both saccharine and rancid. The sweetness seemed endless, pressing down until her lungs ached as though stuffed with spun sugar. Beneath it, sharper notes rose — burnt ginger, scorched butter, and a charred tang that reminded her of roasted flesh. The air was a trap, designed to lure, then suffocate.

Each of these gingerbread cottages was a ruin and a warning, as though some malignant spirit had reached in and dissolved every hint of joy. It was as though the village had been designed not to house, but to consume. Morana could almost hear the whispers of Hansel and Gretel, the tale of children lured into sweetness only to be consumed, and now she understood that the story had never been a tale at all—but a prophecy.

Her gaze snagged on chimneys, not merely smoking but belching with the rhythm of breath. The bricks pulsed faintly, as though the houses themselves were lungs inhaling and exhaling. The smoke that rolled from them carried undertones she knew she should not name — the fat-slick aroma of roasting meat. For an instant she thought she heard voices carried in the smoke, high and thin, like nursery rhymes sung through teeth.

Figures moved inside some of the cottages, shadows twisting with their grotesque shapes. Elves—but not the small, helpful kind of storybooks. Their faces were grotesque masks of glee and malice, teeth sharpened to jagged shards of glass, lips pulled back in eternal sneers. Their eyes, bead-bright and cold as buttons, tracked her. The elves did not rush their movements.

Each carried a tool once benign: rolling pins, piping bags, pastry brushes—but transformed, perverted into instruments of pain. Nails protruded from the wood, molten sugar dripped from the cloth, and every tool seemed to breathe cruelty. This cruelty had rhythm, ritual, almost artistry. Morana thought of folktales told by firelight — of witches who ate children, the hidden folk of the North, the trows of Shetland. Those beings had been mischievous, dangerous, tricksters at the edges of human sight. Here they had been unmasked, stripped of whimsy, forged into tormentors. If they had once stolen butter or bewitched cattle, now they stole innocence itself, binding it in sugar and fire.

Yet even in its the village seemed alive, its decay a mockery of festivity. Gumdrops shrivelled into pits of molten black, Starlight Mints snapped and splintered like the brutalised shrapnel of firewood on the chopping block; and walls bore the clawed and bitten marks of something hungry. Morana's stomach lurched. She felt the pull of memory—the image of gingerbread houses from her childhood, warm and welcoming: but this was no longer a Christmas scene for a bakery display—it was a mausoleum of childhood memories of warmth and safety.

The weight of folklore pressed upon her. Each cottage seemed built not of gingerbread alone but layered with memory — a thousand children's stories condensed, baked, and blackened. The witches' ovens of old tales had multiplied; whole streets of them yawning open: mouths hungry for the next Hansel; the next Gretel. She thought of breadcrumb trails: how easily they were scattered, how quickly the forest swallowed them. Here there would be no breadcrumbs, no path back. The village itself was the oven, and she had already stepped inside. The very air carried the weight of folklore: they came to her mind first as whispers: the kinds of fireside warnings meant to keep children indoors after dusk. The hidden folk of Nordic legend had always lived in thresholds: caves, barrows, hollows in the hills. They were said to mimic human households — smoke curling from unseen chimneys, laughter heard but never found. To step too near their dwellings was to invite sickness, madness, or the quiet theft of one's soul. Here, the echoes of those tales had sharpened. She imagined them crouched within the gingerbread cottages, watching through the seams in sugared shutters, their laughter no longer faint, but shrill, no longer hidden but flaunted.

The trows of Shetland surfaced next, those squat tricksters who crept into homes to steal food, milk, or newborns. Of how they danced in stone circles, their music irresistible yet deadly: anyone who listened too long was lost to their revels. In this place their revelry had curdled. She saw their shadows jerk behind frosting windows, limbs too long, movements too spasmodic to be merry. Their dance was a parody of joy, bodies jerking to rhythms that cracked like bones. The sound that followed was not the drone of fiddle or drum but the scrape of knives across sugar-crusted tables, the hiss of boiling syrup.

What had once been mischievous became predatory; what had once been feared in whispers was now screamed aloud. The hidden folk and the trows had always belonged to the twilight margins of human imagination. Here they had been dragged into firelight, stripped of ambiguity, and forced to serve cruelty openly. Their myth was no longer a warning: all were here, repurposed as agents of torment; their mythologies perverted into instruments of horror.

She stepped over the remnants of a half-melted snowman; its frozen body twisted into unnatural angles. Carrot noses broken and blackened; mouths of coal cracked into expressions of agony. Some elves passed by, dragging portions of another snowman behind them: the other half lost over the hills and far away. Morana felt herself pulled forward, despite the terror that gripped her—each step a surrender to the infernal choreography of this place.

She heard the elves laugh, not giddy but ritualistic. Their laughter rose and fell like carols, though each note bent and broken, a sleigh bell cracked in half. The sound skittered across her nerves. She thought of village squares at Yuletide, choirs with lanterns, children pressing sugared nuts into her palm. The memory soured instantly: here the nuts would be teeth, the lanterns ovens, the children fodder.

Morana felt the fairytale echo—the witches' ovens, the breadcrumb trail of horror—but here it was enacted in three dimensions, in real time, a world turned upside down where innocence had been enslaved to cruelty.

She moved carefully, unwilling to touch the sticky, sweet-sludge in the streets, but the smell followed her relentlessly. Broken gifts littered the corners: smashed, boxes warped, and ribbons shredded. Each package was a promise of terror. A doll lay on its side in the sludge, its porcelain face cracked, eyes filled with congealed marshmallow cream, browned and blistered like pus. Its painted smile had run: streaking down into the muck until it resembled a weeping wound. Nearby, a rocking horse bent under the weight of something writhing in its hollow belly, each creak of wood accompanied by muffled sobs. Wrapping paper clung to walls like wilted banners of forgotten feasts. It was an inversion that cut into her, fairytale magic turned cruel: a brutal reminder that joy could be so easily weaponized.

The candy, the sweetness, was everywhere. But it was toxic: the sugar that should have promised delight now poisoned every sense. Each breath she drew was both intoxicating and sickening. Each sound—the crackle of frozen sugar, the laughter of blackened elves—was a melody of horror. She realized the village itself was alive, feeding on memory, feeding on nostalgia, and feeding on her fear.

The path she had been following through the decaying village twisted unexpectedly, leading her away from the crumbling gingerbread cottages and into a grove of towering candy-canes, their striped trunks arching overhead like the vaulted ribs of a cathedral. A wall of red-and-white spears stood sharpened to cruel points, planted deep into blackened earth like a palisade raised over a graveyard. Their hooked tips curved inward as though to catch intruders in their jaws. From afar they might have passed for festive arches, peppermint-striped pillars meant to welcome children into delight. Up close they revealed their truth: enamelled spirals crusted with gore, their stripes less candy than sinew, each drip of syrup indistinguishable from blood. The sharpened points still wept, drops hissing as they struck the soil. Where syrup touched, smoke rose in tendrils that smelled less of sweetness than of cremation.

Morana hesitated only a breath before stepping forward. The Candy-Cane grove swallowed her.

The canes grew taller as she entered, some still curving like vertebrae overhead; their shadows knitting into a vaulted canopy. Their sticky enamel glistened wetly, streaks of red darkening as though freshly painted. Syrup bled in thick ropes, dripping along her path in a rhythm like a funereal metronome. Her boots sank into treacle veins that sucked and clung, each step a minor struggle, each withdrawal making a sound like lips parting from flesh. The air pressed close, cloying and suffocating. Breathing was like swallowing glass dust mixed with sugar, every inhalation stinging her throat. Beneath the cloy came sharper scents: iron, rot, scorched marrow. Every sound—the pull of her soles, the hiss of dripping syrup—felt amplified, as if the grove itself were listening.

She moved with care, crouching low when shadows stirred ahead. Elves patrolled here, their silhouettes flickering between the striped trunks. They bore themselves with ritualistic poise, each movement deliberate, almost theatrical. On their faces they wore twisted masks with lips pulled into carved sneers. They passed in clusters, their blackened costumes rustling like scorched parchment, dragging prisoners behind them as though drawing offerings toward an altar.

Morana pressed herself into shadow, ducking behind one cane as they paused to work. Through a gap she saw their task: bodies raised like offerings. The victims were hoisted onto the sharpened candy stakes, through torsos, arms, even jaws, their small bodies displayed like grotesque ornaments; limbs twitching. Syrup dribbled down over them, hardening into glassy crusts that sealed their wounds without mercy. Some twitched faintly, fingers jerking like marionettes pulled by unseen strings. Children sagged like broken dolls; their mouths stuffed with candy until muffled screams bubbled from their throats. A veiled bride was forced headfirst down a cane, lace fusing to her body as it split apart. Her legs jerked, then stilled, while the elves licked the dripping syrup as if it were frosting.

The elves tended them as one might tend a festival tree. One ascended a crooked ladder, adjusting the angle of a girl's head so her eyes stared outward toward the path, a glassy welcome for the next traveller. When she whimpered, the elf cooed and stroked her cheek. Then, with a flourish, he drove a nail through her temple, pinning her silence in place.

Morana's stomach tightened. This was no parody of Christmas— it was the revelation of what Christmas had hidden: delight inverted into sacrifice. Candy had become the cross, and children the offerings. She ducked beneath a leaning cane, the laughter of the elves ringing like sleigh bells cracked in half.

Further in, the canes grew denser, forcing her to slip sideways through narrow gaps. Here she stumbled upon another circle of elves engrossed in their craft. A man knelt lashed to a stake, mouth pried open with hooks. One elf held a piping bag swollen with molten sugar, squeezing slowly so the viscous heat poured into his throat. His belly ballooned grotesquely, skin stretching to translucence as the sugar seared him from within. His veins lit red, his chest quaking with muffled screams that became bubbling gurgles.

When the bag was emptied, the elves applauded. One whispered into the man's ear as though passing down a recipe, then split his belly with a sharpened cane. Syrup and viscera spilled steaming onto the ground. The elves scooped ladles of it, tasting as bakers might test icing. Their faces split into ecstasy as though they had sampled perfection.

Morana pressed her fist against her mouth to smother her gasp. Her teeth clenched until her jaw ached. If they saw her, she would be next—piped full, bursting sweetness. She crawled between the bases of two leaning canes, sticky resin clinging to her hands, forcing herself not to tremble.

At last, the grove opened into a clearing strung with silver garlands. At first glance they glittered like holiday decorations, strung from cane to cane in drooping arcs. Then she saw the truth. The garlands were made of human hair, braided and stretched taut. From them dangled ornaments that gleamed in the dim light. She ducked beneath a swaying garland, holding her breath as it brushed her hair. The scent was unbearable, a mix of scorched marrow and syrup boiled past sweetness into rot.

Faces.

Victims had been dipped alive in molten glaze, lacquered until their skin shone like porcelain. Their mouths were forced open by sugar wedges, frozen in eternal smiles. Their eyes bulged, trapped behind hardened gloss, some still flickering faintly with life. They swung gently in the air, clicking against one another like baubles in the wind.

She watched as elves dragged a new victim forward, a woman shrieking until her voice broke. They hoisted her by the arms, plunging her into a cauldron of syrup. Steam roared as her skin blistered. She writhed, her form stiffening as the glaze sealed her. When they hauled her up, she gleamed wetly, her scream trapped forever in the sugar casing. With ritualistic care, they hung her on the garland among the others.

Morana crept beneath the swaying row, the sweet stench clinging to her lips. She ducked low, her back brushing the hair-strands as the "ornaments" turned blindly above her. She could not save them. To try would be to share their fate. The grove demanded decorations, and it would take them until every cane glittered with lacquered faces.

She forced herself onward, clinging to the fragments of breath still hers. And as she moved deeper, she realized this grove was no accident, no fresh cruelty invented for her torment alone. It was older. She remembered fragments of stories told in winter: warnings of groves where children vanished, where candy grew wild and bright, where laughter was heard but never seen. The "Striped Grove," some had called it, though no one could say where it lay. In Alpine villages it was whispered that Krampus hung his prizes there, stringing the wicked for all to see. In the North, tales spoke of hidden folk luring children with sweet stalks, only to bind them forever in the marrow of trees. The Shetlanders told of trows weaving hair into ropes to hang their prey until solstice fires consumed them.

All those tales had been dismissed as fancies. Here, she walked among them. The Candy-Cane grove was not a parody of Christmas, but its black heart laid bare. A cathedral to cruelty, where merriment had been revealed as sacrifice.

The sound of singing drifted closer—a carol, cracked and distorted, voices breaking into sobs and guttural wails. Morana froze, pressing herself against a stake. The singing wasn't the elves. It was the victims, forced into chorus. Their cries rose and fell with the rhythm of a hymn, the grove itself conducting them into a mockery of worship.

Another procession passed. She dared a glance. Prisoners were dragged by the wrists, their feet skidding through the sludge. The elves moved with grim precision, painting stripes of molten sugar across their skin, branding them like meat. One prisoner—an old man with a crown fused to his skull—tried to resist. A candy hook yanked his head back, another pierced his chest, and he was lifted, still alive, onto a waiting cane. His scream broke into the carol, a high note that rang until it dissolved into wet gurgles.

Morana's legs shook. She forced herself onward, weaving between stakes, her breath shallow. A shattered ornament crunched under her boot and she nearly cried out. She bent to see it: a glass globe, its surface scorched, inside a miniature village painted in detail. But the village was wrong. Its houses leaned, snowmen clawed at the sky, and tiny figures hung from minuscule candy stakes. The reflection warped her face across the glass; mouth stretched in horror. She dropped it, heart hammering, and crept forward before the elves could notice.

The deeper she went, the closer the canes pressed, their sticky surfaces brushing her shoulders. Syrup dripped onto her skin, searing like acid. She stifled a gasp, wiping it away, but a welt bloomed across her arm, red and raw. The grove was not passive. It punished touch, punished intrusion.

Her mind betrayed her with memories: Christmases by candlelight, peppermint on her tongue, carols sung by lantern. Each recollection twisted under the weight of this place. The candle became dripping cane. The peppermint a splinter slicing her tongue. The carol a scream. Childhood itself had become a trap, weaponized against her.

She moved in silence, crouching behind a stake as another ritual unfolded. An elf held a piping bag, forcing molten sugar down a victim's throat until his belly swelled, blistered, and burst. Others danced around him, jingling chains of ornaments strung with bones. Their laughter braided into the carols until the grove felt like a congregation at mass—its pews the stakes, its saints the impaled.

The canes began to lean outward, their ranks thinning as though to form an aisle. The treacle underfoot hardened to black glass, cracking with each step. Smoke thickened, tinged with a dull glow. Ahead, upon a rise, the grove gave way to stone.

She saw it then: a hall rising jagged and black: burnt gingerbread, its roof a crown of fused candy-canes, their points twisted into grotesque pinnacles. Smoke poured from its eaves, lit from within by a sullen red. The air pulsed with a low hum, a rhythm like a heartbeat deep in the stone.

Morana's breath caught, shuddering. But she walked onward— because stopping meant surrender. Because stopping meant succumbing. Because looking away meant letting these stories consume her entirely. Because, deep down, she knew that to witness this was to survive—but survival also meant not being the same again.

And as the ground sloped upward towards the blackened hall, Morana steeled herself for worse.

At the heart of the grove, the hall loomed vast and monstrous: a cathedral of blackened gingerbread, walls sagging inward; fused sugar, and scorched bone. Spires of hardened syrup clawed skyward like skeletal fingers, their tips fused with candy-cane shards twisted into grotesque pinnacles. Smoke poured in restless currents from its eaves, a and light bled from wounds in the rafters, a dull arterial glow that made every surface pulse as though alive

Morana's breath faltered. Each step up the slope felt heavier, her boots sticking to the treacle-blackened stones, her chest tightening beneath the weight of dread. She told herself she had survived the forest, but even as she thought it, she knew the forest had only been prologue. Here was the destination, the reason the path had guided her. Here was the Court.

The doors yawned wide, not carved but melted open, their frames drooling sugar tar that hardened into serrated curtains. Beyond lay an expanse of shadow and crimson glow. She slipped inside, swallowed by the air. The air was unbreathable: burned sugar, incense that smelt of frankincense, myrrh, baked apple, souring wine, clove, and rotted orange: all congealed into a sweetness so foul it coated the tongue. Morana drew shallow gasps, each one a knife in her chest. Sticky rivulets of Dutch liquorice dripped in long ropes, dangling above the feasting tables like half-formed stalactites, with hardened jagged chocolate points that threatened to fall with each shudder of the structure.

The tables were laid not for guests but for displays. Melted confections glazed bones into centrepieces; once-white frosting had bubbled into black crusts; broken gingerbread men lay scattered, their heads gnawed away, their icing features scorched. Here and there organs glistened beneath sugar lacquer, veins crystallized into red candy threads, ribs candied into grotesque ornaments. Candles guttered in holders made from jawbones, their wax dripping in great globs like pale fat.

Dark elves scuttled toward the throne. They bore gifts wrapped in skin, ribbons of sinew stretched tight, bows knotted from blood vessels. Some packages pulsed, as if beating faintly from stolen hearts within. Others groaned as though something inside still lived. Each box an offering to the darkness presiding at the hall's end. These gifts the elves set down reverently as they muttered their inverted carols.

And upon the throne, Krampus waited.

Krampus sat upon a throne of fused femurs and peppermint twists. He was massive, his horns curling outward to rake the rafters, tangled with strands of broken lights. His fur was mangy, black matted with patches of ash-grey, revealing the raw topography of old wounds beneath. His face was a ruin between beast and corpse, one eye dull as stone, the other a coal that smouldered fitfully. A tongue black as pitch hung idly over cracked fangs. His claws, long as daggers, tapped slow rhythms against the arms of his throne, the sound more weary than threatening; as though boredom eroded even his appetite for cruelty. His gaze heavy-lidded, half-turned away. Every new shriek, every display of torment, slid off him like rain against stone. The court persisted because it must; the rituals were obligations, not entertainments.

He was terrible, yes—but more terrible still was the weight of weariness about him. His eyes, burned not with rage but with something colder: the exhaustion of centuries, the ennui of a god who had seen every permutation of human folly and flesh and found none of it surprising anymore. The rituals continued, but he did not lean forward. He watched with the vague interest of a man enduring a performance he had already seen a thousand times.

Next came the living gifts: people stripped and their skin decorated as if it were wrapping paper. These were the remnants of last year's catch, Morana realized, the leftovers of a past feast. What she saw paraded before him was not for his pleasure but his maintenance—a reminder to all that his dominion never slept.

A woman was dragged into the chamber—painted head to toe in crimson and gold, her entire body lacquered until she shimmered like gilt parchment, a living ornament. She glowed with a ritual, sacrificial sheen: sacred and obscene in equal measure. Her lips were sealed with molten wax, her eyes wide, ringed in kohl and fear.

Across her bare back stretched a great, ceremonial bow, tied tight enough to make the muscles beneath tremble. The satin loops, once decorative, had long since fused into welts and scars, dyed a deep, deliberate vermilion, the colour of both power and punishment. They forced her to her knees before Krampus. He didn't speak. He didn't need to. She tried to move—but the paint had hardened, cracking at her joints as she trembled. One languid gesture of his clawed hand, and the elves leapt; their hooked candy-cane knives flashing, cutting through her painted skin 'wrapping' as though peeling ribbons. She screamed, ripping open her mouth as the bow unravelled, strips of her flesh curling away like torn paper as the golden 'wrapping' split beneath their knives. The lacquer ran red, paint giving way to blood, and the once-perfect patterns painted across her body dissolved into viscera and ruin. A portion of ribbon fluttered free. An offering in pain. A gift undone.

Another victim, a boy no older than twelve, followed; harlequin diamonds in green and red painted across his body, eyelids gilded shut. Elves unwrapped him with deliberate slowness, tugging until the paint blistered, until his skin tore at the seams of their decoration. His muffled cries broke when they slit his mouth open again, peeling the lips back into a parody of a smile. The elves sang as they worked, their cracked carols rising in shrill chorus as if they rehearsed for a nativity long despoiled. Krampus merely drummed his claws upon the throne, eyes hooded with disinterest.

Then came the unlucky-lucky: those forced to unwrap gifts for themselves. A merchant was handed a parcel that writhed in his arms. When he tugged the sinew ribbons loose, the skin-sack split open and a head rolled free, lips still working as if to form words. He screamed, dropped it, tried to flee, but the elves shoved it back into his hands and made him kiss it, chanting *"Goodwill* to men" in mockery as sleigh-bells clattered. A young woman unwrapped a gift that was her own child, bound and broken, eyes dimming. They crowned her with a circlet of hardened sugar that cut into her scalp, rivulets of blood tracing her face like crimson lace. She collapsed, but the elves propped her upright with candy-cane spears, presenting her as a macabre idol. Her cry tore the air, and she clutched it to her chest as the elves dragged both away. Krampus barely moved. His claws flexed once. His eye flared, then dulled again. He had seen this for eons. Nothing surprised him anymore. Then came a king, dragged in chains, his crown pried from his skull with candy hooks. The elves laughed as they replaced it with a crown of gingerbread, studded with nails of crystallized sugar. They nailed it into his flesh, hammering with glee until blood streamed down his temples. He roared in pain, but the elves only cheered, chanting his name as though acclaiming a sovereign. Here power itself was mocked, crowned not with gold but with candy rot.

The court pulsed with noise: chains rattling, elves shrieking, victims sobbing, the scrape of horns, the hiss of syrup dripping from rafters. Every sound was both ritual and torment, ceremony and cruelty.

And still Krampus watched without expression, his great body shifting only to roll a shoulder or flex a claw. He was not Justice, nor Wrath. He was Continuity—like a god who remains when all meaning has rotted and only spectacle endures. When a victim screamed too long, he gestured once, and the elves silenced them with hooks. When an elf presented a particularly elaborate cruelty, he gave the faintest nod. But there was no hunger in it. No joy. Only the weariness of ritual, a monarch too ancient to be stirred by the suffering that once defined him.

The hall itself seemed to sag with him. Sugar dripped sluggishly from the rafters, less fire than before, more rot. The gifts piled higher on the tables, their twitching, their moaning, forming a chorus of despair that thickened the air like smoke.

Morana felt her heart pounding as if the Little Drummer Boy was playing; each beat a plea for silence. She had thought the worst was the elves, their artistry of pain, their theatrical delight. But this—this sovereign ennui, this cold, unshaken sovereignty— was worse. For it suggested that all agony, no matter how extreme, was finite. It suggested that cruelty itself could become stale, that even horror had its seasons, its repetitions.

And yet, he endured it still.

Krampus' presence pressed on her mind like an avalanche of folklore. He was older than Christ, older than Saturnalia, older than any saint. He was the marrow-deep truth behind all tales of winter punishment, the face glimpsed behind the masks of

Saturn, Odin, the Wild Hunt. A being not of malice alone, but of inevitability. He was hunger made sovereign.

Morana's knees threatened to buckle. She was not yet seen, not yet called—but she felt the truth already: she was one more offering, one more ornament to be displayed, one more parcel in the endless parade of pain.

And Krampus would watch, and Krampus would not care.

Morana felt the weight of it all pressing in, the inversion of every carol, every festive story she had once loved. What had been comfort in childhood now revealed its true face: the tales had never been innocent. They had always been warnings, omens, dark truths softened for children's ears. But here the softening was stripped away, and only the truth remained. This was the living inversion of Christmas. Morana realized, with a certainty colder than ice, that she was not merely watching. The court had already claimed her. She was another note in its carol, another line in its scripture, an extra footnote in the twisted Christmas tale being rewritten before her eyes, another victim wrapped and waiting to be unwrapped.

The elves danced their macabre ballet, their carols splintered into howls, their laughter sharp as broken bells. The throne loomed vast at the end of the hall, Krampus' chains trailing into the dark, his horns scraping higher, higher. He did not need to move to command. His will filled every stone, every breath, every trembling heart.

Morana pressed herself deeper into shadow, yet the hall seemed to draw her in. This was not a place to witness and escape. This was memory, myth, inevitability. Every victim had believed themselves outside the story until they found themselves centre stage.

And then he saw **HER**.

Morana crouched in shadow behind a pillar of fused candy-canes, pressing herself into its curve, heart pounding. She thought she had snuck herself in unseen, but the gaze of the old god found her, slow as dawn. His coal eye burned brighter, and a sound rumbled from him—not hunger, not rage, but something more dangerous. Amusement.

The elves noticed his attention and turned, their heads cocking, eyes gleaming. One hissed, "A stray." Another chittered, "Fresh meat."

From the shadows behind her came the scrape of burning hooves on stone. Morana froze, breath catching, but too late—something vast had already closed the distance. Two reindeer overseers had crept upon her in silence. Charred fur brushed her shoulder, embers falling like sparks from a forge, and then a clawed hand clamped down on her arm. Morana thrashed, boots slipping in syrup-slick ash, nails raking against coarse fur. The reindeer only laughed, its grip bruising, dragging her backward as though she were no more than a doll. She wrenched once, twice—heard something tear in her shoulder—but still she fought, kicking against its shins, her breath raw in her throat. The second guard pressed closer, antlers pricking her skin, a bead of warmth rising beneath her collar as it seized her waist, hooves grinding scorch marks into the sticky floor as together they lifted her effortlessly, her own struggles no more significant than a moth thrashing in flame. And still she fought—because surrender felt like erasure. Each kick, each claw of her nails against their ember-crusted hides, was meaningless, yet to stop would be to concede that she was only material, a thing to be wrapped, unwrapped, and discarded. Terror swarmed her chest, but beneath it pulsed something colder: the dread certainty that this was ritual, and she had no more agency than a lamb brought to the altar. Her body strained uselessly; her mind screamed at the inevitability. Their twisted antlers loomed above, pulsing with veins of fire, faces screaming in their branching black coral as though the forest itself had reached out to seize her. For an instant she thought she recognized those faces—old kings carved from saga, maidens from nursery tales, saints from church murals— all screaming, all trapped in antler-bone like insects in amber. These were no mere beasts but avatars of a winter far older than Christmas, guardians of the Wild Hunt shackled to Krampus' leash, their nobility warped into servitude. Their grasp carried not only brute strength but the weight of centuries of corrupted myth.

The elves chittering built into a frenzy: Their voices rose like a choir of nursery rhymes sung backward, each promise of cruelty half-taunt, half-liturgy. The air shivered, and Morana felt the whispers crawl beneath her skin—not only threat but prophecy, as if in naming torments they began to stitch them into her fate. Their words bent around her, squeezing tighter than the reindeer's grip, until she could almost feel the transformations they imagined: her ribs clicking like sleigh bells, her shadow torn free to dance without her, her veins hardened into striped candy that split with each heartbeat.

"She's soft," hissed one, licking syrup from its fingers. "I'll carve her skin in stripes—red and white—make her into a cane."

"I'll hollow her bones," another giggled, "fill them with sugar, let her walk until the sweetness leaks out."

"I'll stitch her hair into tinsel," crooned a third, "hang her scalp from the rafters and let it sway when the bells ring."

A fourth leaned close, its voice low and venomous: "I'll crack her ribs like walnuts, suck the marrow hot. We'll bind her limbs into bows, make her unwrap herself."

The whispers tangled, overlapping:

"Her eyes for baubles—glass orbs for the tree."

"Tongue into a candy ribbon—stretch it, tie it, pull until it snaps."

"Paint her nails with lacquer, let children pull them like sugar pearls."

"Her teeth ground to powder, dusted over cakes we'll feed to children."

"Her lungs filled with boiling chocolate—she'll drown in sweetness."

"Bind her in heated foil, shake her when she screams—gift-wrap music!"

One shrieked with sudden glee, "No, no—let her unwrap *us*! Let her peel our skin and find her face inside!" The others cackled, slapping the floor.

Another hissed sharp as a blade: "I'll pour boiling syrup into her ears. Let her head fill and set—solid, sweet, silent."

And one, smaller, more vicious than the rest, whispered what made even its kin recoil for an instant: "I'll sew her into her own stomach. Wrap her in herself. Make her the gift and the giver both."

Their laughter rose, a cracked carol, sleigh bells jingling somewhere above as though mocking the chorus. The chamber shivered with their hunger, their delight at imagining the hundred ways she might be undone. Even the hall itself seemed to participate. The tar-dripped walls bent inward, their runnels hardening into shapes that resembled letters, runes from sagas half-remembered, sigils of sacrifice older than Christ. The pillars leaned like vertebrae, vertebrae slick with syrup, curving in to witness her capture. Somewhere above, the rafters groaned, releasing a single drop of molten sugar that landed sizzling on her cheek, as though the building itself wished to mark her for the feast.

But Krampus stirred at last. His massive hand lifted, claws spread, and everyone froze mid-step. His gaze lingered on Morana, the ember eye burning with faint delight. The corners of his mouth curled—not a smile, not yet, but the ghost of one, a twitch unused for centuries. He rumbled a laugh, deep and dry as a cave's collapse.

"Not for you," he said, voice cracked, ancient, the words scraping like stone dragged across stone. The elves whined but fell back, clutching their gifts as if afraid they'd be taken away. The entire hall seemed to flinch. The reindeer froze mid-breath, smoke curling from their nostrils; the elves shrank like whipped dogs, their glee curdling into sulk and silence. For centuries, his voice had been a hammer only of judgment, never of reprieve. That he would deny them, that he would single her out—not as prey, not as spectacle, but as something else—was a miracle so perverse it terrified her more than their promised torments. His ember eye lingered, brightening with the faintest gleam of curiosity, as though the monotony of ages had cracked for an

THE GOBLIN OF ADVENT

instant. That brief amusement, that flicker of diversion, was worse than cruelty. Because it meant she was now his diversion. And diversions did not end gently.

Krampus' ember eye did not leave her. His horns shifted against the rafters with a sound like mountains grinding. At last, his voice rumbled out, slow and deliberate, each word like a stone placed upon her chest.

"Few cross this threshold by will. Fewer still stand unbound before me. So, tell me, mortal—why have you come? What prize could draw you into the maw?"

Morana forced the words through the weight in her throat. "Because something was taken from me."

The ember eye brightened, narrowing to a furnace-point. "Taken," he echoed, the word coiling in the rafters like smoke. "And *so* you seek redress? Then tell me—was it flesh? A child, a bride, a sinner plucked from the snow? If so, you come too late. I claim only what is owed, and the world offers me more each passing year. Their greed, their cruelty, their wanton hunger— each summons me. None undeserving."

Morana shook her head, desperation threading her voice. "Not a person." She faltered. "A gift."

Krampus stirred, his vast bulk shifting with the slow groan of chains. The air seemed to still. Then, with the faintest curl of disdain, he whispered: "Ah... a gift. Then the Advent Thief has crept through your door."

The shadows flickered as his antlers pulsed faintly with fire. He leaned forward, voice lowering to a resonance that felt older than the hall itself. "How far the season has fallen. Once, mortals sang the midwinter carols to me—yes, to me. Hearths glowed with flame in my honour, and bells tolled with a weight of reverence, not mockery. They laid offerings of grain, of blood, of song upon the snow, that I might spare their houses. There was fear then, yes—but it was the fear that made joy precious, life sharper in the frost. They remembered the cost of light."

His claw dragged once across the throne's arm, scoring the sugar-crusted stone. "Now they leave nothing. Not prayer, not fire, not song. They gorge, and forget. And I am left to rot in this parody of festivity, a monarch of ashes and tar."

The great head lowered until his ember eye pinned her like a brand. "Yet here you stand, daring frost and flame for a gift. Not for life, not for power, not for flesh. A trifle. A bauble. And yet unbroken. You have travelled far. You have even seen the Court and still drawn breath. This is more than bleeding, mortal. This is pilgrimage. Ordeal. Descent."

His ember eye burned brighter, and for the first time in centuries there was something more than weariness in it—something like reverence, reluctant and begrudging, but real. "You bleed for it. You endure. Perhaps, in this small defiance, joy is not wholly dead. Perhaps the old songs were not lies. That one might suffer for a gift—not power, not dominion, but a gift—may yet mean the world remembers what it has lost."

Krampus leant, his bulk shifting with a groan of chains. He pointed one claw toward the far wall. A door there sagged open, narrow and steep, exhaling a fetid draft.

"Down," he rasped, the word like a cavern groaning. "To the dungeons. To the Goblin's burrow, where even oubliettes are forgotten, where memory itself is starved and chained. Few who descend recall their own names, fewer still return to speak them. It is the grave of stories. The place where hope rots."

His claws tapped once more against the throne, then stilled. "Yet perhaps you will walk it differently. For you have borne the forest's hunger, the Court's pageantry of ruin, and still you endure. This is not the march of cattle to slaughter. This is the step of one who knows that descent may yet be answered by ascent."

The elves hissed their disappointment, gnashing their teeth, but none disobeyed.

Morana trembled, torn between terror and the faintest thread of hope. He had spared her from their claws, but only to deliver her to something worse. The Advent Thief.

And for the first time in an eon, Krampus sat straight upon his throne, chains groaning, ember eye fixed upon her. Not as one watches another victim, but as one beholds a figure out of half-remembered legend. His great jaw slackened, the ghost of a grin pulling the scarred muzzle, as though he savoured not just her fear, but the strangeness of her courage.

The reindeer seized her once more, their ember-veined antlers casting writhing shadows along the walls, and with hooves striking sparks on the sugared stone, they carried her toward the waiting dark.

CHAPTER TWELVE

JOY IS FOR THE DYING

The reindeer carried her downward. Their antlers scraped the narrowing ceiling, sparking light where veins of fire ran through stone. Each step of their burning hooves left seared tracks on the spiralling stair, and Morana felt the air grow colder despite the heat. The draft smelt of mold and ash, a sweetness gone sour, like fruit long rotted in its rind.

At last the creatures halted before a gate of black iron, crooked on its hinges. Without warning, they threw her to the ground. Stone split her lip; heat seared her palms. One beast kicked her in the ribs as if to remind her she was less than freight. Their eyes glimmered with nothing of reindeer gentleness — only contempt, as though she were already half-claimed by the pit below. Then, snorting ash, they climbed back into the dark, their hoofbeats vanishing up the endless stair.

Morana staggered to her knees. The gate sagged before her, rust streaking it like dried blood. Beyond lay a cavern vast as a cathedral, its roof smothered in smoke. Stalactites hung like fangs. Veins of pitch ran down the walls and bled into pools that hissed where molten stone broke through.

She pushed the gate; it moaned like something waking unwillingly.

Inside, the air pressed heavy as a grave's weight. Shadows shifted of their own accord. Worms, fat with ash writhed along the floor; rats with too many eyes skittered among heaps of wreckage. Shattered toys, burnt paper, bones charred to brittle black. Ornaments dangled from iron chains above, dripping molten glass in slow beads.

And in the centre, on a dais of jagged stone, crouched the Advent Thief.

He was smaller than Krampus, yet infinitely worse to look upon. Intimate. Knowing. His limbs were knotted like roots, his spine hunched, his belly sagging with the plunder of stolen feasts. His skin cracked and flickered like burned parchment. His furnace-red eyes smouldered beneath a dripping brow, blinking open and shut like oven doors. His grin was thin as a razor, every tooth different — some bone-white, others jagged copper, others glinting with fragments of stained glass.

Chained to a ring at the dais's base slumped a brown bear. The iron links bit into his shoulders, crusted with dried blood and ash. His fur, once thick and golden, hung in clumps. His eyes followed Morana wearily, but there was recognition in them — recognition and a sorrow deeper than any human gaze could bear.

The Advent Thief stirred, stretching as if he had been waiting only for her. His skin cracked, leaking embers that hissed against the stone.

"Ah," he hissed, the word curling into her ears like smoke. His voice was both whisper and rasp, a lullaby curdled into mockery. He prowled in slow, deliberate circles, tapping a clawed finger lightly on the stone — a counting of losses, a fey-like habit. The bear flinched at the noise but did not react when some of the stolen gifts were kicked in its direction.

"You thought you ended me?" His head jerked, vertebrae cracking like knuckles. "You thought me drowned, snuffed in fire? Fool. Shadows return when the sun dies, when winter lays her pall again. There is always more night."

The Advent Thief's grin twitched wider, the stained-glass teeth glinting. "And what do you bring me this time? Not claws, not fire. Only yourself. Only the scent of borrowed courage." He inhaled, nostrils flaring. "It reeks of grief sugared over. A taste I know too well."

He prowled the dais's edge, shadows coiling around him like hounds, but his motions held the sly precision of a thief, not the brute approach of a predator.

"You hear it, don't you?" His words dripped, thick as venom. "The emptiness. The silence between carols, the stillness after bells fade. You cannot silence it. It has always been there. And it has always been mine."

Morana straightened, her ribs aching from the reindeer's kick. Her lips parted — dry, cracked.

"It is not yours," she said. Her voice sounded small.

The goblin's eyes flared, and his grin sharpened.

"We shall see."

The air thickened as the Advent Thief regarded her, eyes glimmering like embers beneath stone.

"You are far from home, little candle," he rasped, his words curling like smoke around her ears. "And yet... you come willingly. Foolish, or brave? Perhaps both."

Morana's mouth went dry. She forced herself to breathe, her hands tight at her sides.

The Advent Thief leaned back slightly, tilting his head. "Do you know why I watch?" His grin split thinly, revealing teeth like jagged glass. "Because hope is a fragile thing. So sweet. So fleeting. And I... I collect it. I savour the stumble, the falter, the gasp when joy cracks and fails. There is a delicious warmth in another's misfortune; *SCHADENFREUDE* — *ah*, a spice that never cools."

A shadow passed across the cavern as he tapped his finger again, each strike echoing in rhythm with the unspoken rules of the fey — careful, deliberate, never a lie, always a counting of debts and losses.

Tap... tap... tap.

"Why wake to joy when you know it dies?" His voice dropped, soft, intimate, a whisper that crawled along her skin. "Why sing carols when voices will be silenced? Why feast when the table will be empty again? Tell me, child. Why suffer the wound of joy, when apathy is balm?"

The words wormed inside her mind. She pictured her mother's laughter, warm and gone. Her grandmother's bent frame, fragile and fleeting. The Advent Thief's voice pressed her toward apathy, toward surrender.

"You see," he hissed, circling, claws scraping a rhythm on the stone, "joy is a luxury. A fleeting, foolish dream. Better to let it go. To care nothing. To stop the pain before it ever begins."

Morana shivered. The cavern seemed to shrink, the firelight flickering in her eyes as if uncertain whether to burn at all: molten shadows licking upward like dark sermons. Morana's chest tightened. For a moment, his promise pressed close — tempting. Yet somewhere in her chest, a spark refused to dim.

He circled her now, voice dripping into her ears like venom. "Your mother's laughter made her loss heavier, did it not? Joy sharpened grief's knife. And your grandmother—ah, yes. Bent and brittle. One year, two at most, and she will be gone. Why fight for a holiday already lost to the grave?"

Morana trembled. His words dug deep, prising open wounds she had carried silently. She saw her grandmother's hands, fragile as parchment, trembling as she lifted a cup of mulled wine. She saw her mother's smile, radiant in memory, gone too soon. The Advent Thief's whispers wrapped these images in shadow, whispering that it would be easier to stop caring. To stop fighting.

Her lips parted, and her voice, though cracked, broke the silence. "To lose joy is sorrow," she said. "But to refuse joy is despair."

The Advent Thief laughed, shrill and cruel. "Poetry. Fool's poetry." He leaned close, breath rank with the rot of sugared meat. "Do you not see? Joy is illusion. A bauble dangled to distract you from the void."

Morana's breath shuddered, and the weight of his words nearly broke her knees. Was it true? That joy was but a bauble, a fleeting trinket for selfish hands to hoard? The cavern swayed with his promise, molten shadows rising like sermons of despair, each echo whispering: take, take, take.

She closed her eyes, and memory opened like a hymn. Her grandmother's voice carrying stories of shepherds and angels. She saw the soft glow of lanterns, each flame trembling as if bowing to the newborn king. She pictured the manger, simple and humble, yet radiant with the presence of God, a light that would not be extinguished. She remembered her family gathered close, silent for a moment, eyes lifted as if glimpsing the wonder of angels above the manger. In that quiet awe, even the smallest gift — a token, a word, a smile — felt charged with mercy, a reflection of the dawn from on high breaking into a darkened world. Laughter and whispers rose together, pure and unforced, carrying the truth that God's tender love enters even the coldest, loneliest places. In that instant, she felt it: Emmanuel, God with us, and the enduring light of heaven touching the earth through hearts open to joy

"The world is broken," she whispered, more to herself than anyone else. "Since the Fall, we have known it. Sin claws at everything we love. We lose. We grieve. And yet..." Her eyes opened, steady now, their reflection kindled by the candle flame. "Yet God has not abandoned us. He delights in us. He gives Himself into our frail hands, as once He was given to Mary's arms. At Christmas, He puts His faith in us, and calls us to do the same — to hold joy tenderly, to guard it for one another."

The goblin's grin faltered, ever so slightly. The hiss of the cavern dimmed. She pressed on.

"You forget," she said, voice small, hesitant, yet gathering weight, "that joy is not only for the strong. Sometimes it is all we have against the night. It is defiance. It is mercy. It is the dawn that breaks upon those who sit in darkness and in the shadow of death, guiding our feet into the way of peace. Even grief cannot extinguish it. Even death cannot conquer it."

The Advent Thief chuckled, the sound brittle and cruel. "Little candle, you think you can defy me? You think a single spark can withstand centuries of shadow?"

He stopped, tilting his head with curiosity now, the first pause in his taunting. For a fleeting heartbeat, his sly, thief-like self, watched her as if gauging a trick — perhaps expecting aid she may or may not summon. For a moment, the predatory rhythm faltered — just enough for her to find her footing, to breathe against the encroaching darkness.

Morana drew a shuddering breath, the heat of the cavern crawling up her throat like molten iron. The Advent Thief prowled, flicking his claws, each tap on the stone counting losses she would not surrender to. Yet in the rhythm of his tapping, she discerned a pattern — a pause, a subtle hesitation, a sly creature who thrived on mockery yet recoiled from acknowledgment of truth. He produced from the shadows a small, wrapped package —

a gift, **HER** gift: offered back. Held out like a prize. "Here," he hissed, claws curling around it, "yours, if you dare. Take it. A trinket, a bauble, a spark of delight — all for you. Why share? Why struggle? Why care for others when the world offers so little to repay your efforts?"

Morana's pulse thundered. The package gleamed in the firelight, innocent, inviting — yet heavy with implication. The gleam of a trap. Not freely, but as a snare, a test: take it for yourself, he seemed to whisper, and abandon the rest to darkness. He fed on temptation, on the sight of hearts twisting under the weight of choice, savouring the falter before surrender, the spark of greed before hope is lost.

"See how easy it could be," the Advent Thief crooned, his furnace eyes glinting with malice. "One choice, one act, and you need not worry for anyone else. The village, the children, the waiting hearths — forget them. Take what is yours. Let them find joy without you, or not at all. The world does not care; why should you?" He tapped the package lightly, as if counting her hesitation. "A human will always pick themselves if given the chance. Always. One gift, one selfish act... and proof is written in your own hands. Do you crave proof?"

The village, forest, lake, beasts, shadows, crypt, hellscape, the court—everything coalesced into a single vision: childhood innocence annihilated, folklore made flesh in grotesque forms. All around, the world melted together — sugar, fire, smoke — a single grotesque testament to corrupted joy. Morana's body moved on its own, drawn forward by the weight of history and memory. The blackened sky above reflected the burning, melted sweets below. The snowmen, the elves, the victims—each was a living testament to the perversion of joy. Every Christmas story she had ever heard, every whispered fairy tale, had been warped, melted, and reassembled into this single, endless horror.

The gift tempted her. It called to the small, aching desire for ease, for relief from the crushing world. She swallowed hard, her fingers twitching toward the gift, almost yielding. Yet in that moment, memory pierced the choking haze: the crackle of the hearth, her mother's flour-dusted hands, the smell of baking bread. The thrill of unwrapping a gift with her grandmother's warm gaze watching, pride and love shining in her tired eyes. The laughter of children she had never met but could not abandon. These moments, fleeting, yes — but alive. Burning, shared, and infinitely greater than any gift hoarded for selfish ends. Her own selfish desire faltered beneath the weight of shared love, and the Advent Thief's delight in human frailty only sharpened her resolve. To claim it would be simple — but the price was unthinkable: the suffering of others, the surrender of hope, the betrayal of love. A surge of *weltschmerz* — sorrow for the world, for children waiting, for the village she could not abandon — rolled through her chest, almost buckling her knees.

She opened her eyes, and her voice, small at first, gained clarity and weight. "Joy endures where shadow cannot tread; it defies even your hatred."

The Advent Thief hissed; smoke thinned; edges faltering... then flared, a storm of molten shadow, yet her words had begun to cut. His claws raked the stone, sparks flying. "You dare? Joy cannot last! Winter always returns!" His furnace eyes dimmed, edges crumbling as if the very outline of him could not hold.

Morana's heart battered her ribs. His gaze pinned her, sly and cruel. He was dangerous not like a beast but like a whisper in the dark — already inside her head. Perhaps he had never known warmth, never sung, never been welcomed. That absence shaped him. And yet, even in the hollow of his malice, a thought could take root... if only gently. She remembered Krampus, how he had not killed her when he might have. She recalled the fae's rules — never lie, never thank aloud, always honour deeds quietly. Had he done her a twisted favour? Fairies hated an unacknowledged gift. Perhaps the goblin thought her now indebted to his rival. That, she realized, could cut both ways.

Her gaze flicked on the chained bear, and a pang of grief clawed at her chest. Memories stirred — her mother's little wooden bear amulet; its carved face a quiet sentinel of protection, buried with care. She felt, as if in some delicate dream, her mother's hand wrap around hers while holding it, warm and steady, pressing a quiet love into her palm. The weight of that lost warmth pressed deep into her chest, and a tear slid down her cheek, mourning what was gone yet never truly lost. Her grandmother's voice whispered through her mind, telling of the Brown Ones of the forest: kings of the woods, guardians against darkness, sacred and untouchable. Now here, chained in iron, humiliated, a deliberate perversion. The fae despised iron, and yet the Advent Thief bound what was sacred, thinking to snuff the light of reverence itself.

A frostbite of insight bit through her fear: the Advent Thief could twist joy, manipulate desire, even tempt her with selfish delight — but he could not undo what was sacred, what endured in memory and in heart. The bear, noble and bound, was still a sentinel; its quiet dignity resisted corruption, and so too could her spirit. She inhaled sharply, grounding herself. The image of the bear fused with the memories of hearth and gift-giving, a reminder that defiance and care were intertwined. Even in the cavern of malice, some light remained untouchable, and she would honour it.

"You say joy is illusion," she whispered, loud enough for the cavern to drink it in. "That laughter is fragile, that celebrations crumble. But you... you destroy it because you never had it. You were denied warmth, denied welcome, denied the songs that make the heart rise. That is your choice, not the world's. You collect grief like a miser hoards coin, yet joy... joy is given freely, even to those who would steal it."

Morana straightened, trembling but resolute, drawing strength from memory, the sacredness of the bear, and the warmth of countless Christmas mornings. "And so we light it again. And again. Until the end."

She advanced, each movement deliberate, letting the weight of her love, her memories, her defiance, press against his darkness. The cavern throbbed with centuries of joy and hope, fragile yet unbroken, pressing against the weight of his malice. The Advent Thief's grin faltered, the rhythm of his claws stuttering — for the first time, she sensed that her courage, and the defiance it embodied, was piercing through the shroud of his malice.

The Advent Thief hissed: like a sharp wind tearing through stagnant heat. His furnace eyes glowed, shifting, suspicious, as if her words had slipped past his defences.

Morana's mind raced, recalling the fey rules she had learned from Krampus' aid. Never lie to a Fey. Never thank them for gifts aloud. But acknowledge their deeds in quiet reverence. A plan blossomed: she would not give him false praise, but she could plant a seed of thought.

"I could place a gift for you," she said softly, deliberate. "A token, left in secret. Something small, unnoticed, yet known. Not for fear, not for obedience — but for the joy of giving. Even to you, even to a creature who has never known it."

For the first time, his grin faltered. His claws stopped tapping; the rhythm of despair stuttered. He leaned closer, scent of charred sugar heavy, yet wary. Morana pressed onward.

"Joy is not illusion. It is a defiance. Against sorrow, against death, against the shadows you weave." She stepped closer to the bear, tracing the iron with her gaze, imagining the sacred reverence of brown bears guarding the world. "And though you chain what is sacred, though you think to twist it into your mockery, it remembers. It endures. And I... I remember, too."

A pause. The cavern seemed to hold its breath. Even the blackened smoke swirled slower, curling around him like a hesitant cloak. The Advent Thief's furnace eyes narrowed, suspicion and something else — fear, almost — flickering beneath their glow.

"Joy is for the living," Morana said, her voice rising, a spear of defiance in the oppressive heat. "It does not bow to fear. It does not bend to bitterness. It is the warmth you have denied yourself, yes — but not the warmth of the world. Not the love given freely, the laughter that survives, the songs that echo beyond your reach. You cannot take it from those who will hold it still."

The Advent Thief hissed, smoke thickening like storm clouds. Yet in the cracks of his fury, Morana glimpsed the truth: he was not infinite. His malice was bound to memory, to his own grievance, not to the world itself. And she stepped forward, closer to him, voice steady, a blade slicing the tether of his anger, testing the limits of a creature that thrived on despair. "I will not let your shadow fall here. Not over me, not over those I love. And perhaps... perhaps even you can still receive what you were denied."

The furnace glow in his eyes wavered. The claws twitched, uncertain. Morana's chest rose and fell with deliberate breaths, each one a fragile anchor against the oppressive air. Shadows quivered unnaturally, coiling like living smoke, and the cavern itself seemed to breathe, steeped in the suffering and malice of centuries.

The bear stirred.

Her gaze flicked on the chained bear, and a pang of grief clawed at her chest. Its eyes—dark, ancient, and knowing—held a sorrow that reached beyond the mere cruelty of the Advent Thief. "Ah, do you recognise him? He is not just any bear; this is Veles! Let me tell you his story, and tremble for we speak of beings that had walked the world long before humans carved settlements into the woods. Legends said he could summon storms, command beasts, and speak the language of roots and stones".

Morana felt the tremor of a tale older than memory as the Advent Thief began the tale:

"Long ago, in the age when the world was young and gods still walked among men, Veles had interfered with a ritual of Czarnobóg, god of misfortune. The people believed — as mortals so often do — that only the spilling of human blood could appease a god. They did not see the truth: Czarnobóg hungered not for appeasement, but for ruin — death of body and soul, the quiet extinguishing of hope.

In that age, Veles had acted with compassion. He had sought to spare the innocent, to shield those who laboured under the shadow of Czarnobóg's relentless malice. For this, the god of misfortune struck, binding Veles to the shape of a mortal beast, stripping him of divine radiance, chaining him with iron as a mockery of the power he once wielded in a hole beneath the land he commanded: never again to feel the apricity again. The ritual ground, the forests, the rivers he once commanded, were now scarred by fire and ash. His voice, once the wind through treetops and the rush of rivers, was reduced to the sigh of fur against iron".

The cavern seemed to pulse with the moral horror of the act: iron biting into fur, the scent of ash, the molten veins glowing like blood under stone, and the weight of centuries pressing on Morana's chest. And yet, even bound, Veles's presence radiated a quiet dignity, a reminder that no chain — mortal or divine — could entirely snuff the enduring light of protection he embodied.

His essence endured. Within the weary, bloodied eyes of the bear, Morana glimpsed the eternal vigilance of a guardian who had dared defy a god, who had chosen the welfare of mortals over his own glory. He was a sentinel of a world that Czarnobóg sought to rend, a testament to resistance against despair. The iron chains bit into him, molten streaks of stone ran like veins beneath the cavern floor, and the Advent Thief prowled nearby — a warden, a mocker, a creature corrupted by the long shadow of grief and cruelty. Yet even in his chains, Veles's presence pressed on the mind like a story remembered in whispers across centuries: that courage and protection could endure, even in forms that seemed broken, even beneath the weight of divine wrath.

Morana's chest ached as the truth of it pressed into her mind. This was no mere beast. This was a god who had borne the injustice of another deity's spite to safeguard the living. The bear's dignity was a quiet, unwavering defiance, a myth incarnate. And if she could honour that, if she could see and act with the reverence the world had long forgotten, she might yet carry some fragment of that ancient, enduring light into the darkness that threatened to swallow her. Morana grounded herself. She traced the iron with her gaze, imagining the sacred reverence of brown bears guarding the world. Even in this cavern of malice, some light remained untouchable. And now she understood: freeing Veles was not merely an act of courage—it was a restoration of justice, of memory, of the balance between the mortal and the sacred.

"You chain what is sacred," she whispered, voice threading through molten air thick with ash and heat, "but you cannot break it. Even you cannot snuff that light."

The Advent Thief stiffened. His furnace eyes flickered, not with rage, but with something darker—memory, loss, and the weight of centuries without warmth. In the molten light, the scars along his flesh shimmered like a grotesque tapestry: marks not merely of battle, but of exile, hunger, and neglect. Twisted sinew and jagged bone hinted at transformations he had suffered to survive the long winters, to mimic the cruel fey and hide from the wrath of those he had once betrayed.

Morana knelt, running her fingers along the iron that bit into the bear's shoulders. Rust flakes, like dark snow, fell into molten pools. The bear shifted, its matted fur flickering like sunlight in smoke, eyes impossibly deep with patience and sorrow. Morana could feel the echoes of a god in that gaze whose memory outlived tyrants and tormentors. The cavern's molten veins pulsed as if in resonance, tremors running through the floor, walls, and ceiling.

She knelt lower, pressing her hands against the iron chains. They shrieked like bone splitting under pressure. Whispering, she offered warmth and reverence, invoking the forest kings, the spirits of hearth and gift, and the small, enduring joys of her childhood. Slowly, almost imperceptibly, the chains broke. With a groan like cracking bone, they fell away. Iron split as if torn by the jaws of the earth itself, shards hissing molten in the air. The cavern roared with a thunder older than stone, and from the bear's chest rolled a sound so vast it was not a growl but the memory of creation itself. His breath burst in a gale of ash and snow, scattering fire like frightened birds. The walls bowed as though in worship, and every shadow fled before the terrible dignity of Veles freed.

The bear rose. Its fur, burned and matted, shimmered with the dignity of survival. Muscles flexed like living maps of legend, sinew and fur entwined with mythic power. The goblin recoiled, furnace eyes reflecting both malice and a glimmer of recognition—he saw, perhaps, what he had never known: courage and care unbroken by cruelty. For a heartbeat, his grin faltered, and Morana saw not the monster but the creature he had been.

"You were not always like this," she said softly to the Advent Thief, voice carrying through the molten gloom. "Once, you were small, warm, perhaps loved, perhaps protected. And they—whoever they were—took it from you. You were denied hearth and home, song and laughter. You learned cruelty because kindness was denied."

The Advent Thief's jaw twitched. Smoke curled from cracked lips. Furnace light flickered across twisted bones and gnarled joints. He hissed, almost inaudibly, a sound caught somewhere between anguish and fury. "Do you think pity will save you?" His words were rough as burned parchment. "Do you think understanding will undo what has taken centuries to carve into my flesh?"

Morana pressed on. "I do not offer pity. I offer acknowledgment. You were shaped by suffering, yes, but you are not its master. You can choose another path. Let it begin with this bear. Let it begin with one small act that honours what you were denied, not what you hoarded."

"You... would give," he rasped, voice a twisted lullaby of longing and spite, "to one who has never known warmth?"

Morana nodded. "Not because you deserve it. Not for obedience. But because the act itself matters. Even for you, even for a creature denied joy, there can be the spark of giving."

For a moment, silence. Then the goblin, as if testing the fragile truce, discarded the small wrapped Advent gift toward her, letting it tumble, indifferent yet deliberate. His furnace eyes softened slightly; flickers of recognition betraying centuries of longing and loss. The unspoken pact lingered: and if she inspired other children to leave gifts, he would avoid taking from those households too.

The cavern convulsed violently, as though the world itself was tearing open. Walls split in jagged arcs; veins of molten stone yawned like serpents seeking escape. Black stalactites quivered like fangs, dripping with fire. From the fissures, molten light spilled across grotesque reliefs carved by the earth itself: cages, shattered toys, phantom children frozen in eternal fear — twisted monuments to stolen warmth. The bear-god stepped beside her, a sentinel of earth and storm. His presence made the fissures widen, molten rivers hissing in fear whilst also grounding her against the quake. Behind her, the goblin watched, crooked grin trembling at its edges. He was not defeated, not silenced — but for the first time, he hesitated. Perhaps even tasted, faintly, the spark of what he had never possessed. Even as the ground trembled and the cavern groaned, she understood something fundamental: the peril was not just around her—it had been within her all along. And she had endured.

The Advent Thief prowled in the trembling dark, smoke curling from him like the residue of centuries of grief. His grin was sly, but beneath, Morana saw the boy he had once been: abandoned at the edge of winter, hollow-eyed, left to freeze while others feasted. Warmth had been withheld, joy denied, until his wound had festered into hunger with teeth. Now he fed upon faltering, upon despair, for it was the only feast the world had ever left him.

"You risk all for what cannot last," he hissed, smoke billowing from his furnace eyes. "Perhaps all this was for nothing. Even if you freed your precious beast, even if you spoke your clever words — still, you must return. Still, you must cross your hearth before the night dies. That is part of the Law of Advent. And Mundilfari... he is not your ally." His words coiled like molten smoke, half threat, half bitter delight.

The ground split wider, fissures exhaling fire. Shadows reached up like smoke-born hands, clutching, whispering in the voices of children long devoured by despair. Morana's chest constricted, but she forced herself forward, drawing on every memory she carried: the crackle of the hearth, her grandmother's voice telling of the Brown Ones, her mother's hand pressing the wooden bear amulet into hers. Warmth, love, reverence — these were her armour.

The gatefold shivered into being, its outline glowing like a wound in the fabric of the world. Time pressed at her back like a blade. Morana stepped toward it, each movement deliberate, bearing warmth, defiance, and memory as her only shield.

The G Advent Thief's laughter followed, dwindling, whispering even as it vanished into the quake:

"Joy cannot last forever."

But Morana did not falter. She stepped into the gatefold, into the bitter bite of winter, the night stretching on before her — alive with peril, yes, but also with the enduring light of memory Veles rumbled, following behind her, the sound of mountains shifting in their sleep — a promise and a threat carried in one breath. The Advent Thief watched, his crooked grin stretching thin — not defeated, never defeated, only amused at the race she must still run. Girl, beast-god, and goblin — bound together by bargain and defiance, suspended in that narrow instant before the night devoured all. Thus was a pact of fire and shadow struck in the deep places of the world, where a child bore joy against despair, and the bonds of gods and monsters alike were broken.

Yet such victories are never without cost, and the echo of that night would tremble through every winter yet to come. And above, the first snow of dawn began to fall.

JOY IS FOR THE DYING

CHAPTER THIRTEEN

LITANY AGAINST THE LONG NIGHT

The first snow of dawn had begun to settle, whispering across the jagged teeth of the winter landscape like ash falling from a ruined sky. Morana stumbled forward out of the gatefold, her limbs heavy with the weight of exhaustion, the memory of the Advent Thief's furnace eyes still burning behind her skull. Each step pressed her deeper into uncertainty. Her home was over hills and far away.

The first touch of false dawn licked across the horizon, threatening to erase the night and all its secret wonders. Paths twisted and dissolved into shadow; the forest seemed alive, the trees bending and groaning as if mocking her, roots writhing underfoot like snakes, grasping to trip her.

The footprints of Veles' great paws disappeared in the powdered snow. The iron chains that had bound him were gone, yet every step he took was measured, ancient, as if he carried the memory of mountains in his bones. Morana pressed closer, gripping his fur, feeling the warmth of life and legend beneath her fingers. A sharp wind tore through the trees. The wind smelled of iron and burned sugar, thick with the memory of fear. Morana shivered. She had no map; and there was no Christmas star to guide her. She was lost. Crest-fallen Morana sank to her knees in the snow.

Veles roared.

The roar erupted like the cracking of the very firmament, a sound older than trees, older than the mountains themselves, as though the bones of the world had been strung into a gargantuan, primal, cursed instrument of the gods. It poured from the beast's throat—a churning, guttural furnace of fury—twisting flesh and sinew into shapes no living eye should witness. Each note was a clawed hymn, scraping against reality, vibrating through roots and stone, shivering through the marrow of every living thing that dared to exist in the shadow of its ancient lineage. It carried the weight of countless predator-lords whispered of in long-forgotten myths; whose names, never spoken, were enough to inspire dread. The voice of the first predators: the blood-forged guardians of forests; fury encoded into the very warp of the land. The trees recoiled; their bark split like old, cursed parchment, leaves shivered with the memory of sacrificial rites long since buried. Shadows bled into one another, writhing across gnarled roots and moss-covered stones like dark rivers of sentience. The forest itself seemed to inhale in terror, awaiting the ruin promised by that monstrous hymn of some vengeful god.

The sound was a living thing, hungry and intimate. It clawed through Morana's chest, rattled her teeth, and pressed against her lungs with the inevitability of an old curse. She could almost SEE the shape of the roar: coiled, tendrilled; the edges flickering with green fire and crimson ichor, as though the air itself had been stitched with threads of wrathful magic. And in its wake, silence became a grave, thick and suffocating, pregnant with the memory of horrors that had walked these woods long before humans even had a name for fear. This was no mere animal. Veles was THE Ἄρκτος — 'The Bear' of old legend, a myth incarnate; a living echo of terror written into the bones of the earth; and this roar carried not only fury but judgment, morality, and the exquisite, unbearable beauty of ruin itself. It was a summons, a challenge, a prayer cast into the void of eternity. Morana flinched; half-certain the sky itself would answer.

It did.

Above, the aurora tore open the heavens; flowing like liquid flame, tracing a luminous path between treetops. Not gentle ribbons of light, but a cataclysmic bloom of green, violet, and bruised red, arcing and pulsing like the lungs of some slumbering god. The night's black canvas quivered under the brilliance, shifting and breathing, alive with the memory of eons. Waves of colour crashed across the sky like molten rivers, burning and freezing simultaneously, each fold of light whispering the names of heroes and monsters, of sacrifices made and denied.

It was a bleeding tapestry of motion: green veils rippling like venom through oil, bruised reds bleeding at the edges, violet fingers curling into the black. The night stretched taut beneath it, like a drumhead held fast by the bones of the world. The aurora did not dance.

It rode.

The Valkyries came first — terrible and bright, armoured in ice and star-metal, their helms slick with the memory of war. They thundered across the heavens on steeds whose hooves struck sparks from the void, spear-points gleaming like comet-tips. Their hair blazed like wildfire, whipping behind them as they roared across the firmament, shrieking battle-hymns in a tongue that tasted like iron and blood.

Behind them arched the *Bifrost* — not a gentle bridge, but a living artery of the cosmos, pulsing with molten colour. A road of flame and frost, curving across the sky to where the gates of Valhalla yawned wide. The fallen followed, their spirits torn from flesh still warm, eyes wide with awe or terror as they were swept up by the hunt — into light, into legend.

But the sky held more than the gods of one people.

From the north came the fire-foxes. Great beasts with eyes like suns and fur that sparked when it touched the frost-bound peaks. They ran across the dark with wild, joyous ferocity, their tails trailing sparks that bloomed into flame and coiled upward into the sky. Each time their bodies brushed the edge of the world, the heavens flared.

Elsewhere, the sea broke its silence. A whale breached in the pitch-black arctic waters — not flesh, but something older: a leviathan wreathed in ghost-light, with scales that mirrored stars. It turned in the deep, and its glistening hide scattered starlight like salt, flinging it into the void where it hung — radiant, aching.

The Inuit whispered that the spirits of the dead were playing — chasing a walrus skull through the heavens, laughing with a sound like wind through hollow bone. In some villages, it was not the dead, but the walruses themselves who played — great tusked beasts whose games with human skulls summoned the sky to burn.

Further still, where the aurora visits like an omen, the dragons awoke. Vast serpents — older than empire, older than name — coiled through the clouds. Their jaws unhinged, and from them spewed violet flame and golden smoke. The lights were not decoration. They were war. Dragons in battle, thrashing across the horizon, their scales scraping sparks from the dome of the world. It was a duel beyond time — not for territory, but for the soul of the sky.

Each people carried a tale, and within each tale the same truth pulsed: the aurora is not light.

It is passage.

It is power.

It is the skin of the veil between what is, and what hungers just beyond.

To stand beneath it is not merely to witness beauty — it is to be watched.

By gods.

By beasts.

By your ancestors long dead.

Morana felt it — that prickling in her scalp, the deep itch in her bones. Not awe alone, but exposure, as though she were naked before myth itself. She clung tighter to Veles, her breath frosting in ragged bursts, her heart thundering with the certainty that something vast and unseen had turned its gaze upon her.

Morana's breath froze in her throat. She felt the aurora pulse through her chest, pressing against the ribs that ached from her flight through shadow. The tapestry above seemed to break apart and descend, its legends no longer distant myth but living presences. A Valkyrie wheeled low over the treetops, spear trailing sparks that hissed as they struck snow. The fire-foxes darted close enough that their tails scorched the drifts into brief rivers of steam. A dragon's coil pressed against the Prussian blue sky itself, so vast that for a heartbeat she felt trapped inside its ribs, the stars burning like embers between its scales. In that instant she understood that myth was not a thing of the past but of the present — that she was not a girl watching legends, but a girl being judged by them.

These were not stories now. They were witnesses. She could feel their gazes prickling along her skin, ancient eyes marking her as part of something older than blood or bone. The aurora was not only a path — it was a tribunal, a host of myths gathered to watch whether she faltered or endured.

She knew, with an instinct older than fear, that this was her path—etched by fire and memory, an unbroken thread of myth calling her home. The Northern Lights a living thread sewn through the wilderness. She faltered, uncertain of her footing. The snow was deceptive, hiding roots and rocks, but the aurora called, a promise of guidance that demanded trust.

Veles shifted beside her. Before she could steady herself, he lowered his massive head, and with a single motion that was both terrifying and tender, he gathered her onto his shoulders. The rush of his movement sent her hair streaming behind her, and the cold stung her cheeks, sharp as glass.

"Hold on," she whispered, trembling, uncertain whether the words were to Veles or herself.

The iron chains had left scars, but now he was a living engine of motion, a mountain with a beating heart. His fur bristled like winter pines in a storm, sparks trailing from his paws as he bounded forward. Each leap tore the frozen ground, sending shards of ice and snow spraying like molten crystal, yet he moved with terrifying grace, instinct woven into sinew.

The forest blurred. Trees became monstrous silhouettes, their branches writhing like clawed arms. Frozen rivers shattered beneath his feet, splintering into shards of light that reflected the aurora above. Morana clung, heart hammering, mind reeling from both terror and awe. The wind tore at her face, carrying whispers of the dead, of gods and beasts, of stories etched in blood and frost.

She looked up. The aurora had become a living conduit. Curtains of green and violet bent and shifted, guiding them, forming a luminous river in the sky. The fire-foxes darted along its currents, leaving trails of flame that pulsed with unspoken instruction. Morana realized she had never seen the world like this: every myth, every tale she had heard in whispers or dreams, suddenly burning bright, woven into the very air she breathed. **TRUTH**.

Veles roared again—a deep, resonant sound that split the silence. The aurora answered. Colours intensified, folding into arches and spirals, the sky opening into a cathedral of light. Red bled into green, violet surged into gold, and the air vibrated with something ancient, something hungry, something alive. The patterns above were a litany, a map of memory and hope, guiding her across wilderness that would have otherwise swallowed her whole.

Branches whipped past, jagged and grotesque, scraping at her coat and skin. Her knuckles bled from gripping Veles, but she did not care. Each pulse of the aurora illuminated a path previously hidden, each flicker a whisper of where to leap, where to turn.

The forest was a nightmare, but the sky was an oracle, cruel and beautiful, terrifying and merciful all at once.

Morana was even sure she could hear it singing; the aurora's echo etched forever in her soul.

A mountain rose before them, its peaks serrated like the broken teeth of some ancient leviathan. Veles's paws struck with the force of falling glaciers. Snow and ice flew in molten arcs, splintering into crystalline shards that caught the aurora and refracted it into madness. The sky's colours bent, coiling into luminous ribbons that wrapped around the peaks, guiding them along a path invisible to mortal eyes.

Morana screamed—not in fear, but exhilaration, the sound caught in the gale, lost in the roar of wind and aurora and the thunder of Veles's charge. The earth itself seemed to quake under his might. Trees twisted into grotesque forms, their bark melting like candle wax under the aurora's gaze. The landscape itself had become a dark, beautiful cathedral, a testament to cruelty, survival, and the mythic resonance of the world.

The horizon brightened with the faintest threat of dayspring. The aurora flared once more, a final, brilliant command. Veles leapt, landing with a crunch that shook the earth, and they rose over a valley of frozen rivers and snowdrifts: the Northern Lights painting every crevice with divine fire: as if attempting one final act to ignite her very path home; as if the sky itself conspired to see her homeward. Her vision blurred with snow and the sweat that ran in rivulets down her temple. Each breath felt like inhaling fire and frost together, a searing cold that lodged in her lungs and turned to ice with each exhalation. The world around her shivered in muted colours, twilight greys pressed into shadowed whites, the pale hints of dawn chasing her across the frozen fields.

The village rose before her like a fragile promise, a constellation of warm lights in the frozen dark trembling in the pale fingers of dawn; delicate against the relentless sweep of winter. Rooves were dusted with snow, windows glowing like lanterns in the infinite void, but they still seemed impossibly far; small and fragile, breathing in the last hush of winter's night. Chimneys smoking, hearths flickering, and she knew that each house held warmth and vigilance, gifts protected by those who loved. The aurora held on; a spectral blessing above the village. Morana pressed her palms together, whispering a silent prayer of gratitude: for Veles, for the enduring light of joy, for courage found in the bleakest places.

With each heartbeat a hammer, Morana felt herself starting to falter, her body cramping under the weight of the journey, her lungs raw from the cold that scraped them like glass. Morana lifted her gaze, snow streaking her cheeks, lungs burning with every ragged inhale. Each house was a promise and a threat: if she faltered, if the cold, the snow, or the exhaustion claimed her, Christmas would vanish, along with all its joy and light, leaving only the hollow echo of failure. The gift in her hands—the carved bird, delicate and impossibly precious—felt heavier than the world. She pressed it to her chest as though it could anchor the fraying threads of hope itself; a fragile jewel against the storm of her exhaustion.

The aurora above, once a living river guiding her through myth, began to curl and fade, folding its arms back into the unseen heavens: into the black like the closing of a cosmic eye; as if warning her, a final act to gain her attention, that the stories would retreat if she could not claim them in time.

She could see the church spire, the bakery's crooked chimney, her grandmother's porch—a single point of home—but she could no longer deny the changes in Vele's footfalls. Veles's great form was a living gale beneath her, but storms, she realized, could not rage forever. Even mountains had limits. Even myths had endings. Each paw strike, throwing up spires of ice that glittered in the remnants of the aurora's light, was falling heavier than the last.

The last stretch seemed to stretch into eternity. Morana's heart pounded against the cage of her ribs, her mind rattling with the thought that she might not make it. The village grew, then shrank in false proximity as the snow rose in drifts that stole their footing. The weight of the morning pressed against her, a tide of white and cold and myth, and she knew the gift, and the hope it carried, might slip through her hands. Morana's muscles trembled; her fingers, curling around the gift, ached as if she carried a fragment of the aurora itself. She feared she might drop it; apprehension sharp and sudden like the crack of ice underfoot, and the thought alone made her chest constrict until she thought she might collapse. Morana felt the changes in the aurora above, once a living river of guidance, a luminous tribunal of myths and monsters, had nearly completed its curl back into the heavens, fading like a lover's sigh. Its brilliance—green fire, violet flames, bruised reds—shrunk from her eyes, leaving her exposed. The stories were retreating, retreating into a realm she could not follow, and her heart seized with the knowledge that the last living traces of magic, of wonder, were slipping beyond reach.

Veles surged forward, lungs heaving, claws tearing the frozen earth as if trying to carve the very snow out of existence. For even he, ancient as the mountains, felt the press of impossible urgency. His leaps grew less graceful, more frantic: each stride an effort against the inevitability pressing toward dawn. Morana clung to him, an arm tightly wrapped in the fur of his neck, hair whipped into her face, skin scraped by the brambles that struck like cruel hands. She felt his muscles tighten and quiver, a tension that spoke not only of weakness, but of divine desperation.

Then, through the white haze, Morana felt a shift. The world narrowed to a single point, and she saw her:

Her grandmother.

For all this while, far across the snow-draped village, her grandmother had waited; hands pressed together, murmuring prayers that had not ceased all night long. Her breath had fogged in the morning cold, whispering names and pleas into the sky, a litany of hope and fear that tangled with the aurora itself. The wind had carried whispers of the aurora, cries of ancient creatures, and she thought of it all as signs of divine intervention, threads tugged in her favour to bring Morana home. She had heard the roar of Veles, had felt the tremor of the mythic beast through the soles of her boots; and had left the comforts of warmth to stand vigil. She scanned the horizon, eyes flicking over the white drifts, searching for the dark, impossible silhouette of her granddaughter.

Her grandmother stood now upon the porch, wrapped in her shawl, trembling in the cold yet immovable, face carved with worry and faith alike. Arms raised, fingers curling against the invisible threads of hope, lips parting in a cry that split the air, "Morana! Hurry! My child! Hurry!"

The sound of her voice pierced the snow and wind, raw and human, and yet it carried something older—a command, a prayer, a summoning. Morana's chest constricted; tears froze on her lashes as the distance between them seemed to stretch impossibly. Every muscle screamed; lungs searing with the effort to breathe. She saw the porch, the glowing windows, the curve of the roof—but each moment felt like moving through treacle, each second a lifetime: in which universes came into being, lived and died; each second a millennium closer to the last and dreadful YOM HADIN.

Time itself seemed to tremble as Mundilfari spun time ever forward.

On the porch, the woman's eyes were wide, luminous in the pre-dawn light, reflecting both the fear of a grandmother and the certainty of a believer who has lived long enough to know the impossible can be wrought by faith: faith so powerful that it can hold a hope even when the darkness has already triumphed and the grave holds its victory. She saw Morana faltering, her tiny form lost amid the sweep of snow, the shadow of mountains, and the retreating aurora. She knew, as one knows fire or blood, that her granddaughter could not make it alone. She could see the exhaustion in every line of the Brown One's frame, hear the stuttering rhythm of his breath; and could feel the dread in her bones the impossibility pressing toward them.

And yet the grandmother's heart flared, a furnace of determination. Not a faint hope, not a whispered plea, but a searing, all-consuming invocation. She lifted her hands, trembling, and let the prayer pour forth—words for God, for the saints, for the old gods of the forest and snow, for the spirits whose names had been whispered across generations. Each syllable was a spark, each breath a flame. The words were not only for heaven — they were for Morana herself, cast like a lifeline through the storm, something for the girl's failing heart to seize upon. She did not merely speak: she wove her faith into the world, braided it into the air, pulled it into the snow and wind and aurora itself. Her voice rose in a crescendo of desperation and love, shaking the trees, stirring the spirits, tugging at the heart of the universe itself: *Bring her back. Keep her safe. Let her live.*

She could feel the threads of the impossible weaving in response. Snow swirled like silvered smoke. The aurora, sensing the fire of true belief, brightened and trembled, extending a trembling path of light and a prayer of its own. Morana's grandmother did not falter, even as the cold cut to her bones. Every ounce of her being strained, every fibre of muscle, every beat of heart was a command to the unseen forces that she would not, could not, allow Morana to fail. She invoked all the names of God, older powers, a harmony of mortal and mythic, and let the act of her soul's prayer pour outward like a tide against despair.

Vele's eyes glimmered with the knowledge that the edge of time was near, that he could not outrun it—for even gods cannot outrun the inevitability of time; and in that terrible recognition, he made the choice that only a creature like him could conceive: she must fly.

Veles reared, the power in his legs coiled like a glacier about to split. His roar shook the heavens again, and Morana, pressed to his thick neck, felt the vibration thrumming through her bones, a tremor that was fear and blessing entwined. His eyes, molten and ancient, met hers for a fraction of a heartbeat: reflecting dawn, fear, and fury, desperation and love; and she understood the decision made in that glance. In that gaze, she saw what he had seen—the impossibility of reaching the porch alive, the fleeting seconds that demanded a choice no mortal could conceive.

There was no more time for gentle motion; no path would suffice. If she was to reach the door, it would be by faith, by flight, by surrender to force that bordered on divinity itself. Veles groaned, a chord that reverberated through snow and sky. She felt the force of his muscles coil, then uncoil like a catapult of the impossible. With a motion that was at once terrifying and pure, he launched her into the air.

She was airborne, suspended between myth and mortal terror. The wind tore past her face; the snow became a blur; the aurora flickered above like the last spark of a dying world.

She flew.

Morana screamed with raw, human terror.

She screamed, not for fear but because the universe had narrowed to this single, impossible act. It was not flight but hurling, not grace but desperation, and yet in that raw, violent trajectory there was a kind of faith: that love could throw you further than your own strength ever could. Flight was not freedom—it was the last chance for survival, hope made flesh, faith made tangible. Every instinct in her body screamed against the terror, against the burn in her lungs, against the relentless pull of gravity and dawn and exhaustion. And yet she flew.

The snow below became a blur, a mosaic of white and shadow. The wind tore past her face, whipping her hair and stinging her skin. Screams tore from her throat; a sound caught between fear and exhilaration. Time seemed to fold, the world contracting and stretching with her arc through the air. She glimpsed the aurora above, green and violet fingers curling into nothingness as if trying to grasp her and pull her forward as its last glows dimmed above her like a dying ember. She clutched the gift to her chest with every ounce of strength she had left. The house grew larger, its windows glowing like distant stars, the porch a beacon of warmth and hope. Her grandmother's shawl-wrapped figure leapt to her mind, a vision she held onto with trembling certainty.

But she could see her grandmother's eyes and knew she would not make it.

Her grandmother's voice, lifted in prayer and love, followed her across the snow, a living thread that seemed to reach her through the air, through the storm, through myth itself: *Come, child. Come. You are not alone. You are seen. You are loved.* Grandmother did not know if God would bend time back for her, but she trusted in the miracle of it: for it had been done twice before, and in stories things are always better in threes. And thus, her soul screamed in yearning to **ETERNITY**.

And עוֹלָם אֵל the *ANCIENT ONE* moved. Across all realms. Across all time. Across the existence of realities that were; that will be; that could have been but never were and will never be;

ANCIENT ONE REACHED OUT AND HELD BACK THE SUN. And all gods, archons, and emanations across dimensions were afraid and trembled.

The air cracked with tension. Morana felt the world holding its breath: not daring to move. Every second stretched like a blade. Every heartbeat was a universe. And then—the impossible: the snow and porch rushed up, warmth and light and human touch waiting at the end of the impossible arc. She braced herself, heart hammering, lungs raw, gift still clutched, ready to meet whatever fate awaited.

The culmination of faith, love, desperation, and myth had conspired to bring her here, and she was alive.

The landing was chaos incarnate.

The first collision hit like a hammer. Her body slammed against the porch railing; wood groaned and cracked beneath the weight. Veles's momentum carried them forward, unstoppable, and Morana felt herself pressed into the sharp curve of the steps, then over the threshold. Snow flew in violent arcs, spraying into the hearth and over the floorboards. She could hear the thud of boots against the boards, the scream of splintering timber, and the impossible, heart-stopping knowledge that the gift could be crushed beneath her.

Breath left her lungs in a violent gust; pain lanced through her shoulders and spine. Yet, despite the bruising force, the warmth of arms around her followed instantly—soft, protective, insistent. Her grandmother's arms wrapped around her in a surge of desperate love. The old woman fell backward onto the floor, dragging Morana with her, bodies twisting, hair tangling, breath knocked out in a chaotic, sharp explosion. The warmth of her grandmother's body collided with the cold, wet storm that still trailed from outside, and for an instant, Morana could only feel the violent shock of survival—the thrum of impact, the bite of cold, the weight of her own terror.

Her grandmother held her, clutching her, kissing her hair, murmuring her name over and over like a chant against the impossible. Morana's own sobs joined hers, a mingling of relief, terror, and the absolute surrender of fear. For a long moment she did not dare move. The silence between heartbeat and heartbeat was unbearable — as though the universe itself waited to see if she had succeeded. The storm, the aurora, the myths—they had led her here, and she had survived to witness it, to hold the tangible proof of perseverance and hope. Morana had made it home and across the hearth in time. She was there, gift in hand, able to open it on this new day of Advent.

She lay there for a heartbeat, stunned, afraid to move, afraid to look at the gift lest she find it broken or lost, a symbol of failure. Morana gasped, pressed against her grandmother's chest, teeth chattering, eyes wide. "The gift...?" she rasped, voice raw, breaking in the echo of adrenaline. Her fingers flexed around the carved bird, as though sheer will could keep it intact. Morana's own hands trembled as she opened the gift. The carved bird gleamed in the firelight, a miracle of wood and craftsmanship. She traced the lines with her fingers, overwhelmed by relief, by awe, by the almost unbearable joy of completion.

Yet it was safe, still in her hands; the carved bird intact, a testament to her perseverance. The carved bird, delicate and perfect, had survived unscathed, wings etched in tiny, impossible detail. In its survival she felt the survival of everything — of hearths and hymns, of laughter, of every fragile moment of joy that had ever been threatened by the dark. The realization hit her like a wave, a tidal surge of joy and relief so fierce that it almost knocked her over again. She clutched it to her chest, tears spilling free now, streaking frost and ash across her face, washing away the rawness of cold and the ache of muscles, leaving only the quiet, searing joy of having arrived.

Her grandmother held her tighter, rocking slightly in the aftermath, murmuring names and prayers over and over, as though repeating them could anchor the miracle of life. "God, all the saints, the old spirits, help us give thanks... my child, my child," she whispered, voice trembling, vibrating with every beat of her heart. Morana pressed her face into the shawl, drinking in the warmth, the smell, the pulse of life that radiated from her grandmother's body.

Her grandmother laughed, a wet, trembling sound caught between relief and disbelief. She pressed a hand to Morana's cheek, then kissed her hair, murmuring, "You are here, and you are safe. You are alive, my child—you are alive." The words poured over her like warm water, flooding away the terror. But it was not gentle; it was fierce, urgent, the sound of a lifetime of love and prayer finally given form.

Her grandmother's hands smoothed the snow-damp hair from her face, cupping her cheeks with deliberate, careful strength. "You are home," she said, and the words carried the weight of every prayer she had ever spoken, every myth she had ever believed, every impossible hope she had held in the dark. For the first time, she dared to breathe fully, to let the terror slip out of her chest. Every sensation—the snow still clinging to hair, the splintered wood beneath them, the heat of the fire, the faint, lingering sparkle of aurora fading outside—sank into her bones, grounding her. She realized she was not merely safe. She had survived the impossible. She had returned.

The fire crackled violently as if it, too, had felt the collision, sparks leaping from the hearth into the air, mingling with the drifting snowflakes that clung to their hair and clothes. The fire began to burn as if awakened by her return, casting dancing shadows across the walls. Warmth flooded through the house, spilling into her bones, seeping into the numbness left by snow and flight. The scent of bread, baked and golden, mingled with pine smoke, and the lingering scent of snow that had followed them inside. Morana let herself breathe, truly breathe, for the first time in what felt like an eternity. Snow still fell lightly against the windowpanes, a faint echo of the world outside, but inside, the warmth of hearth and love wrapped around them like armour.

Morana pressed herself into her grandmother's side, letting herself collapse in the aftermath, their bodies melting into the fire's glow, and felt the pulse of love and safety that was older than the aurora, older than Veles, older than fear itself. Morana wept and laughed in a single, uncontainable expression of survival and joy. It was a mortal echo of the mythic: the gift, the hearth, the embrace, each a tiny universe of certainty and devotion. Myth and mortal met in that small room: the aurora's passage folded into the domestic miracle.

Her grandmother pressed her closer, murmuring words of home, of safety, of endurance. Morana felt the weight of the journey lift in the warmth of the hearth and the arms of the woman who had waited for her. Dawn crested fully now, gentle, inevitable, but no longer threatening. The aurora had faded, folding its brilliance back into the sky, yet its blessing lingered in the warmth that filled the room, in the pulse of life and love that could survive even the most mythic terror.

In that quiet aftermath, Morana thought of every step, every gasp of breath, every furious leap of Veles across the frozen forest. She understood, with a clarity sharpened by exhaustion and exhilaration, that joy was resistance; that love and hope were acts of defiance against a world that might try to snatch them away. They had been given, then fought for, then claimed in full: the gift intact, her grandmother safe, herself alive.

She closed her eyes for a heartbeat and then opened them, daring a small, steady smile. This was home. This was triumph.

This was the quiet miracle of survival, of love preserved against the impossible. The fire flickered, casting shadows that danced like ancient creatures across the walls. The gift lay between them, a bridge between legend and life, a talisman of all that had been risked and all that had been won. And in that light, in that warmth, Morana understood fully: the mythic could bow to the mortal, and the mortal could embrace the mythic in turn.

Above, the daylight burst and spilt forth, and for a heartbeat, the wind stilled, the snow hushed, and the world seemed to exhale. The first light of dawn stretched across the horizon, pale but insistent. The snow glittered as if pricked by hidden stars, each flake flaring briefly before folding back into the drift. For an instant, Morana imagined she saw shapes in them—faces peering out, watching, remembering. The old ones, the keepers of stories, who had seen children falter and endure, who had waited for some ember of joy to survive another winter.

Veles' eyes reflected the dawn, not golden, but the bruised blue of night reluctantly retreating. He did not step forward, nor did he vanish, but lingered between worlds like a hinge in the door of myth. His presence was both benediction and burden: he reminded her that courage had a cost, that promises tied the living to the realm of gods and monsters alike. And yet, in his vast silence, she heard gratitude—an animal prayer that required no words. Veles rumbled low, a promise and a warning. From the doorway his shadow lingered, vast and trembling, as though myth itself was reluctant to leave her hearth. He had carried her home, and that was enough. The Advent Thief had not been defeated; the dark had not been vanquished; but then, perhaps darkness was never meant to be vanquished. It was older than men, older even than the gods who bound themselves to guard against it. It dwelt not only in the frozen forests and whispering voids, but in the deep recesses of the human mind—the corners where fear curled, where grief lingered, where cruelty waited for its hour. It was not an enemy to be slain once and for all, but a shadow that pressed at the edges of every hearth, every heart.

Morana understood this now in a way she had not before. The Advent Thief was not merely a creature that prowled the snow; it was the hunger that gnawed when kindness faltered, the whisper that said love was too fragile to endure. In the black of his eyes she had seen not just fangs and claws, but the reflection of every doubt she had carried in her own chest—the belief that she was too small, too late, too powerless to matter. And yet, she also knew this: darkness did not need to be destroyed for light to exist. It needed only to be faced, resisted, named, and sometimes even pitied. Perhaps that was why such stories always returned in winter. Not to promise the end of shadow, but to remind the living that shadow could be borne, carried through, and met with something fiercer. A covenant of courage and defiance.

Morana's chest tightened, not with fear, but with something fiercer: the realization that she had carried light through dark, and in doing so, had changed the shape of her own story. She was not only a child who had fled, but one who had returned bearing memory. In her palm, the weight of the carved bird seemed to pulse once more, as if answering dawn itself, reminding her that gifts, once recovered, never ceased to speak.

Somewhere deep inside, Morana felt it: even in the shadow of monsters, even beneath the weight of cruelty, light could always find a way. Perhaps it was the aurora's last sigh, transformed into music; perhaps it was only the bells of men. Either way, it was sound answering silence, a mortal echo of cosmic song. And in that echo Morana felt herself part of something vast and unbroken, as though her small breath had joined with winds that had carried tales for centuries. And on that note, the air filled with tintinnabulation.

EPILOGUE

The snow had softened, not melted, but hushed; the drifts lay like quietened spirits across the world. Morana's breath came in ragged, visible bursts, crystallizing in the air between the trembling of her heart and the warmth of her grandmother's arms. She had never felt the small human body so simultaneously fragile and infinite—diminished by terror, yet expanded by relief. Her knees gave, her hands unclenched the gift that had almost been lost, and she sagged forward, sinking into the familiar weight of life that had waited for her in the dark.

Her grandmother held her close, as though closeness itself might mend what winter had tried to steal. Tears spilled unchecked, tracing paths along snow-dusted cheeks. Morana pressed her lips to her grandmother's in a kiss that tasted of smoke, pine, and hope returned. The embrace held centuries, as if each pulse of warmth was a heartbeat of the world itself.

"Invite the Brown One in for breakfast," her grandmother whispered between breaths, voice carrying both gravity and mirth. "I feel like making honey gingerbread pancakes... and hot cocoa. Thick. Sweet. The sort that sticks to your fingers and leaves warmth on your tongue long after the cup is empty."

Morana blinked, half-laughing, half-gasping, and turned toward Veles. He knelt beyond the porch, enormous paws pressing lightly upon the snow, dark fur glittering faintly with remnants of frost and aurora, eyes deep ink-black gemstones in the dawn. He lowered his massive head, the rumble of his throat speaking with clarity, though in tones deeper than the earth: a quiet acknowledgment of gratitude. Freed, yet bound still by duty, his dignity shimmered like the echo of constellations long forgotten.

Her grandmother laid a hand upon Morana's shoulder, steadying the trembling girl who had faced impossible darkness. "Thank you," she said softly, almost to the wind, eyes fixed upon the massive bear. "Thank you for bringing him back into the world of the living... and for keeping our hearts warm while the darkness tried to reach in."

Veles shifted, deliberate, careful, impossibly graceful. The chains that had once bound him were gone, leaving scars no eye could see, yet lessons remained in sinew and memory. His gaze fell upon Morana, then her grandmother, and his voice—low, resonant, tinged with ancient sorrow—carried words almost like prayer. "I must return to the underworld," he said. "There is disorder, chaos that has spread unchecked. Angra Mainyu whispers where he should not, Mictlantecuhtli laughs through corridors that belong to silence. I must restore what is broken, reclaim what has been lost."

Yet even as he spoke of duty, Veles hesitated, paws shifting against the snow. The dawn painted his fur with mortal firelight, and for a heartbeat he allowed himself what gods and beasts are rarely granted: a pause. "But first," he rumbled, almost shyly, "I will share your hearth." His gaze softened, not less vast, but nearer, and in that nearness, Morana saw what it meant for myth to be weary—and to seek warmth, just for a little while.

Morana pressed a hand to his muzzle, trembling as warmth met her palm. "Will you... come back?" she asked, voice tiny against the immensity of all that had passed.

He lowered his massive head to her height, eyes locking with hers, measuring courage and heart alike. "Perhaps," he said, and the single word carried the weight of mountains, rivers, and nights spent waiting for the aurora to return. "For a Christmas Eve. A gift yet unimagined, a surprise yet to come; but one born of hope and courage alike."

Inside, the cabin smelled of ginger and honey, the cocoa thick and sweet. The gift sat upon the table, small, carved, yet pulsing with the courage, danger, and joy that had been fought for tooth and claw. Her grandmother kissed her temple again, lingering, memorizing the shape of her relief. "You see," she said, almost to herself, "joy is not given freely. It is an expression of love. It requires patience, courage. It is the heartbeat of the hearth, the voice of those who will not turn away, even when the dark presses close."

Veles lowered himself carefully into the cabin, the floorboards groaning beneath the weight of myth made flesh. He curled close to the hearth, fire reflecting across his glossy fur, and the room seemed to hum, vibrating with the song of the world itself—life and myth interlaced, danger and comfort balanced upon the same fragile thread.

Breakfast was quiet at first, each bite of gingerbread pancake a small victory over the terror of the night. Laughter came slowly, tentative, then more freely, rolling across the cabin like the first thaw of spring. The snow outside glinted, touched here and there by the last whispers of the aurora, and candles burned steadily, wards against forgetfulness and fear.

Morana's gaze returned to Veles, wondering if the magic of that impossible night had truly ended or merely shifted form. The bear's eyes, deep and knowing, answered without speaking, as though the underworld itself lay behind him, yet he had chosen this hearth, these humans, this fragile, fleeting warmth.

Her grandmother leaned close, brushing snow-matted hair from her granddaughter's face. "Remember this," she said, voice low but unwavering. "Every act of love, every courage faced, every gift returned becomes joy—the truest magic. It binds hearts, builds worlds, feeds flames that no darkness can quench."

Outside, the wind whispered softly, no longer menacing, carrying hints of ancient stories still untold. Morana felt the weight of myth and home pressing together in her chest, warmth that required no fire, no candle, no hearth. Veles shifted, the sound like distant thunder softened to a purr, and the girl snuggled in once more. "I will wait for Christmas Eve," he murmured. "But today... today we celebrate what has been won. This day, the darkness recedes because hearts held fast."

Her grandmother's arms wrapped around her again, grounding and eternal. "You are home," she whispered, "and safe. And now, let us eat, let us drink, and let us remember... joy is our gift to one another. Always."

The world lay still beneath the snow's muffled silence, the forests and fields wrapped in frozen taciturnity. And beside the front door, a small gift Morana had placed for the Advent Thief, a simple offering, a promise kept, left with a whisper of hope— that even in the coldest night, the smallest act of kindness could light the way.

Later, as the fire lulled and laughter faded into a soft quiet, Morana's thoughts drifted back to the gift she had left at the door. In her mind's eye, it still lay there, small against the whiteness, waiting. Earlier, the snow had accepted the gift without judgment, its surface unbroken but for the faint outline of her boots. The silence had folded in around her, vast and listening, as though the trees leaned in to see what had been given. She wondered if the Advent Thief had found it by now, if the silence outside carried not only threat but a strange new promise. The memory settled into her chest like a second heartbeat, a reminder that kindness was itself a kind of defiance.

Now, Morana's breath clouded the glass of the window as she peered out one last time, half-expecting a shadow to move, a claw to extend, a furnace eye to ignite from the black. Yet the night remained still. Instead, the hush seemed to soften, as if some unseen presence had acknowledged the gesture. Perhaps nothing would come of it. Perhaps everything.

Her grandmother's hand closed around hers, warm and trembling. "It is enough," the old woman whispered, her voice both reassurance and invocation. "We do not play with monsters—we remind them of mercy."

Morana swallowed, throat raw from cold and crying. She did not trust her voice, so she only nodded. The weight of the carved bird pressed gently against her palm, and she realized that survival had not demanded bitterness. Even here, on the edge of terror, she could choose generosity. The Advent Thief had taken so much, but it would not take that.

Behind her, the house breathed warmth. Fire cracked, snow melted in their hair, and the faint creak of the rafters felt like the exhale of a tired but living thing. She lingered one heartbeat longer at the threshold, between the endless hush of the world and the fragile, golden glow of home. Snowflakes drifted like silent prayers around the little package she had set down, each one catching the starlight before vanishing into darkness. She wondered if dawn would still find it there. She wondered if a shadow would lift it away before morning. She wondered if the

Thief himself would pause, and remember, and spare some other child.

Her grandmother squeezed her hand more firmly, pulling her back. "Come," she said. "The night is watching, but the hearth is waiting."

Wood and iron shut out the cold. In the marrow of her bones, Morana felt it: something unseen had shifted. The gift was not only a plea—it was a declaration. That even hunted, even exhausted, even nearly broken, one could still choose to give.

Inside, the hearth roared, the aroma of gingerbread and cocoa filled every corner, and the small, carved bird rested safely upon the table, a testament to courage, endurance, and love returned. Morana nestled into her grandmother, fingers entwined, hearts beating in unison, while Veles, the Brown One, rested beside the fire, a guardian at once fearsome and tender, his eyes reflecting distant stars and the warmth of the world he had helped preserve.

In that quiet, sacred moment, the tumult of the long dark of Advent seemed to recede, leaving only the glow of survival, hope, and the unbroken bond of family and myth. Every shadow that had pressed close was now held at bay, not by magic alone, but by hearts that had dared to endure, to trust, and to love fiercely.

And in the peaceful glow of hearth and snow, as myths receded and hearts held fast, they found the world once more bent to love— not in triumph alone, but in endurance; in small warmths carried through vast darks. The tale would not end, not truly; but for this night, they were whole. And, in the way of all stories worth telling, they endured happily ever after.

THE END

ABOUT THE AUTHOR

Walter Firth is an educator and priest with a rich background in history, theology, and human behaviour. His work spans diverse and often challenging ministry settings, including communities deeply affected by trauma.

Drawing on these experiences, Firth explores the complexities of human nature—especially its shadow side—with compassion and unflinching honesty. He believes that by confronting difficult truths, we can illuminate the path toward healing and transformation.

Through his writing, he seeks not only to tell compelling stories but to contribute to a world more whole and just than the one he inherited.

www.ingramcontent.com/pod-product-compliance
Lightning Source LLC
Chambersburg PA
CBHW032206030726
47494CB00020B/641